BLACK C

Champagne dripped off the face of the man who'd had the audacity to grab my arm. "How dare you! Do you have any idea who I am?"

"Mmm, no," I purred, leaning in closer. "Do you have any idea who I am?" I put my lips right next to his ear and grabbed his arm. He grunted and tried to pull away, but I didn't budge. "I'm not a lockpick for hire, and I'm not just a pretty face. If I have to go to the trouble of figuring out who you are after I already said I'm not interested, I will ruin you. That's a promise." I drew back and let go of his arm. We stared at each other in silence for a long moment, then he lowered his eyes, turned around, and walked right out of the museum. A few yards away, a little crowd of ladies clapped.

Yeah, girls, I feel you. Good riddance to him.

"I've already got his name, social security number, work history, and credit score," Boris said over my earpiece. "How should we ruin him?"

ALSO AVAILABLE

MARVEL CRISIS PROTOCOL
Target: Kree by Stuart Moore

MARVEL HEROINES
Domino: Strays by Tristan Palmgren
Rogue: Untouched by Alisa Kwitney
Elsa Bloodstone: Bequest by Cath Lauria
Outlaw: Relentless by Tristan Palmgren

LEGENDS OF ASGARD
The Head of Mimir by Richard Lee Byers
The Sword of Surtur by C L Werner
The Serpent and the Dead by Anna Stephens
The Rebels of Vanaheim by Richard Lee Byers
Three Swords by C L Werner

MARVEL UNTOLD
The Harrowing of Doom by David Annandale
Dark Avengers: The Patriot List by David Guymer
Witches Unleashed by Carrie Harris
Reign of the Devourer by David Annandale

XAVIER'S INSTITUTE
Liberty & Justice for All by Carrie Harris
First Team by Robbie MacNiven
Triptych by Jaleigh Johnson
School of X edited by Gwendolyn Nix

MARVEL HEROINES

BLACK CAT DISCORD

CATH LAURIA

ACONYTE

FOR MARVEL PUBLISHING

VP Production & Special Projects: Jeff Youngquist
Associate Editors, Special Projects: Caitlin O'Connell and Sarah Singer
Manager, Licensed Publishing: Jeremy West
VP, Licensed Publishing: Sven Larsen
SVP Print, Sales & Marketing: David Gabriel
Editor in Chief: C B Cebulski

Special Thanks to Nick Lowe

First published by Aconyte Books in 2022

ISBN 978 1 83908 134 7

Ebook ISBN 978 1 83908 135 4

Cover art by Joey Hi-Fi

Distributed in North America by Simon & Schuster Inc, New York, USA
Printed in the United States of America
9 8 7 6 5 4 3 2 1

ACONYTE BOOKS

An imprint of Asmodee Entertainment Ltd

Mercury House, Shipstones Business Centre

North Gate, Nottingham NG7 7FN, UK

aconytebooks.com // twitter.com/aconytebooks

*To Lottie, Gwen, and the crew at Aconyte –
there's nothing better than working with
people who believe in you, and I'm
sure Felicia would say the same.*

CHAPTER ONE

Everywhere I looked – gold.

Jewels.

Fashion so high it could probably see its house from up here.

It was like walking into a dream tailored exactly to me, a dream where I was surrounded by all the wealth of New York's most elite, laid out and mine for the taking.

Diamonds winked playfully in the bright overhead lights. Chandelier earrings dazzled. Pendants and pocket watches alike rested against chests like little welcome signs: "Hey there, Felicia! Come and get me, girl! You know you want to."

I did want to. Oh lord, how I wanted to. But unfortunately, I *wasn't* in a dream right now. I was, in fact, at the Met Gala, dressed like the hottest member of *Ocean's 8* – *not* the pink one, pink wasn't my best color – and surrounded by the contents of some of the finest, most secretive, most challenging vaults in the entire city. The real kicker was that I wasn't here to steal anything. Not this time. Epic shopping lists took time and effort to compile, after all.

Restraint of any sort was the exact opposite of my normal

MO, but there's being an unrepentant thrill-seeker, and then there's pulling off a heist in a museum packed with ninety percent of the Big Apple's super heroes. I might be bold, but even I knew the value in choosing your moment, and tonight? Tonight wasn't for stealing. My clutch was tiny and I barely had room underneath this dress for my Spanx, never mind somebody else's big, beautiful, bulky gems.

That didn't mean that the evening was a *waste*, though. I mean, firstly, I looked absolutely fabulous, and stealing someone's attention was almost as nice as stealing their Cartier bracelet. Secondly, did I mention that there was a lot of bling on display? Things normally kept locked away where no one could admire them or, say, valuate them? Oh, I had every intention of making tonight into a shopping expedition *eventually*, but first I had to put together my wish list! Diamonds might be a girl's best friend, but if they didn't crack the five-carat marker I wasn't interested in them.

Sorry, pretties. You've got to do better than that to catch the Black Cat's eye.

I extended a hand, and three separate trays of champagne curved toward me like my fingertips were magnetic. Ha, nope, just sharp enough to slice and dice anyone who got on my bad side. I picked out a glass and winked at the young woman who'd brought it, who blushed as red as the guy dressed up like a sparkly blood clot on the other side of the Metropolitan Museum of Art's great hall.

"Will you stop flirting and get a move on? There are over five hundred people here and you've only cased thirty of them so far!" The voice came through the com hidden inside my diamond earring loud and clear – almost too loud.

"Will you stop worrying and relax?" I murmured around the rim of my glass as I took a tiny sip. Mmm, delicious – I loved champagne. There was a lot I didn't like about the wealthy elite, which made stealing from them a very potent form of therapy for a firmly middle-class girl like me, but the drinks were something I could appreciate. "The event has hardly started. You can't expect me to march around here like I'm a grand marshal and muster them all into parade rest. This is a delicate crowd."

Boris Korpse, my henchman extraordinaire, huffed on the other end of the line. "Delicate, my butt. Half of them came here drunk and the other half will be that way before the end of the night. Just swan up to some randos, throw out a few compliments to get their attention, and let the necklace do the work. Like that guy! The tiepin alone must be worth a quarter of a million dollars!"

"That wasn't a rando," I said, resisting the urge to roll my eyes. "That was Tony Stark." Who hadn't noticed me, thankfully, because I wasn't quite ready for that level of chattiness yet. Maybe by the time I got to my third glass of champagne.

"Was it really?" Boris hummed. "Huh, I didn't recognize him without the helmet on. I should have guessed, I suppose. He walked like a man used to wearing concrete boots."

"The armor is actually very light!" At least, the set I'd sort-of-OK-*very*-illegally-fabricated was. I hadn't ever actually worn it, just used it to distract Tony Stark for a while, but it had looked very aerodynamic.

"His armor is a disgrace to science! And don't get me started on the–"

I tuned out most of Boris's rant; I knew his opinion of Tony

Stark, and manipulating his dislike to give me a few moments of peace was child's play. A few of his lines were enough to make me chuckle, but I restrained myself to a distant smile as I began to wander the Temple of Dendur.

Smiles were one thing, laughter quite another at the Met Gala. We were supposed to be living up to a somber and reflective theme, after all, which was – get ready for it – Celestial Bodies: An Exploration of Fashion and the Universe. There was a time when a theme like this would have had people dressing as stars, or planets, or maybe some daring designer would try to find a person who could embody the stultifying terror of a black hole and deck them out in all Vantablack. I'd met plenty of people here tonight who were very stultifying and would be vastly improved with a black bag over their heads.

Abstracts like that weren't anywhere to be seen tonight, though. The number of people I'd passed who were dressed like Asgardians alone was as staggering as it was uninspired, and let me tell you, most of them couldn't pull off the armor. A breastplate, to my mind, should be more suggestive of what's underneath the plates, but hey, what did I know?

At least they'd decorated their fashion missteps with their sparkly best.

I made a slight adjustment to the gorgeous emerald brooch situated in the middle of my chest, making sure it was displayed to its finest advantage. It really was a work of art – a lab-created emerald with a microscopic computer literally grown into the crystal structure that used the emerald itself with the versatility of a microscope/camera hybrid. Oh, and it had its own Wi-Fi! No cadging from coffee shops for me.

"You need to stop lookin' at the guys," Bruno Grainger, my

other partner in crime, chimed in. "Get a load of the dames instead. They're the ones who're really dressed to impress, right?"

"*Dames.*" Boris scoffed. "What decade do you think you're in, sir? When did you start preferring your galas hard-boiled and drenched in the desperation of Prohibition?"

"Questionable nomenclature aside, you make a good point," I said, and turned toward the snack bar.

Yes, the snack bar. Trust me, after working out and eating in for months to fit into these dresses, the first thing anybody who'd been avoiding carbs and sugars did once they got past the photographers on the main staircase was fill their mouths with as much canapé as they could, and I didn't blame them one bit. I pulled in behind the deputy mayor's wife, a woman with some sort of Celestials thing going (if the rows of lights in her massive headpiece were any indicator), and tried to get a bead on her... well, beads. Were they pearls, or white jade? I sidled closer.

"–course I'm here by myself, like I am every night lately," she was saying in bitter tones to the man next to her as she piled miniature crab cakes on a plate. "David has been working himself to the bone at the office, the *bone*, I tell you. I can't wait for this awful trial to be over. Joseph Manfredi should never see the light of day again as far as I'm concerned, and if there were a jot of justice in this world his father would be joining him behind bars."

"Take it easy, Barbara," the man at her side said, making a soothing motion with his free hand. "It's all for show, you know that. Silvermane is just flexing in his old age, hoping to spring his son loose before he finally kicks the bucket."

"He'll never kick the bucket," Barbara snapped. "That man practically *is* a bucket, with all of the metal parts he's got these days. A retrial is an absolute farce. The motion should never have gotten past a judge in the first place, but the Maggia has half the judiciary in its pocket."

I really shouldn't linger – especially not after my brooch informed me that the beads were plastic – but I was interested despite myself. Silvio Manfredi, aka Silvermane, was one of the oldest and most established power brokers in New York City. His super villainous heyday might have passed, but the Maggia crime syndicate he was a member of was still going strong. Silvio's only son and former heir was Joseph Manfredi, who'd done a brief stint as the villain Blackwing before one of his guys ratted him out to the FBI. He'd been locked up ever since, but apparently his father was reconsidering his son's usefulness if he'd gone to the trouble and expense of buying him a second chance.

I'd heard a little about the new trial – it was hard to avoid it when it was splashed across every headline at every newsstand in the city – but I hadn't heard that Silvermane had deep enough pockets to buy out so many judges. Was he hiding a special treasure vault somewhere? It had been, oh, *months* since I'd stolen anything of note from the Maggia, and all I'd gotten away with last time was a measly million dollars. A million dollars was barely enough to keep my mad scientist and NASCAR-wannabe driver in equipment for a month, never mind pay my rent. A penthouse apartment in New York City cost a mint, and *healthcare?* As a very specialized small business owner? Ridiculous.

"Move along from the cheap seats already," Boris said.

"You're not going to get anything worthwhile out of the civil servant section, you need to go swimming with the big fish! Find the corner where the billionaires are all pulling out their–"

"Rude," Bruno interrupted. I could practically see the frown across his broad face. He and Boris had been with me from the start of my illustrious thieving career, and were as loyal as two crooks could be. They also bickered like an old married couple.

"I was going to say *wallets*," Boris replied, sounding far too smug for that to be true. "Pulling out their wallets to see whose is the fattest. Or really, in this day and age, comparing the size of their personal rocket ships. Is it just me, or is everybody going to space lately?"

"Only the ones we don't want to come back," I murmured as I made my way through the crowd. "It's such a waste of time, too. There's plenty of fun to be had right here on Earth." The idea of roaming the galaxy for the biggest scores posed its own temptations, for sure, but I wasn't about to be beholden to a billionaire or offer to host a Klyntar to get there. There were plenty of temptations here on Earth… like this delicate little morsel of a human being right up here.

Ah, now this was the fashion statement I'd been yearning to see. This well-heeled young woman had come dressed as the sun, and what a fine choice it was. Her costume was absolutely resplendent with gold – a gold dress, heavy gold bracelets with an Egyptian air to them stacked practically up to her shoulders, a gold collar-style necklace that mirrored the crown on her head… and all of it, my little computer informed me via Boris, was at least eighteen carats. She didn't quite manage *elegant*, but she was definitely striking.

"Get closer," my loud-mouthed minion said, "I think these actually might be genuine antiquities. I can cross-reference the museum database with the–"

"Get *out*!" the center of the solar system exclaimed to the person nearest to her, smacking one of her well-rounded hips with a bejeweled hand. "Are you kidding me? There's totally gonna be a golden apple in New York City! It just doesn't make sense otherwise."

"Jasmine, honestly," the older woman at her side said in a lower voice, like she was embarrassed. She was dressed to look like the moon, but this was no Beyonce/Solange comparison of excellence. This lady was doing little more than reflecting the big, bright personality next to her. I sidled a little closer – I might as well get a good look at the moonstone choker around her neck anyway. "This is hardly the place to be discussing something so… crass."

"Oh please, how's it crass, Mom?" Jasmine of the golden regalia asked. "Why shouldn't we talk about what everybody wants to talk about anyway? And I'm telling you, deada–"

"Jasmine!"

Jasmine sighed. "Dead*booty*, is that all right? I'm telling you, deadbooty, once an apple shows up here? I'll be punching my way to the front of the line to get my hands on it. Can you imagine? The answer to any question you want! Totally accurate! Isn't that amazing?"

"I'm sure it's some sort of gimmick," another person in her circle said. "Watch, it'll be some big corporation's marketing ploy, or some kind of mass hallucination spurred on by an out-of-control mutant, or–"

"No! No, they're real!" A new voice entered the conversation, a gentleman dressed like a ... like a ... was all that latex supposed to make him look like a symbiote?

Jeez, insensitive much?

I wanted to punch him in the face on account of his bad taste alone, but I restrained myself. After all, he'd done some sort of opal overlay for the eyepieces, and to say they looked expensive would be a gross understatement, emphasis on *gross*. I breathed a little heavier, so the camera would tilt up and get a better angle.

"They really are," the man went on, oblivious to my appraisal of his otherworldly goods. "I know someone who knows the man who found the one in Sydney. He took it to a casino and won over five million dollars in a single night!"

"What an idiot," Jasmine moaned, and I had to agree with her. "He could have gotten so much more if he'd just focused on the motherfu–"

"Jasmine, watch your mouth!"

"The mother*freaking* stock market, is that all right, Mom?" she snapped.

"I imagine he had to work fast," the man said, sounding a little miffed. "Once you've found an apple, after all, you're marked."

Oh, you were marked, all right. Marked as an epic rube, the person everyone else was going to be hustling to hustle once you made your choice. It was pure idiocy to use one of the mysterious golden apples as an oracle. These weren't just the next Sugarcrisp or Honeybee: a strange, magical-looking object appears out of nowhere with the words *For the cleverest* on it and prompts you to ask it anything as soon as you pick it up? Terribly suspicious, in my opinion. I didn't mind magic, but I also wasn't about to invite it to play in my mind if I didn't have to, especially when nobody seemed to know its provenance.

There had been golden apples found in Shanghai, Madrid, and Sydney so far, at least as far as the press had been able to find out. Each one had been picked up by a small-minded opportunist, and each one had been used to make money in some way. *Money.* Like there weren't a million more interesting things they could have gone for... but no. They'd all asked for the quickest way to make a load of cash.

The first guy had ended up with something like sixty-five million Chinese yuan – about ten million US dollars, nothing to sneeze at. No sooner was it in his hands than the government stepped in to remind this citizen that gambling was illegal in China and he'd be lucky if they just confiscated it and he didn't end up in jail. Now he was completely broke.

The guy in Madrid also got himself a pile of cash, which he immediately spent on an absolutely gorgeous, hideously expensive Bugatti. He almost as immediately crashed it joyriding on a narrow mountain road in the Sierra de Guadarrama range north of the city. Another waste, and one that ended with him dead in a ditch. The guy in Sydney had just found his apple yesterday, but I didn't doubt he was also on a quick road to ruin.

I rolled my eyes as I listened to the little crowd in front of me keep going on and on about what they'd do with a golden apple, then decided for the sake of my brain cells to sidle elsewhere. I could always come back to Jasmine later... or preferably skip her and head straight for Daddy's vault.

I moved through the crowd like the cat I was – relaxed, but predatory. It was a good balance to strike; no one shied away from me, but no one was quite ready to seek out my company either, which was how I liked it. Cats were careful when it came to who they spent their time with, and any fool who thought they could press the issue? Well, that's when the fur began to fly.

"Excuse me, Miss Hardy?"

Like now.

I turned to face the man who'd come up from behind to accost – I mean, question me. "Yes?" I said, as coolly as I could manage, looking him up and down without bothering to hide the fact that I was judging him.

"I, uh, I was wondering if I could have a moment of your time to discuss a… potential *business* opportunity."

Yep, judging him, judging him so hard. "I don't think so," I demurred, turning back around.

"Miss Hardy, wait!" Then he reached out and had the audacity to–

Grab.

My.

Arm.

I let him turn me, his mouth already running a mile a minute. "I represent a group of investors who are looking for someone with your special skills to help us acquire a – *gah!*" He let go of me and staggered back as I threw the contents of my champagne glass into his face.

Hey, it was that or go for the jewels – the *family* jewels. I was being reserved, under the circumstances.

"This is a party," I said politely, handing my glass off to a dumbstruck waiter. "Not a job fair. Trying to talk to me about your little business dealings here is bad form. And walking up to someone you don't know and grabbing her by the arm? *Very* bad form. Now." I smiled brightly and with complete falseness. "You can either leave this party with nothing damaged but your dignity and your cummerbund, or we can do things a bit more directly. What do you prefer?"

"I... I..." Champagne dripped off the end of his graying beard, his eyes wide with shock – shock that was gradually turning into anger. "How dare you! Do you have any idea who I am?"

"Mmm, no," I purred, leaning in closer. "Do you have any idea who *I* am?" I put my lips right next to his ear and grabbed *his* arm. He grunted and tried to pull away, but I didn't budge. I might not be super strong, like half the super people in this room, but I was more than a match for a pudgy Wall Street desk jockey. "I'm not a lockpick for hire, and I'm not just a pretty face. If I have to go to the trouble of figuring out who you are and what you want with me after I already said I'm not interested, I will *ruin* you. That's a promise." I drew back and let go of his arm. We stared at each other in silence for a long moment, then he lowered his eyes, turned around, and walked right out of the museum. A few yards away, a little crowd of ladies clapped.

Yeah, girls, I feel you. Good riddance to him.

"I've already got his name, social security number, work history, and credit score," Boris said with a sense of satisfaction. "How should we ruin him?"

"Oh, let him go," I said, looking for another glass of champagne. I was less interested in drinking, more interested in having something in my hand. You had to have something in your hand at an event like this. Alcoholic or not, it acted as the social lubricant necessary to start conversations with people you otherwise might not approach.

I'd approach anyone – with a few exceptions – but not everybody was as naturally charming as me.

"You're losing your edge, letting someone get away with disrespecting you like that." Bruno sounded disapproving.

"He didn't get away with anything," I said loftily. "I'm here, he's gone. And also, this isn't the Maggia, Bruno. You don't go breaking people's kneecaps for being jerks. If I started doing that I'd have to graft a baseball bat onto one of my arms." Dealing with jerks was a simple fact of life when you were a single female in the big city – in the big world, really. If you were alone, it must mean that you were fair game.

Now that I thought about it, picking up an escort wasn't a bad idea. Walking around with a partner provided you with a very particular type of shield, the kind that could be both good and bad. If I'd actually come here to work a job or, god forbid, to *solicit* one, my efforts would be hampered if I had someone else around to cramp my style. But since I was here to window shop, having the right sort of person on my arm could be the perfect entrée into plenty of conversations that I might otherwise have more of a challenge entering.

Let's see, let's see… who was the best choice for me? Single, obviously – I wasn't interested in providing onlookers with a catty moment tonight, and it didn't get much cattier than stealing someone else's escort. I also wanted someone with an in to the super hero community – either someone who was a part of it or someone close enough to it that I'd have an excuse to stare at the rest of the bright and shining stars who'd come down to the lowly firmament today.

Stealing from the super-powered community was honestly easier than targeting regular people a lot of the time. Mostly because of ego – there was nothing more satisfying than pulling off a job on someone who thought they didn't need basic security because they were so awesome that no one would dare. Even more satisfying, though? Finding ways to pull off jobs on people who had *maximum* security for their special something – whether it was diamonds, technology or magical artifacts. I'd stolen from an alien invasion, for crying out loud. I was *good* at it, and more, I liked the challenge of it.

I had my goals. Now I needed the right target to help me achieve them. I looked around the vast room, doing my best to identify people who'd gone out of their way to look less like themselves tonight. Fortunately, I had a lot of experience when it came to identifying super heroes. Everybody wears a mask these days, but that's just a minor stumbling block. You have to look at the other things: the way they walk, the tilt of their head, how they carry their shoulders, the volume at which they're accustomed to speaking. Don't just know a face – know the whole body, that's my motto.

Let's see… oooh, Johnny Storm was here! He was always up to play escort duty, and as long as I didn't mind listening to him talk about his latest rebuild, we could have a pretty good time together. And it looked like he'd come alone too, so–

Oh, whoops. Nope. No. I was going to be keeping my distance while his sister was in visual range. It wasn't that Sue Storm and I had beef, necessarily. We were sensible enough to know that there was absolutely nothing anyone could do to make us into people who could get along, so we didn't bother trying. But she would take it personally if I commandeered her little brother to hang out with me for the evening, so the Human Torch idea burned out before it really had a chance to light.

Who else, who else... Janet Van Dyne was just a few yards away, looking slightly murderous as she sipped her drink and stared at all the designs that hadn't been made by her. She'd make for interesting company, at least, and had enough clout that no one was interested in upsetting her by shutting her out of a conversation. But, eh... maybe too much work. I kept looking.

Hmm, Namor was here as well. Fascinating. I'd always wanted to learn more about his underwater kingdom, and there was a lot of privileged information I could get out of him if I played my cards right. On the other hand, it was probably no accident that he was alone, and less of an accident that no one seemed to be hanging out within five feet of him. He had turned annoying people into an art, and from the look of things I was more likely to be ignored than invited in if I had him on my arm.

I turned back toward the stairs to expand my search, and saw the most perfect specimen of masculine physicality other than Spider-Man appear at the top of them. *Thank you for joining us tonight, Mr Rand.*

Tall, blond, and built like a martial arts master – go figure – he'd gone with what looked like a basic black tuxedo at first, but upon closer look, was studded with thousands of tiny glinting shards of light. Diamond chips, perhaps. And an even closer look revealed–

"Oh, Danny," I said, tucking myself in by his side and ignoring the way he startled, like he hadn't heard me approach. Which he hadn't. "I've always admired a man who's not afraid to wear a little glitter."

He ducked his head a little shyly. "Yeah, do you like it? It wasn't my idea, but it kind of went with the suit, and..."

"Whoever helped you with your makeup is a saint, because it would be a crime not to highlight those cheekbones," I assured him. "Frankly, I think you should wear glitter more often. Have you thought about incorporating some into your costume?" He laughed, and I decided to press my advantage. "So, no escort tonight? No tiny, terrifying girls and their gorky green dragons?"

He shook his head. "Nah, no Pei. And you, no breaking into my building and stealing my stuff?"

"That was one time!" I protested. "And you said yourself that it was fun."

Danny grinned. "Yeah, it really was. Nice dress, by the way."

"Thanks." The dress was azure blue fading to a matte black on top, simple but striking, while the mermaid-style skirt had each of the twelve constellations of the Western zodiac embroidered in silver thread on it. "Say. How do you feel about having some company while we make the rounds before dinner?"

He blinked in surprise. "You mean, you?"

I resisted the urge to roll my eyes. "Well, unless you have a secret admirer that you expect me to be passing a note from, then yes. Me." I fluttered my eyelashes a little. "Is that a disappointment?"

Danny held out his arm and gallantly said, "You could never be a disappointment, Miss Hardy."

"Could he be any more of a pushover?" came Boris's disgusted tones over my jewel-encrusted earpiece.

"Shut up and let the boss work," Bruno scolded him.

Both of you shut up, I wanted to say, but I ignored them instead.

"Gotta love a gentleman." I laughed as I wrapped my hand

around Danny's elbow. "Clearly you've never discussed me with Daredevil." Who *wasn't* a disappointment to that man in one way or another? Some people were impossible to please.

"Actually, I have, and he was really nice!"

God, I just wanted to pinch Danny's cheeks and get him a Shirley Temple. I settled for passing him a glass of champagne. "No, *you're* really nice. Thanks for the company." I smiled brightly at him. "So. Where shall we wander first?"

CHAPTER TWO

Danny Rand, aka the Iron Fist, aka my pickup for the evening, really was a cinnamon roll of a human being. There was nothing quite so gratifying as getting invited into conversations with people who usually wouldn't give you the time of day, but who couldn't try kicking you to the curb without making your date upset on your behalf. In his civilian identity, Danny would have opened enough doors just because of his business contacts, but thanks to there being no secrets in the super hero world – seriously, I didn't even bother trying to hide who I was these days, the mask was just because it really set off the color of my eyes and gave me a bit of probable deniability when it came to video evidence – everybody with a hint of a super- power in New York City would chat him up too.

I got my eyes, and the camera in my helpful brooch, on all sorts of beautiful things – heirloom jewelry, fancy wearable tech, more than a few magical artifacts. It was fantastic. The conversations? Not so much.

It was the exact same thing, over and over – "Crazy about the retrial, huh?" or more often, "How about dem apples?"

Everybody wanted to talk about golden apples, golden apples, golden apples. I had to field three more refusals to steal the next one that popped up in the space of half an hour, at which point even Danny pointed out that some of these people were being "kind of rude, huh?" to the chagrin of the folks around us.

"You get used to it," I said, trying to keep a good face on the whole situation. "After all, I *do* have a reputation when it comes to stealing the unstealable."

"I don't think it's possible to steal one," someone piped up. "I mean, these could be gifts from some sort of god, right? They seem that way to me, at least. If the gods are delivering the apples to their chosen ones, then surely you can't just steal one."

"Are you kidding me?" someone else – it might have been a random Avenger, there were so many of them these days – scoffed. "*Literal* gods leaving all-knowing trinkets around for people to pick up? That would never happe – oh hey, there's Thor! 'Scuse me, everybody."

He left, and I leaned in closer to Danny and whispered, "Do you think he knows how ironic he's being?"

"I kind of hope so, because otherwise he's oblivious."

Ah, I knew there was a bit of an edge to the Iron Fist somewhere in there. "Very true." I glanced around the Temple room, which was hosting the cocktail party. There was still half an hour until dinner, and I was feeling a little "funned out" when it came to schmoozing. "I've heard there's a new show opening soon at the museum," I said, carefully turning Danny in the direction of the Great Hall. "Do you think they'd let us look at it if we asked them nicely?"

"Oh, are you talking about the Crown Jewels?"

"Is *that* what they're hosting?" I asked, knowing full well that it was *exactly* what the Met was hosting right now. How the curator had talked the Tower of London, much less the British monarchy, into sending them over was a mystery, and one I'd like to solve, because it paid to know who the power brokers were in the art world. For now, though… on to the razzle dazzle!

There were a few other people milling about the hall that led to the collection, but almost everyone was back at the Temple, where they could see and be seen. The only person of interest we passed along the way was a stunning woman in a long gold dress with dark brown hair pulled back in a cross-tie style, something I didn't see a lot of. I winked at her on the way in, and she smiled and winked back as she returned to the social fray.

My fingers itched as the lady passed – she had some gold bangles hanging from her wrist that were positively exquisite. It had been, oh, *hours* since I'd stolen anything more substantial than someone's pride. I'd promised myself I wasn't going to compromise my time here by working a job, but surely getting a little practice in was just the smart thing to do?

I playfully leaned a little harder against Danny and patted his chest. "What does a guy like you really enjoy about coming to a thing like this, huh? You can't be hurting for company, and I didn't think you were the gala type."

"I've been trying to get out more lately," he said a little shyly, as I deftly lifted his wallet, his valet slip, and the little dragon-shaped pendant around his neck. I'd polish the pendant up before I returned it to him; it could use some TLC. "Misty says I can't do all my socializing with my fists."

Ah yes, Misty Knight. I wasn't sad that she didn't come to the Gala – we hadn't talked much since our Heroes for Hire days, and that was just fine with me – but I was a little curious about whether they were on or off right now. "Any reason she didn't accompany you?"

"It's not really her scene."

There was a lot to unpack there, but I wasn't a baggage handler. I was here to drink someone else's champagne, get the goods on a lot of other people's finery, and generally look fantastic. "It's not for everyone, true."

"I'm surprised you came," Danny commented, which… Huh? What about the Met Gala wasn't *my* scene? Was I not important enough for this kind of shindig? Did he think I couldn't *afford* it?

"Why?" I asked, as calmly as I could.

"Because everyone automatically assumes that you're here to steal something," he said, then quickly continued, "Not me! I'm not talking about me, I wouldn't think that. Don't, I mean… Think that… Um."

Given that I had a handful of his personal belongings in my clutch right now, his defense of me was extra ironic, but I took it graciously. "If I lived my life based on other people's expectations, I'd never get anything done," I said with perfect honesty. "Everybody wants something, right? In my case, they usually want me to work a job for them, or they want access to my privileged information, or they just want to be seen with me to increase their street cred. With you, well…" I smiled again. "I can't speak to what everybody else wants, but I was definitely looking for a friendly face to make passing the time here a little more pleasurable."

"I'm glad I could provide," he said, perfectly at ease, and my *god*, he was so much like Peter sometimes. Who would have thought I'd ever take a liking to such sweethearts?

"I'm glad you could too," I said, then let my attention be distracted as we entered the Michael C. Rockefeller Wing, where the Met had the Crown Jewels on display.

Well, I say "entered"; we hopped over the red velvet rope with a sign in the center of it that read "Wing Closed" but we were hardly the only ones to do it. A few other couples were milling around, staring at the pretties. And why wouldn't they be when the pretties in question were so exquisite?

We stopped in front of the case that held the Imperial State Crown and looked it over in silence for a moment, Danny because he was being polite and me because – oh, how could I not?

Boris, on the other hand, didn't care to stand in silent reverence when he could be doing math instead. "There are almost three thousand diamonds on that thing."

"Eh, most of 'em are tiny," Bruno said dismissively.

"Do you know how many semiconductors I could buy with those?"

"I repeat – tiny."

"You never know when the semiconductor market is going to tighten up again. I need to lay in a substantial inventory before IBM or Stark Industries gets a stranglehold on the market. And look at that hideous thing – it would be a service to all mankind to repurpose those diamonds. And all those pearls, not to mention the sapphires."

"Why not go for the big ruby right in the middle?" Bruno asked. Boris snickered.

"That's not a ruby, it's a *spinel*. Practically worthless."

"It surely has some historical value," I said before I could help myself. Danny glanced at me.

"Hmm?"

"I was just thinking about the history of a crown like this," I said, picking up the thread like the pro I was. "And the value getting to see it might have for whoever comes and views this exhibit. It could teach them a lot about–"

"The powers of oppressive and violent colonialism," Boris said with his trademark frankness.

He wasn't wrong. I opened my mouth to repeat his line but something else, something so beautiful it made my lungs seize in my chest, caught my attention.

"Oh, you've got to be *kidding* me."

"What?" Danny looked around. "What is it?"

"Nothing." I pulled him away from the case and turned us toward the wing's exit. "Let's head back to the main room, shall we?"

He jerked his thumb back toward the Crown Jewels. "You don't want to see the rest of the display?"

"No, I'd rather–" *Gouge my eyes out*, I wanted to say, but I didn't get a chance to.

A scream pierced the air. Not the sort of scream that came from someone being chased by a mugger, or the scream of someone's nails being pulled out, or even the scream of an unhappy infant. Any of those, all of them, would have been preferable to the scream we'd just heard.

This… *this*… was the scream of a person who'd just seen the most amazing, marvelous, fantastic thing in the entire world. This was the scream of a person who'd just noticed the shining golden apple sitting on top of the case that held the Sovereign's Orb. The orb was rather golden apple-ish itself, but it had absolutely nothing on the work of art next to it. I'd seen pictures, of course, but those were nothing in comparison to seeing the real artifact in the flesh, so to speak.

It was an apple, if apples were the most perfectly proportionate pieces of fruit in the universe. It was golden, insofar as it had a luster that shone so brilliantly it could have been lit by an internal light, an aura that somehow gleamed through the gold itself and left it looking just a little bit brighter than everything around it. It was magical, because there was no way that something looking like that couldn't be magical, and the power of that magic was practically palpable.

It was a golden apple, small enough to fit into the palm of my hand, no more, no less. It was the single most elegant thing I'd ever seen in my life, and when I looked at it, really *looked*, part of me couldn't help but want it. I could just barely make out the glint of the writing around the middle of it before the screaming woman ran into the case so hard that the apple fell onto the ground. It rolled, easily, almost as though there was a driver inside of it, some tiny being maneuvering it around the other cases and the desperate, lunging stomps of the one... two... three people who were now chasing it across the floor.

It came to a stop right at my feet, settling on its side. I stared down at it, my lips parted, my fingers twitching like crazy. *For the cleverest*, I read on the apple, and oh...

Oh dear...

CHAPTER THREE

For the cleverest.

I had never felt more worthy of anything in my life. I reached down, and–

"Look out!" Suddenly I was scooped up in a pair of strong arms and held close against a hard chest as an absolute *horde* of people fell on the apple, shrieking and scratching and shouldering each other out of the way as they all tried to be the one to grab it first. I looked around, a little dazed, and realized that Danny had grabbed me and gotten us both out of the fray in the nick of time.

"Dang." I stared at the teeming crowd, glad now that he'd pulled me out of it before I was crushed. "Where did all of these people come from?"

"I don't even know!" He sounded as flustered as I felt. "One second there were just a few of us in the whole hall, the next a crowd of people is running in from the Great Hall!"

"Someone must have snapped a picture." Ugh, social media had almost gotten me stampeded by a swarm of apple-craving jerks. "Well, hopefully someone will grab the darn thing soon and we can go back to what we were doing."

That was seeming less and less likely by the moment. As the crowd that had gathered around the apple rolled and punched their way across the floor, they managed to knock several of the display cases completely over.

Ooh, this is my chance to grab that pretty Sovereign's Scepter!

No, stop it, Felicia! I wasn't here to steal, darn it! Besides, there was no good way to run back into that mess of people without getting dragged into it, and I couldn't think of much I wanted less than to be part of a public scrum. Cats didn't *do* riots, thank you very much. Especially not riots where the security guards who were tasked to look after the Crown Jewels were practically trampling people in their hurry to be part of the group of apple-grabbing wannabes.

At the rate apple fever was spreading, I wasn't going to have the choice to stay out of it for much longer. The crowd was getting bigger and bigger, no one able to hold onto the prize for more than a few seconds before it was knocked out of their hands or snatched from their clutches by the burgeoning ranks of the over-eager apple believer.

That was it. I was calling it for the night. I turned to Danny and shouted, "Let's get out of here!"

"Good thinking!" he shouted back, and headed for the exit.

That's when the ceiling came down almost right on our heads. Literally, the freaking *ceiling*. Who had just smashed a hole through the ceiling of the Met? I didn't want to stick around to find out. "Come on!"

Between the two of us, we managed to skirt the edges of the

onrushing horde without throwing more than a few punches here and there. I could hear walls cracking behind us, more roof and an occasional hoity-toity column falling to ruin. And people were running into that fiasco. *Into* it. All for a stupid wishing apple.

You wanted it. Don't deny it.

Maybe I had, a little bit. When it had been right there at my feet, ripe for the taking. If I'd had a question ready to go, or better yet, an exit strategy that didn't involve imitating a battering ram, I might have. But I didn't regret not taking the chance… much.

"Is it the Green Goblin?" someone yelled in fear.

"Is it Doctor Octopus?" someone else sobbed.

"Is it Loki?" The man in question – he looked like an Asgardian but that didn't mean anything, half the crowd here tonight was dressed like an Asgardian – grinned as he raised a sword high into the air. "Hail, Loki! Come test your mettle against me!"

Mad. Everybody here was utterly mad, and I wasn't playing that game tonight. "I think it's time we made our graceful exit."

"I'm not sure we'll be able to," Danny said, pointing toward the main entrance. It was surprisingly empty – the security force and police were doing *something* right, at least, by not letting a whole horde of people run inside. Getting *over* to the entrance, though, would be impossible in the current press. Heroes and regular people alike were still jockeying for position. I saw Iron Man rise out of the crowd, and there went the Wasp, and… oh lord, was that Deadpool throwing himself into the air? I'd *really* rather he didn't see me, given how things went down the last time he and I tangled. "Unless you can fly?"

"I can't," I said with a frown. "You?"

"No, but maybe I can–"

"Mine!" someone with a slightly familiar voice squealed. I turned my head and saw the inimitable Jasmine doing her version of a happy dance, jumping around in her stilettos like a circus performer. And in her hand? The golden apple. "It's mine, it's mine, I – *hey!*"

No one even had to grab it from her – it simply slipped from her grasp, although with the points on those nails of hers, I wasn't sure how. A second later someone else came up with the apple, and a second after that –

"I'll take that." Iron Man swooped down from the air, grabbing the apple out of its momentary guardian's hand and leaving them cursing his name. "This is too dangerous to be left in a place where it could – *gah!*"

A bolt of bright red energy hit him in the shoulder, and the mechanical arm holding onto the apple dropped, fingers forcibly releasing and dropping the golden fruit to the ground. It managed to find space to roll again, as if there weren't a hundred pairs of feet moving around it, a hundred hands trying to grab it. It rolled until it was picked up by Nighthawk, who was immediately tackled by three different civilians.

It took a lot for a guy like Nighthawk not to lash out and start swinging, apparently more than he could handle while still holding on to the apple. "Cage!" he shouted, and threw the apple across the room to the tall Black man standing by the wall.

"What am I supposed to do with this?" Luke Cage snapped, looking at the apple like it was poison. Interesting – he really wasn't tempted by it? I wondered what the breakdown in this room was of people who could hold onto the apple without being drawn in by it, and people who would fight to the death to hold onto the thing. A hundred to one? Two hundred?

"I'm not – hey, get off me, you–" Cage was taller than most of the people in the room, which was good, because right now at least five of them were trying to climb him like a tree.

"Use it or throw it, don't just stand there gaping like a numpty!" Elsa Bloodstone yelled, and – my goodness, Bloodstone was here? This really *was* the place to be seen tonight. She never did formal events. Judging from the excited look on the face of the dark-haired, almost-identically featured woman next to her, she'd probably come because her sister had badgered her into it.

"You take it, then!" He threw it to her, but she didn't bother to actually grab hold of it, just jerked a sawed-off shotgun out from under her jacket – how had she gotten it in here past the metal detector? That was what I wanted to know – and smashed the apple like she was playing cricket, sending it sailing into the air. There it was picked up by –

The Human Torch. Of course. Johnny never could resist getting into the thick of things, and he had the whole "engulfed in superhuman flames, don't touch me if you want to live" thing going for him. Plus, he could fly. "I've got it, Sue!" he yelled triumphantly, waving the apple above his head. It looked … fine. Intact. Which was kind of weird, because it had undoubtedly been scratched, trampled, beaten, and now burned over the past five minutes. It should be in tatters, or at least mushed or dented some.

Magical. So, so magical. This looked like a job for Doctor Strange, except he wasn't here tonight.

But the Enchantress was. Greeeeeat. "Give me that, insect!" Amora howled, and all of a sudden Johnny's flame was gone. So, apparently, was his ability to fly, because a second later he was falling to the floor. Sue Storm and the Thing managed to catch him, but a second later they too were buried in the mobile pile of aggressive partygoers.

"It's mine!"

"No, it's got to be mine!"

"Give it back to meeeeeeee!" I watched Jasmine throw herself into the edge of the group and start punching way more fiercely than I'd given her abilities credit for. To the right of her, her formerly staid mother was doing the exact same thing.

This was my chance. The crowd around the edges of the room had thinned, and between the two of us, Danny and I had managed to shoulder enough people out of the way that, finally, we were on the edge of the Met's vast and empty steps. Below us, by the street, a thick line of security staff held back the teeming crowd, a mix of curious onlookers, paparazzi, and people who paid attention to social media and were desperate to try their hand at getting the apple for themselves.

"Whew." I blew a stray platinum-blonde hair out of my face. "That was a mess."

"Yeah, it – I really should go back in there and help make sure it stays under control," Danny said apologetically. "Are you going to be OK from here on out?"

I smiled at him. "What a gentleman you are. Of course I'll be OK. You go look after your friends." I was sure he wanted to check on Cage, among others.

"Thank you!" He was back into the Great Hall in a flash, leaving me by myself. I could hear dozens of clicking cell phones, see flashes from the professional cameras in the street. I needed to get out of here.

"Boris, where are you guys at?"

"Too far away to be any use," he said, sounding supremely irritated. "The streets are closed off for five blocks in each direction; people are only getting through if they're leaving the area, not going in. There's no way we're going to be able to pick you up without driving up some walls, and..."

"And you made us give back Spider-Man's car," Bruno added petulantly. "Bet you wish you hadn't now."

"Don't whine, boys, it's unbecoming." I should have let them know to head home the moment I saw the apple – chaos was sure to follow. I could walk to meet them... but honestly, in these shoes? I was light on my feet, but even a cat might turn an ankle in six-inch Balenciaga heels. I tapped my clutch against my hip thoughtfully, then remembered my little pilfering spree from not long ago.

Oh, but should I? Well, why not? I'd get the car back to him... soon. "You guys can get out of here. I'll catch a different ride. Valet!" I called out, and a young man in a black polyester tuxedo ran over to me. I handed over the ticket to him, along with a hundred-dollar bill and a dazzling smile. "Please grab my car for me."

"Yes, miss!"

"Thank you." He ran off just as fast as he'd arrived, and since I was the only one out here waiting for a car – because I was the only person at this party who wasn't a nincompoop, apparently – I expected him to be back quickly. All I had to do was–

"Hey!" A young woman at the front of the line of people

being held back by police – more of a girl, honestly, if I was going off her youthful attire – shouted toward me. "Hey, Felicia Hardy. I need to talk to you."

Oh, great. Sure she did. And I needed to talk to her... like I needed another symbiote in my head. I ignored her, and everyone else clamoring from fifty feet away.

"Hardy! I'm talking to you!"

And I'm ignoring you. I pulled my phone out of my purse and pulled up my tracking app. Boris and Bruno were heading away from the museum, taking the circuitous route back to my apartment – we went to a lot of trouble to keep people from connecting us with our home base, because I hated having to pack up and move when someone I didn't care for found out where I lived. With some people, it was a lost cause – Spider-Man was always going to be able to find my place, he knew me too well, and a piece of work like Odessa Drake had too many goons working for her for me to hope to escape her notice and stay in the city. She'd learned that messing with me meant going to war, though, so she was surprisingly circumspect – as much as someone who called herself "the queen of thieves" ever could be.

"*Hardy!* Stop pretending you can't hear me and get over here!"

I wasn't getting a call, but I put my phone to my ear anyway, just to give me an excuse to ignore this annoying child even more. Her voice was grating, and oddly familiar.

"Black Cat! I *said* I've got to *talk* to you!"

Oh, we were resorting to super identities now, were we? So petty. Where on earth was my – I mean, Danny's – car? Was I going to have to hunt it down myself?

The roar of an overdeveloped engine entered my life, and a bright green, late-model Ferrari convertible sped onto the scene, coming to a screeching halt just a few feet away from me a moment later. "Ah!" I said brightly. "Perfect. Thanks so much."

"Don't give that to her! That's not her car!"

Geez, did this kid ever shut up? I handed over another hundred as I traded places behind the wheel with the valet. "Thanks again."

"*Hey!*" It was the girl again, but this time she wasn't talking to me. "She's got the golden apple!" she shrieked. I'd never wanted to be able to silence someone with a look so badly before in my entire life.

A murmur spread through the crowd outside the museum, half curious, half considering, all completely intrigued. "Are you serious?" one of the paps asked her, putting his camera down and reaching for his keys.

"Dead serious," the girl said, and her face was… well, dead serious. What a devious little brat. "She's got the apple. Of *course* she's got the apple, Felicia Hardy is the Black Cat! The best thief in all of New York City. You think she'd let something like that within arm's length of her without grabbing it for herself?"

Rude! Not entirely incorrect, but I hadn't actually gotten my paws on it. Good thing, too – black and blue were for costumes, not skin.

"Cat!"

"Hey, Black Cat!"

Oh boy, all the paparazzi were getting in on it now.

"Felicia, is it true? Do you have the golden apple?"

"Come on over and talk to us, Miss Hardy, we'll be nice!"

"Don't make us come over there!"

I revved the engine, enjoying the power of the machine I was sitting in, the speed inherent in it, the freedom. I turned to the watching crowd and winked. "Catch me if you can." Then I sped off into the darkness, laughing as I left the chaos of the evening and all its unpleasant surprises behind.

CHAPTER FOUR

That should have been it. My big middle finger to the evening, racing off in a cloud of exhaust that only the glitter of my gemstones could penetrate… I mean, that was a quality move, a real showstopper. They should have been gaping after me, jaws dropped, eyes dazzled. They should have been left holding their hearts in their hands, unable to get over the sheer magnificence of my exit. That was the general expectation, at least.

That was *not* what happened. I had severely underestimated the allure of those freaking golden apples. It wasn't but a minute later, cruising down Park Avenue in the opposite direction of the terrible traffic for once, that I picked out the first tail. I recognized him from the museum, one of the professional photographers who'd gone there to shoot outfits that were out of this world and ended up deciding that chasing me down was a better use of his time.

"Oh, for the love of…" I picked up the pace, zooming around the cars in front of me like they were standing still and leaving the photographer, in his quaint little sedan, in my metaphorical dust. *Take that, you–* "Oh, come on!" I shouted as another car picked up where I'd left him. "This isn't what I need tonight!" I needed a shower and a slice of pizza, not a bunch of amateurs following me so they could… what, run me down and take the apple that I didn't even have off my unconscious body? Not a chance!

I swung Danny's car onto East 60th Street, where I knew I could get around people as needed, and then I really let things go. It ought to take me about forty minutes to get home – fifty if I was careful – but at the pace I was setting, I'd be there in fifteen. The Ferrari was fantastic, if not exactly low-key, and it handled like the sweet little ride it was. I knew enough about cars – the expensive ones, at least – to know that I was sitting behind the wheel of well over five million dollars right now, and that if I messed this baby up, Danny would probably have to send it back to Italy to get it repaired.

Don't you worry, sweetie, I'll take good care of you. You and me can just–

I suddenly swerved so hard I almost went off the curb. Cars, more cars, coming in off the side streets like they were being paid to do it. Only these weren't professional drivers. I'd been pursued by professionals plenty of times, and they didn't drive Honda Civics and… was that an *ice cream truck*?

"Apple!" I saw the woman driving the ice cream truck scream in my rearview mirror. "Give me the apple!"

Holy heck, these people were insane. How were they following me? Where did random citizens of New York go to look up "best way to intercept Black Cat when she's just trying to get home from a long day's work"?

"All right, fine," I muttered. This was going to be an even longer drive home than usual. "Let's see how you like this." I made a sharp turn down a side street, zooming past parked cars squished so close together it probably took a crane to get them out onto the road. Some of the cadre who'd been following me turned as well, and then the pursuit turned into a parade of clown cars, bouncing into each other and off the sides of the street as they tried to keep me in their sights.

More cars came, though. There always seemed to be more – worse yet, they were getting ahead of me now, trying to cut me off. Thank goodness that not all of these people had completely lost their sense of self-preservation, because when it came to playing chicken with a Ferrari, most of them backed down.

Not all of them were that compos mentis. There were some drivers who had either lost all of their common sense thanks to that apple, or who had never had any to begin with, and they were coming at me hard. It seemed like they didn't care if they smashed into me or not, or whether anyone got hurt, as long as it meant stopping me. These people... they merited special treatment.

I had to concentrate to use my bad luck power these days. It didn't rest just under my skin the way it had once upon a time, but I didn't mind. It was a sorry super hero who let their powers get the better of them – that was the kind of person more likely to be a villain, from what I could tell. I focused on the car careening down a one-way street – the *wrong* way, I might add – and activated my bad luck ability. Their tires almost immediately began to wobble, and a second later, just as they got close enough for me to read their plates, they swerved hard right into a dumpster.

Their license plate said *2HOT4U.* I shook my head as I drove off. With an attitude like that, it was too bad the dumpster hadn't caught fire, too.

I got another pursuing car to run over a fire hydrant, which resulted in a marvelous spray of water arcing up into the air, like someone had popped a champagne bottle in my honor. The last one who flirted with running into me dropped back, and I figured they'd looked at the odds and re-evaluated their life choices.

A second later, gunfire rang out. Out of the corner of my eye, I saw sparks on the pavement just a few feet away from me mark where the bullet had hit.

Oh, *absolutely* not. How dare they? I focused on the driver's seat, ignoring the next two bullets that flew my way, and triggered my own little bad karma bullet. A second later, the front windshield of the pursuing car blew out completely, and a moment after that it careened onto the sidewalk, finally coming to a halt against one of New York City's beautiful streetside honeylocust trees. The driver had probably gotten a squib round, a round that didn't fire from the barrel, and then followed it with another try. That meant that the bullets, the gun, and probably that gent's hand were all gone.

I tried to care and couldn't. *That's what you get for shooting at me.* Nobody else was going that far, at least, but I was still being paced by several other cars. I needed to get back to my place as soon as possible, and before I ended up running someone over due to their own stupidity.

Gradually but steadily, the cloud of my pursuers became less and less numerous. Maybe it was because it was getting dark, maybe it was because I'd headed back to more populous places where Danny's car, while fabulous, didn't stand out quite as much.

Maybe it was even because I'd slowed down to drive the speed limit. Ugh.

Whatever the reason was, I took it. I wanted to get home yesterday. I was sweaty, smoggy, and supremely irritated by the Gala tonight. I turned on my connection to the boys, then said, "I hope we got enough data from that cluster to make this worth our time, because that was *not* fun."

There was no answer. Odd. Was I transmitting? I checked and – yep, technology was still a go, my voice should have been coming through loud and clear. "Hello?" I tried again. Still nothing. "Helloooooo?" Nothing.

I was getting worried now. Boris and Bruno were professionals, and technically we were still working. They knew to respond to me under the circumstances. Had someone grabbed them? One of my crazy apple stalkers? But no, how would they even put me and the boys together, much less when we were in different cars in different parts of the city? Something didn't add up.

Was it one of my enemies, or worse yet, my frenemies? I had more than enough to go around, and sometimes the frenemies in particular liked to get salty and involve people whom they had no right to touch in their attempts to get to me. If this was Odessa's idea of a sortie, I was going to be paying a very unfriendly visit to her. And by unfriendly, I meant, "I will be stealing another Iron Man suit, flying it through your living room window, and dangling you over New York City from five thousand feet up until you tell me what you did with my crew."

But… there was something else that was odd about this. I could hear something in the background over our connection, a murmur of voices, very regular and loud. A TV show, or a radio program? I thought I recognized one of the voices. What the…

Oh, you had to be *kidding* me. That was an anchor I recognized from the nightly news. Was my crew actually watching the fallout from the Met Gala right now? I could very well imagine what the news was about – they were probably having a lot of talking heads come on to discuss that stupid apple. I hoped someone had finally used it to ask a dang question, because I didn't want a distraction like that messing up my city when it should be focusing on more important things, like failing to hide its secrets from me.

I was going to give the boys a piece of my mind about their laxity, though… as soon as I got through the traffic over Roosevelt Island, that is.

CHAPTER FIVE

By the time I got back to my penthouse apartment, I was sure that I'd shaken all the creepy stalkers who'd followed me from the Met and those who had joined in along the way. It had taken a bit more work than I'd expected, and now I was hungry as heck in addition to being gross from too many people and too much city air. This dress would never be the same, that was for sure.

I liked my building for a lot of reasons, even though it wasn't as close to the epicenter of the city as other places I'd lived. One of the reasons I liked it? It had a car elevator. Yes, every level of the place was its own apartment that had a section dedicated to a garage, and each garage connected to a huge freight elevator that could carry just about anything short of a tank all the way up to the highest floor, which was mine. I drove the Ferrari out of the elevator and into my garage, turned off the engine, and sniffed the air.

"Ugh." Smelled like this beast's engine was running a little rich. I opened a couple of windows to help air the place out, then headed into my apartment, ready to kick some butt and take some names.

I found my crew sitting on the leather couch in front of my wall-sized television, drinking Pabst – not my choice, I assure you, Bruno had probably dug that out of the fridge in his room – and splitting a bowl of popcorn as they watched replays of the pandemonium at the Met tonight. Boris, occasionally known as Dr Boris Korpse when he was bothering to put out a scientific paper, was a demolitions expert of the highest order. I could always count on him for an explosive solution to any problem, and he was almost as creative when it came to infiltrating as I was – a good trait in a professional thief. His jet-black hair might be going grey, but his mind was as sharp as ever.

Sitting next to him was Bruno Grainger, my muscle. Not that I needed help in the muscle arena, for the most part, but it wasn't all about strength. Bruno had three characteristics I loved in a henchman: he was a good fighter, he was a good driver, and he didn't talk back. Boris would talk the ear off anybody who would listen about anything that was on his mind, whether that was particle physics or the latest episode of *Lego Masters*, but Bruno was more the strong, silent, and reliable type.

Which was why it was so irritating that he hadn't bothered to answer my calls. They were just sitting there, staring at the screen, and eating, drinking, and above all laughing as they watched the chaos unfold. "Look at that – three people high!"

"It's like watching a cheerleading competition," Boris agreed. "Except they're not nearly as good at keeping the people on top in the air."

"Nope, not even close. Oh, look out for the – oooh, dang."
Bruno winced. "That had to hurt."

"They took the path of Icarus and flew too close to the
sun," Boris declared. "Only in this case, Icarus was the Human
Torch."

"Yep. Shoulda ducked."

"Indeed."

My irritation was on the verge of boiling over into shouting
territory. Are you done with your reality TV yet? Can I get
some flipping attention now?

As soon as I acknowledged my feelings, they began to
dissipate. It was an old trick the Black Fox had taught me, one of
many meant to help me overcome adversity and emotionalism
by being open about when things sucked, which helped me to
get over them just as fast.

"Time waits for no heart," he'd told me, not with his usual
light-hearted mien, but with a frown furrowing his brow. "A
ticking bomb won't stop ticking just because your feelings are
intense, or uncomfortable, or hard to see beyond. You are the
final arbiter of what you do and do not let your emotions do to
you. No matter how you master them, let me assure you that
it's of the utmost urgency that you *do* master them."

I hadn't always managed my emotions very well. I'd had a lot
of lapses over the years, especially when it came to the big ones:
love and hate. But irritation? That, I could let go. Besides, I was
tired, and that popcorn smelled pretty good.

I quietly set my clutch down on the back of the couch, then
reached over between them and grabbed the popcorn, lifting
the bowl over their heads and into my arms. I inhaled a buttery,
salty bite and sighed with satisfaction.

"Hey, wha – boss!" Bruno was on his feet immediately, his eyes going guiltily to the com lying forgotten on the side table. "Hey, so you're… back."

"So I am." I took another handful of popcorn. "I see you guys made it home OK too."

"Obviously," Boris said, but the mere fact that he didn't snap it let me know that he was feeling sheepish as well. "I see you've stolen our popcorn."

"What can I say? I spent all night denying myself tasty treats, I think the least I deserve is some popcorn." I walked around the end of the couch and plopped down next to Boris, shoving more popcorn into my mouth. Neither of them tried to take any more of it for themselves, so I duly accepted the stolen snack as their apology. I pointed at the few beers still resting in their six-pack by Bruno's feet. "Gimme one of those."

"Sure thing." Bruno grabbed one for me, cracked it open like the gentleman he was, then handed it over. I sipped. Hmm, Pabst Blue Ribbon. It was a million miles from the high-end champagne I'd been drinking not two hours ago, and honestly, it would have tasted good for that reason alone right now.

"So," I said after a moment. "Who has it now?"

Boris refocused on the screen with a scowl. "It's either Tony Stark or the Thing, or possibly Loki."

"Nobody knows, boss," Bruno said with more candor, gesturing to the screen with his own drink as he sat back down. "I don't think anybody's seen the actual apple for half an hour, but there's a lot of chatter goin' on about who *might* have it. It might be used up already, for all we know."

"Nonsense!" Boris said. "If the apple were gone, we would

definitely know. That's not the sort of information that stays quiet after the bookies get involved, and you had better believe that there's some big money riding on who has that apple and what it's eventually going to be used on."

"What would you use it on?" Bruno asked, munching on a handful of popcorn. He was staring at the TV screen with a pensive look, which was unusual for him. Not that Bruno was incapable of introspection, he was a thoughtful guy in his own way, but he didn't usually broadcast that thoughtfulness where other people could see it.

"Confirmation of my grand unifying theory," Boris said immediately. "I won't be one of those scientists who begs extra-terrestrial intelligences for their equations like dogs begging for scraps. Who could trust them, anyway? I'd far rather have confirmation of my *own* investigations."

I frowned at him. "Hang on, so you'd ask a magical apple from we-don't-know-where to give you *its* version of a grand unifying theory, but you wouldn't trust any information you got from an alien? That doesn't make sense."

"I didn't say *a* grand unifying theory," Boris corrected me with his nose in the air. "I said *my* grand unifying theory. It's not solely astrophysics based. There's a lot more inclusion of materials science, and chemical volatility and–"

Bruno laughed. "More explosions, you mean! That's so you, Doc."

Boris scowled. "Well, what would *you* use your question for, if *you* got the apple?"

"I dunno." Bruno stared at his beer. "Not on cash, that's for sure. I've got more than I can spend already, and who've I got to spend it on other than me? Don't get me wrong, I love havin' money to burn, but…" He shrugged. "It's not everything, you know? Maybe I'd ask where my brother ended up. I lost track of him when I was locked up, and after I got out, I couldn't find him again."

Boris looked utterly aghast. "Are you telling me you would waste a question that could potentially unlock entire universes to you on something as trite as the location of a *family member?* Thank god the odds of me witnessing this incalculable mistake are zero, because it might just be enough to give me a heart attack."

"Rude," I chided him. "Not everybody cares about the secrets of the universe, you know. It's all right to have different priorities." Neither of their questions really appealed to *me*, not even Bruno's; I had all the family I needed. But I could respect that they were being true to themselves.

Boris sneered at me. "I suppose you'd ask how to get away with the greatest heist of all time."

"Oh, honey, no." I smiled disparagingly at him. "I don't need a magic apple's help with that. I'm perfectly capable of getting away with epic heists all by myself."

"Then what would you use it on?" Bruno asked.

"Nothing. I wouldn't use it at all." Having gotten close to it, having felt the apple's allure, I was now more convinced than ever that the best place for me to stay when it came to New York's latest must-have accessory was far, far away from it. Magic had *never* done me any favors. "I've got way better things to do with my time than get involved in a mess like what happened tonight over a piece of magical fruit.

"Think about it," I said, warming to my topic now. "The second you pick that thing up, you become a target. If you don't know exactly what you want to use it on in the very first second you hold it, you're screwed.

"And even if you *do* know what you want to use it for, one slip-up could ruin it all. Imagine if you asked for a huge load of cash, but you stuttered and it came out *mash* instead, and the next thing you knew you had directions on where to get the biggest load of mashed potatoes on the east coast. That's the sort of thing that elevates a person to internet meme status, boys, and I'm way too pretty to be a meme."

"I see." Boris nodded. "You're scared of it."

I made a *pfft* sound. "Not even remotely."

"So scared that you can't bring yourself to consider the thinnest of hypotheticals in connection with it," he went on, ignoring my scathing look. "So scared that even Mr Grainger, whom we all know is hardly a paragon of imagination, can do a better job coming up with a purely theoretical question for this scenario, while you hide behind transparent complaints that are nothing but a wall put up around your true fears."

I rolled my eyes at Boris's amateur psychoanalysis. He sounded like every counselor I'd ever had to meet with in juvie. "What fears?"

"That you don't know what you want. Or that you're so scared of what you *might* want, you can't bring yourself to contemplate it and risk exposing your id's sordid underbelly to your higher consciousness."

"Watch whose sordid underbelly you're talking about, mister," I warned him. "I've been tempted before. Yggdrasil, anyone? I know how it feels to be offered everything I could ever ask for, and I didn't care for it then. What makes you think I'd care for it now?"

Boris looked at me intently. "I assumed, incorrectly perhaps, that you'd grown some since then. Learned yourself a little better. Accepted your own psyche." He sniffed. "I suppose I gave you too much credit."

"Eh, knock off the head-shrinking," Bruno said. "The boss is complicated, not like you or me."

Boris huffed in affront. "Excuse you? I'm very complicated, I'll have you know!"

"Oh yeah? Then why are all your shelves filled with chemistry books?"

"Because chemistry is *interesting*, you dolt!"

Bruno shrugged. "Or 'cause you only have one interest. One. Blowing stuff up. You're smart, but you ain't complicated, Doc."

"What insolence!"

"Boys, boys." As much as I loved the banter – and I could sling it myself as well as anyone – I was tired, and the bickering was only making it worse. "Bruno, thanks for thinking the best of me. Boris, thanks for thinking the worst. I don't know what I would do without my shoulder gremlins." I pinched Boris on the cheek before he could pull away, then patted Bruno's hand and gave him the rest of my beer. "But right now, I think I need to clean up and get some rest. Remember to review the footage I got from the Gala – for *jewelry*, not for who might have the apple," I clarified, as newly avid eyes suddenly turned to me.

"Is tomorrow soon enough?" Bruno asked, looking a little sheepish. He held up his can. "Because I've actually had three of these and Boris just had one but you know he's got the worst alcohol tolerance in the world, and–"

"Lies!" Boris shouted, cheeks darkening further as he

flushed. "I just – I'm very *particular* with what I choose to drink, is that such a crime?"

"And you *chose* to drink this? I seriously question your taste." I shook my head and stood up. "Whatever. Tomorrow is fine, it's not like most of those people will even be in a position to take their finery off until tomorrow at this rate." The news program showed a scene at the Met that was absolutely swarming with police and FBI, all the partygoers being rounded up and questioned. At least, all of the partygoers who hadn't gotten out of there early, like me.

"Thanks, boss."

"Don't break the camera."

I rolled my eyes and headed for my room. My apartment had the sort of open floorplan I usually loathed – what was the point in stealing some of the finest art in the world if you had no walls to hang it on? But I'd learned over the years that clear sightlines were more important than ostentatious displays of wealth, and no matter where I lived, I never let myself get too comfortable. How would I feel if my Degas or Yoshimoto Nara was destroyed by some careless ninja or flame-wielding buffoon?

I stepped into my room, which sat behind one of only five doors in the entire apartment, and sighed with relief. Finally, I could let down my hair a little bit – literally too, in my case, but also… Felicia Hardy or Black Cat, I was almost always putting on a show for *someone*. Boris and Bruno knew me better than most people, but I still didn't let them in all the way. How could I? You never knew who would betray you, and the closer you let people get, the worse that betrayal felt when it inevitably came.

I resolutely did *not* think of my former mentor as I took the diamond-studded hairpins out of my coiffure and set them down on my dresser. The comb that was holding the whole updo together came next, and my hair fell down around my face like a platinum curtain, hiding me from the outside world. I could barely see my own reflection in the mirror in front of me, which...

No. I had nothing to hide, not from myself. I pushed my hair back behind my ears and looked straight at the woman in the mirror. She was beautiful, coiffed and elegant, with power and grace in every line of her body. She was strong, a person in control of her own destiny, not under the thumb of anything or anyone. Not a villain, not a piece of a magic tree or a golden apple, not a bad memory from college, not even the caring but confining embrace of a lover. She relied on no one but herself in the end, and she was enough for that.

I was enough for that.

I stuck my tongue out at my reflection to break the moment, then undid the rest of the jewelry, careful to make sure it wasn't still recording before I started getting undressed. The dress took some shimmying to get out of, but I wasn't about to be defeated by silk and taffeta after the night I'd had. I drew a bath, bombed it with something that made the entire bathroom smell like an orchard of orange trees, then settled in with a bottle of ice-cold water from the mini-fridge and tried to relax.

Tried being the operative word. Usually, my post-job cooldown routine involved something tangible, something I could look at and revel in and hold in my hand. A night like tonight, no matter how exciting and unexpected, left me feeling dissatisfied. Information gathering was important, but it was far from my favorite part of the job. Plus, I just couldn't stop thinking about that stupid apple.

For the cleverest. What a ruse. What a silly thing to be able to seduce people into its web with… and yet, it had worked. I'd nearly gone for the thing, and it might have been the words or it might have been the glitter, or it might even have been something truly magical, like the apple having some sort of alluring aura that I'd gotten caught up in. What*ever* it was, I didn't like it, and I didn't like the idea of it rolling around the city somewhere, getting people who didn't know better into mischief. Or worse – getting someone who *did* know better into mischief.

Just because the people who'd gotten their hands on apples so far had disposed of them in dramatic and careless fashion didn't mean that everyone who grabbed one would. A person who was actually clever, for example, could get the kind of question answered that might rock the foundations of civilization – and I wasn't talking about Boris's explosive theories, either.

What if they knew the identity of every super hero in the world? Or every remaining mutant? It wasn't like *that* kind of thing had ever led to pain and chaos before. There were too many terrible examples to choose from, and yet there would always be someone out there who thought to themselves, "But this time it'll be different, because I'm in charge, and I'm better than those other people." And yet, they never were.

Heck, take it down a notch from there and imagine a disreputable CEO having some way of knowing in advance before an employee got sick and letting them go before they cost their company too much in healthcare costs. I knew better than to think that there weren't plenty of jerks out there who would love to take advantage of that kind of knowledge – thanks for the tender loving corporate care, US of A. Technically I "employed" my mother, just so I had a good way to pay for her insurance along with the rest of my crew. Mom's plan came with all the bells and whistles, and it cost me a fortune, but it was better than me worrying about her dying of the flu because she didn't want to deplete her savings on a visit to the ER.

Perks, baby. That was one of the many differences between me and someone like Odessa Drake. She believed in "Render unto Caesar," while I was more of a "Get in, loser, we're going shopping" kind of person.

I shifted uneasily in the water, unable to relax despite the calming atmosphere. It didn't take long for me to give up my good idea as a bad job and get out. I dried off and got into a camisole and pair of sleep pants, brushed my teeth, did my skin routine – because I was fantastic in a lot of ways, but that didn't translate to having a perfect T-zone – and headed for bed. Sleep would do me some good right now. When I woke up in the morning, I'd be able to go on with my life without thinking about that stupid apple or the stupid people who might be getting their hands on it even now.

My thousand-thread count sheets and goose down duvet failed me though. No matter what I tried, whether it was counting sheep or conjugating verbs in Mandarin – which was more like establishing timeframes in Mandarin, since there were no verb tenses – I couldn't get to sleep. I'd moved past the apple and into the realm of everything that might *potentially* bother me, not just the things that definitely did.

Would Danny be upset that I'd driven off in his car with his bling in my purse? Probably not, but I should get it all back to him as soon as possible anyway, or at least text him an apology. Had my mom seen any of the rigmarole at the Met tonight? Had she seen any footage of me? Was she worried? Mom kept things close to her chest, a holdover from when she was accustomed to not asking Dad where he'd been or how he was paying for her new car, our new house, my prep school. I should let her know I was OK, just in case.

Ugh. Caring about what other people thought was such a pain in the butt sometimes.

By 3AM, I knew there was no hope of sleep for me tonight. I got up, grabbed the Empire State University hoodie I'd permanently borrowed from Peter and slid it on, then walked out into the living area. Boris and Bruno had both gone to bed, it seemed, but the computer was still there on the side table, complete with the recording I'd made of tonight's events. I'd get an early start on reviewing the footage, see if I could pick out the best marks.

I settled onto the couch, belatedly pulling a few crushed pieces of popcorn out from under my rear as I sat back. "You two will be cleaning this mess up in the morning," I muttered in the direction of my snoozing crew. This was *not* some frat boy bachelor pad where the dishes were only done once they started spilling out of the sink and onto the floor. We were *adults*, for god's sake. We could do better than that.

Cleanliness might be next to godliness, but it's also a hallmark of personal care. Always take care in everything you do, in every aspect of your life. A cluttered home leads to a cluttered mind, Black Fox had intoned more than once in some of his more esoteric moments. Personally, I just thought he was anal-retentive, but I'd gotten used to picking up after myself while I was training with him, and I wasn't about to stop.

Footage. Get on to looking at the footage already. Staring at a blank screen and fishing in couch cushions for stale popcorn wasn't doing me or my insomnia any favors. I opened up the recording and settled in to do some professional evaluation. Although, geez, we should find somewhere else to hide the camera next time, because the number of people who were looking at my chest like they wanted to have an intimate, one-on-one conversation with it was as repetitive as it was annoying. Not unexpected – my dress was a lowcut showstopper, after all – but still annoying.

I used a custom program to help me pick out the nicest pieces in each frame, getting as much information as I could on the various angles I'd captured at the Gala before I'd moved on to someone else, and evaluating them with my computerized loupe. Gosh, there were a lot of nice pieces in the mix. Nothing that made my heart skip a beat yet, but plenty of things that I wouldn't mind throwing onto my bed and rolling around on for a while. Gemstones of all cuts and clarities, antique settings worth a fortune in their own right, heirloom jewels and priceless artifacts... and then I was looking at the Crown Jewels, and a moment after that...

The camera had only managed to capture the very top of the apple as it rolled to a stop at my feet. I could still make out the top of the lettering, though, could still see the gleam and glisten of that enchanted fruit as clearly as if I was there again. My heart picked up the pace and my mouth went dry. It really was so, so beautiful. Exquisite, in fact. Its perfection made me dislike it even more. *How dare you be so pretty and so dangerous all at once? That's* my *schtick, I'll have you know.*

A second later it was gone, buried under a pile of bodies as Danny pulled us out of the fray. The sheer desperation on display left a bad taste in my mouth. People thought if they could just get their wish, if they could just have the one thing they thought they wanted more than anything else, that their lives would be perfect. But nothing was consequence-free, and even though the apples hadn't been popping up for long, any good that came from them was almost immediately overshadowed by how much worse off they left every person who used them.

Or… did they?

Huh. I knew about three apples that had come into existence before the one that showed up here tonight, but maybe we only knew about them *because* they'd been used so recklessly by the people who grabbed them. Was it possible that there was an apple out there, or two, or more, that had been found by someone and actually made their life better? If so, why hadn't the world heard about it?

Then again, who wants the world poking its nose into their private business?

CHAPTER SIX

Before I could go down that rabbit hole any further, the computer automatically switched over to the home screen for the alarm system. A proximity alert was sounding in the garage. Right, *shoot*, I'd left the windows open in there. Ugh.

I shut the alert down before it could wake anyone else up, then pulled up the camera feed for the garage. I was treated to the equivalent of surround sound in visual, the program already honing in on the only thing moving in the entire place – a person sitting in the front seat of Danny's car, doing something with their hands. But what?

I zoomed the camera feed in for a closer look. Were they trying to hijack… no, wrong motions, and besides that it just didn't make sense. They might have gotten in thanks to my carelessness, but there was no way they could get a car out of here without setting off some serious countermeasures. So what the heck were they doing? It looked almost like… whittling, maybe.

What. The. Heck. If I had a Spidey sense, it would be tingling up a storm right now.

I needed to figure out who this was before I went barging in there. *Always prepare for the unexpected,* Black Fox had told me more than once. I used to argue that that was stupid advice. "How do you prepare for the unexpected if you're not expecting it?" I'd demanded in a *duh* tone of voice as we went over some safe-cracking techniques.

"By anticipating everything that *might* happen and planning accordingly," he'd responded so evenly that I knew he was disappointed in my response. "There are old thieves and there are bold thieves, but there are no old, bold thieves."

"I don't know, you're still around," I'd quipped. That had gotten me a smile – right before he sent me back to figure out yet *another* way to break through a Monument vault door.

OK, so I needed more information. Whoever it was, they weren't trying to get into the rest of the apartment, and they weren't keying the cars or anything, they were just… sitting there, whittling. So, first things first – get a better look at this person, then put a name to a face. I was glad now that I'd caved when Boris had asked for what I'd thought at the time was an over-the-top, ten-camera system for the garage. "It's the most vulnerable room on the entire floor!" he'd insisted, and it looked like he was right. Not that I'd be telling him that.

Right corner… nope, still too shadowed. Left center… better, but I still couldn't quite make out the person's face. Maybe if they–

The person suddenly sneezed, bringing one hand to their face before shaking their head out. I didn't even need to zoom in to figure out who they were after that. It was the kid, the same kid from the Gala, the same kid who, I could now confirm at this closer distance, had been harassing me all freaking week.

It had started on Monday, with the girl approaching while I was casing the cases at Tiffany and Co's and grabbing my sleeve. "Hey, you–" was all she had time to say before security was escorting her out. At the time I didn't think much of it; she was dressed like a ragamuffin, carried a suspiciously big backpack, and clearly wasn't interested in buying, so it wasn't surprising management didn't want her inside their flagship store.

The next time I saw her was during lunch at a fabulous Middle Eastern restaurant called Nur on Wednesday, when my date had been vocally interrupted by this brat stomping up to the hostess's desk and yelling across the cozy little brasserie, "Hey, Black Cat! I've gotta talk to you! *Black Cat!*"

My date had blinked at the girl, then at me. "Is she… talking to you?"

"No," I'd said unconvincingly, as the girl continued to shout. "Definitely not."

"Ah. Um." My date set down her napkin and pushed back her chair. "If you'll excuse me, I don't… think this is going to work out." She'd left before I could start to apologize – for something that wasn't even my fault, too!

Then there was what had happened just this past evening, with the kid not only stalking me outside the Met Gala, but siccing the paparazzi on me as well. I didn't appreciate being played for a fool, and my first impulse was to wake Bruno up and send him in there to take care of things. No calling the cops – I certainly wasn't about to let *them* know where I lived. But…

She had found me. That was the weirdest thing of all – she *kept* finding me. How? I thought I did a very good job of keeping my home base from the public eye. So how was a kid who didn't even look old enough to drive – not that that mattered, since this was New York City – follow me here? What was her deal?

If I kicked her out without bothering to talk to her, I'd never find out. And if I riled her up *before* I talked to her, she might clam up anyway. I might have a pretty hardline stance toward people who disturbed the sanctity of my home, but I wasn't about to rough up a kid.

Well, then. Guess I better go talk to her. I looked down at my outfit and decided that casual was fine. Even without my costume on, I still had my bad luck power at the ready. If the girl had a weapon or tried to attack me some other way, I'd just trip her up with that. I walked over to the garage door and slipped my feet into the pair of flip-flops I kept there for when my suit's shoes got mucked up while I was out. Then I stepped into the coolness of the garage, flipping on the light switch as I went.

The girl's head shot up, and she looked straight at me with wide brown eyes. I expected an apology, maybe, or at the very least an explanation as I leaned against the doorframe, crossing my arms. What I got was–

"It's about time you showed up. I thought I was going to have to set something on fire before you bothered to get out of bed."

Wasn't *someone* in a cheeky mood tonight? "How did you get in here?" I asked, pretty sure I already knew the answer but wanting to verify.

"Climbed up, climbed in." She pointed at the closest window, which… huh? She'd closed it. "For someone who values her privacy as much as you're supposed to, you sure made it easy to get in here."

"Not so easy," I purred, sauntering over. "After all, you did have to *climb* up here." I nodded at her pack. "I take it your harness is in the bag?"

"Nope." The girl's lower jaw jutted forward as she aggressively met my gaze. "I free climbed it."

"Did you really." If she had, that was just stupid. We were ten floors up, and the building might be made of brick but it wasn't like that provided decent handholds. She hadn't used the fire escape – that had an alarm on it set to go off under the weight of a person, so the whole building would wake up and know there was an emergency if it was in use.

Ten floors, freehand, wearing that enormous pack? "Are you enhanced?"

"Nope."

"Are you lying?"

"Nope."

"Hmm." I had to give it to her, at least her story was consistent. Whether it was true was another thing entirely. "What are you doing in my car?"

"It's not your car," she said, then paused. "You don't want to know my name?"

Ah, teenagers. So predictably self-centered. "I'd much rather know whatever it is you're sprinkling around in there. Why don't you tell me?" *Before I take finding out into my own hands.*

"It's magnesium," she said easily, "from a camping match. Did you know that magnesium is one of the key ingredients in thermite?"

"I do know that, actually." It was impossible not to know something like that while sharing space with a person as obsessed with burning and/or blowing things up as Boris. "Why are you spreading magnesium shavings around my car?"

"It's *not* your *car*," the girl said irritably. She pushed herself up out of the seat and onto the trunk – leaving little black skid marks on the paint from her enormous Doc Marten-esque boots, I might add – and then…

She flicked on a lighter. "Do you know how hot magnesium burns?" she asked. There was no waver in her voice, no fear, no doubt in her actions. Her eyes were fixed on mine, her jaw still set at a pugnacious angle. "Would you like to find out?"

Look who thought she was the cat's pajamas. "Are you actually threatening me?" I asked, just to be perfectly clear.

"More like I'm threatening the car, but… yeah. I am." She waved the little flame back and forth. "So, what's it gonna be, Black Cat? Are you going to listen to me *now*?"

Oh my god. I'm being menaced by a teenage hooligan in my own garage.

The image was too good – I just couldn't help myself. I started laughing. I couldn't even focus on the girl, I was laughing so hard, finally bending over to put my hands on my knees as I giggled at the absurdity of it all.

"Hey! I'm being serious!"

"I know," I gasped, "I know. I, um, I take you *very* seriously, too, but…" Nope, I couldn't manage a complete sentence yet. I leaned back against the door, thankfully closed so my guys couldn't hear my bout of hysteria, and laughed and laughed. Holy crap. The only thing that could've made this better was her threatening *me* with bodily harm, not just the car.

"Stop laughing at me!" the girl yelled, actually stamping her foot on Danny's trunk. "I'll do it! You think I won't?"

I finally managed to get a semblance of control over myself. "I think you won't if you really want me to talk to you," I said, breathless and smiling, and also deadly serious myself. "Just know, if you set that car on fire, I'll hand you over to the cops personally, right after I make you apologize to Mr Rand. But you've proven your sincerity to me, so bravo." I gave her a sarcastic slow clap. "Way to go, champ. Now, how about you hop down from there and tell me how you found me in the first place, for starters."

The girl stared at me for a long moment in complete silence, then flicked out the flame and shoved the lighter in one of her pockets. She jumped from Danny's car to the concrete floor and pulled out her phone. "It's not like it was all that *hard* to find you. There are networks on social media dedicated to tracking super heroes, and with all the interest in you after the Gala? It was pretty easy to map out your route and the likeliest places you'd be just looking at other people's posts." She shrugged. "I basically followed you from Twitter to TikTok."

Oh, dang. She had me there. It wasn't that I didn't know there were plenty of people out there tracking the appearance of heroes and villains alike, I just hadn't realized it was so advanced. It was a wonder anyone could keep an identity secret these days, unless they lived in the sewers. "That makes unfortunate sense." I'd have to do better at flying under the radar.

"*Yeah* it does," she said, with a sneer. "Now, are you gonna listen to me?"

Boy, she was just dying for me to ask her about herself. I figured it was time to throw her a line, too, or she might lose it and do something we'd both regret. I really didn't want to interact with any cops today, or ever, and I certainly didn't want to be responsible for handing over a kid who looked like she wasn't even old enough to drive. "Sure, I'll listen to you. What do you want to say?"

She blinked and looked away, then glanced at me sidelong. "It's kind of cold in here," she said in a little girl voice, theatrically rubbing her arms. "Could we go inside? I promise I won't do anything."

Oh, ha. There was no way I was letting her step foot into my inner sanctum. "You get bonus points for trying to play up the poor little girl act to me, but–" I made a buzzer noise. "Not gonna work. Start talking or get ready to get hogtied."

Her hands dropped back to her sides, and her wobbly mouth firmed into a frown. "God, you're mean."

"Yep. Now get on with it."

"Geez, fine." She squared her shoulders and took a deep breath. "My name is Casey Beck, and I need your help to find my father, Dalton Beck."

Dalton Beck... why did that name sound so familiar? I was sure I'd heard it recently, but I couldn't quite place it. Beck, Beck... wait a second... "Are you talking about Firestrike?"

Firestrike had been a member of Joe Manfredi's brief-lived criminal super group Heavy Mettle. He'd worked as one of Manfredi's enforcers, and his background as a firefighter had set him up perfectly to act as an arsonist. In the end, though, *he'd* been the one to turn state's evidence on Joe Manfredi and, ultimately, get him sent to prison.

So what the heck was his daughter doing here all by herself? "Hasn't your father been in witness protection for the past two decades?"

The kid, Casey, nodded tightly. "He was – we were – but he

was brought back to New York to give testimony against Joe Manfredi in his new trial, and now he's gone missing!"

Missing? "Wait a second, shouldn't he be in FBI custody?" Witness protection was a big deal, if I remembered correctly. "How could he just go missing?"

Casey threw her hands up. "I don't know, and the FBI won't tell me anything! They're a bunch of..." She paused and wrapped her arms around herself again, only this time I saw it for the self-soothing movement that it was, instead of a carefully modulated play for sympathy. "I don't know what happened," she said. Her hands tightened around her biceps. "But he's all I have, and I need to find him." She looked me straight in the eyes. "And as of last Wednesday, you're the last person he laid eyes on."

Oh. Oh, dang. All right, that was pretty heavy. If this was a ploy, which it could be since I had no memory of seeing her father anytime last week, then it was working. She couldn't have designed a better backstory to get on my soft side – a criminal father, a daughter who wanted to reunite with him, either not wanting to involve the mom or not *having* a mom to involve... it was like listening to my own biography. "All right, come on," I said, then turned and opened the door into my living space.

Casey's eyes widened, and her hunched shoulders dropped as the surprise from my offer shook her. "Are you serious?"

"Don't I look serious?"

She didn't move. "Is this, like, some sort of reverse-psychology thing?"

Great, so now she didn't trust *me*. "We can keep talking out here if you really want to, but it *is* kind of cold, and there's hot chocolate inside."

Her tongue darted out to lick her lips. "Can I have coffee instead?"

"Do you want to stunt your growth?"

She rolled her eyes. "Oh my god, you sound like my dad." As soon as her brain caught up with her mouth, the hunch came back to her shoulders. She picked up her backpack, slung it over her shoulder, and walked right past me into my apartment. I shut off the light and followed her, silently sending up a prayer to whoever might be listening that they would give me the patience to deal with a teenager, before sunrise, on no sleep.

I closed the door to the garage, then walked past Casey, who was standing stock-still a few feet inside the apartment, and motioned her over to the kitchen table. "Sit." I pointed at an open chair, then headed for the coffee machine. Boris had picked it out, which meant it had more bells and whistles than an Iron Man suit, but I'd mastered it enough to make a basic espresso and its close cousins. I fixed a drink for myself first – extra dry cappuccino with enough sugar to make my teeth hurt – and pounded it before moving on to make one for Casey.

I went deliberately slowly, watching her out of the corner of my eye as I tamped down the grounds and got the espresso brewing, then grabbed the chocolate powder. She was trying to be surreptitious as she stared around my place, but I could see the question in her face. "I don't keep any of it here," I told her.

She looked at me, perfectly innocent. "Any of what?"

"Any of the things that I might *allegedly* steal. I don't keep them here."

"Why not?"

Not the question I was expecting from such a seemingly savvy kid. "It invites trouble. If you have something that other people want, especially if you flaunt it, then sooner or later you're inviting some uncomfortable interest. Not that I always mind a little trouble," especially not if it meant getting a "stern talking-to" from my favorite wall-crawler, "but I don't want to have to be on guard in my own home all the time." My brief stint as a crime boss had cured me of the desire to constantly put on a show of wealth for people who simply didn't deserve my attention.

"But you're on guard anyway, right?" Casey glanced over at my computer, looked up at the cameras in the corners. "That's how you found me. Something alerted you."

I nodded. "True. But that's different."

"How is it different?"

"It's the difference between a crime of opportunity versus a crime that's premeditated."

Casey scowled, brushing wispy, asymmetrically cut brown bangs out of her face. "Are you kidding me? I totally planned this whole thing!"

Oh, you sweet little optimist. "You've been following me around, that's true," I agreed. "And you got the paparazzi outside the Met Gala to chase me so you could track me down, that's also true, and that was very clever." I believed in giving props where props were due. "But would you have gotten in so easily if I hadn't left the windows open? No. Would you even have tried to get in if you hadn't seen those open windows, or would you have stayed on the ground and waited for me to come out?"

I looked at her and raised one eyebrow as I stirred the chocolate powder into her drink. "Judging from your earlier actions, you would have hung out in front of the building until

I showed up, not climbed ten stories to take a chance on getting in through a window that might be locked, barred, or electrified."

She shrugged. "Maybe I wanted to impress you."

She *had*, honestly, but I didn't want to let her know that yet. The last thing this kid needed was more reason to fixate on me. "Whatever your intent was, what you *did* was see a chance and take it, not make your own way in. So yes, I like to have my guard up against people who take the rare opportunities I create and exploit them, but I'm also not inviting people to try and steal from me by leaving all of my beautiful things out where anybody could see them."

"Because you're afraid?" she said, her jaw once again jutting out pugnaciously. She barely had enough jaw to pull it off, and the effect was kind of like watching a bulldog puppy bark at a butterfly.

I rolled my eyes and deposited her drink in front of her with a *clunk*. "My business is my business, my space is my space, and I'd rather not waste my time handling hasslers when I could be planning my next job." I sat across from her and crossed my legs. "Now, down to business. You said that I was the last person who saw your father. How do you know that?"

"I can't tell you."

"Then why should I bother to listen to you at all?" I asked, resisting the urge to start shouting at her. "How am I supposed to know you're not just some weird, thrill-seeking kid wasting my time with a made-up sob story about a guy who may or may not be your dad–"

"He *is* my dad!" She jerked her phone out of the center pocket of her hoodie, unlocked it, and turned the screen around to face me. "Look at us!"

I leaned over to look at her phone, not touching it – you never could be too careful when it came to handling other people's technology. The screensaver was a picture of her, in a Metallica T-shirt that was way too big for her, beaming at the camera as she squeezed the waist of the man next to her. He was on the taller side, with broad shoulders and a barrel chest that was starting to sag a little in his middle age. His hair was light brown, with the same shaggy texture as hers, and his broad hands and forearms were scarred with burns here and there. He was smiling, but despite that, I *did* recognize him.

Huh. Firestrike had gone and had a kid with someone. "Where's your mother?"

"She died last year." Casey looked down into her drink. "Colon cancer. Dad almost had to declare bankruptcy after she died because he was so sad, he couldn't go to work for a while and they fired him."

"What was your dad's job?"

"He was a claims investigator for an insurance company."

In the arson department, no doubt. A funny place for a former arsonist to end up, but then again – who better to catch a thief than another thief? I imagined it was the same for all sorts of crimes.

"He was getting better, though," Casey said, looking up at me again. Her hazel eyes glittered with determination. "We were going to therapy together, and he had two job interviews lined up. He even started cooking Mom's recipes again. We were going to be *fine*, and then the stupid attorney general called the stupid marshals and the next thing I knew, he told me he had to come here to testify at the trial. Then he left, and at first he called every night, but then five days ago… no call."

She scowled and took a gulp of her drink. "And when I called the marshals, they told me not to *worry* about it! That even if my dad didn't come back, I'd still be taken care of! Like they were already writing my dad off! Which is *bull*, and I told them that, and then a few days ago they told me they were going to put me into temporary foster care."

"So you decided to come to New York?" I prompted, after a moment of silence. The expression on Casey's face was… complicated, something I didn't know how to interpret even with all my people skills. The only emotion I could clearly make out was regret, but why?

"Yeah," Casey said, after a moment. She took her phone back and swiped along for a bit, then turned the screen toward me again. "This is the receipt for my bus ticket."

I inspected it for a moment. It looked genuine. "You still haven't explained how you know I'm the last person he saw before he disappeared."

She shook her head. "I can't tell you that yet. But I promise I *will* tell you once we get my dad back. So." She held out a hand toward me. "Do we have a deal?"

Honestly, if this was a con, it was complicated enough that I should be taking notes. And if it was real? Clearly Casey wasn't comfortable telling me how she knew what she knew about me yet – if she really knew anything at all and wasn't just making that part of the story up in order to get my help – but if she was just interested in getting help, she could have gone to the cops. Heck, with her social media expertise, she could have tracked down a bona fide super hero and persuaded them to help her find her dad. There was a reason she thought I was the person for the job, and I was *definitely* curious about that.

"I want honesty from you." Casey frowned and started to put her hand down. "Not about how you know I saw your dad last. You already explained that you're not going to tell me about that yet, and I appreciate you being upfront with it. But if we're going to work together, I need to trust that you're not keeping more things from me. Are the US Marshals looking for you?"

"Probably," she said reluctantly. "I dumped my old phone before I left Ohio, but I'm sure they know I was heading here."

"More honesty, kudos to you," I congratulated her. "I don't have time in my busy schedule to handle heat from the marshals on top of everything else, so if you're going to temporarily join my crew, we'll have to make sure you go out in disguise."

This perked her up immediately. "Join your crew? Really?"

"*Temporarily*," I emphasized. "Long enough to look into this thing with your dad. I don't take apprentices, especially not ones who aren't old enough to legally drink or drive."

"I can legally drive!"

I stared at her in silence.

"I mean … I have my learner's permit."

Uh-huh. "Well, you won't be practicing your skills here," I told her.

"Got it." Casey nodded hard. "So, what kinda skills *will* I be practicing?"

Felicia, stop and get a hold of yourself! My rational mind was catching up with my emotional one, and it wasn't happy. Are you seriously considering going on a wild goose chase all on the say-so of a teenage runaway who broke into your home? Really? What happened to all those magnificent heists you've got in the works? What about all the beautiful jewelry you planned to steal after the Met Gala? What are you doing?

I was doing exactly what any good thief should do when the world seemed out to get her. It made sense to lay low after the disastrous Gala, whether the apple got used up fast or not, and if I could hone my information-gathering skills at the same time, so much the better. And I really did want to know how Casey Beck knew what she claimed to know.

Plus, I might, *miiiight*, just a little tiny bit, feel sorry for the kid. A scosh, a smidge, a soupçon of sorriness.

I grinned at her and lifted my mug in a mock toast. "Buckle up, buttercup. You're in for a crash course on how to be a successful thief."

CHAPTER SEVEN

The first hurdle in my hastily declared plan came from the boys. Neither Bruno nor Boris was pleased to stumble out of bed into the living room and see an unfamiliar person sitting on the couch, laptop open as she trawled back into the digitally recorded past to find out what I was doing five days ago. I could have told her, but learning to work for her keep was Lesson Number One, as far as I was concerned.

"What the–"

"Who in the–" Both of them were going for their weapons, but when Casey looked over, she seemed supremely unconcerned.

"As if," she sneered, before turning back to her computer. My crew looked at me with identical "WTF" stares.

"Boys, boys." I gestured to the breakfast spread I'd laid out on the kitchen table in offering. "Come have some caffeine and something to eat, and I'll explain."

"It had better be a stellar explanation," Boris groused as he sat down, mini-grenade he'd jerked out of his pocket still in hand. What he'd been planning to do with *that*, I didn't know – mini or not, a grenade would still eat up my Corinthian leather couch, and I wasn't OK with that sort of collateral damage coming from the people I lived with.

Bruno, on the other hand, holstered his gun with a yawn and sat down without another word of complaint. "Did somebody send her to you?" he asked, after gulping down his first cup of tea, a special matcha blend he preferred and went out of the way to special order from Japan.

"No, but good thought," I said. "Actually, she's brought something of a little puzzle my way." I told them about her father's disappearance and the probable connection to the Manfredi case. By the time I was done, Bruno looked determined, while Boris looked practically demented.

"You don't want to get tangled up with Silvermane and his ilk right now!" he hissed, spearing a sausage with his knife for emphasis. "The Maggia is buzzing with rumors and insinuations, and a lot of their buried conflicts are going to come bubbling to the surface soon, along with a lot of bodies."

"Getting tangled up with the Maggia isn't a foregone conclusion," I said.

"Are you *joking*, woman? The star witness in one of the biggest cases against the Manfredi family, in history, has been abducted, and you think that somehow you can escape an actual confrontation with them when you go looking for said witness?"

"First off." I pointed a finger at him. "Don't call me 'woman' as if it's my name *or* an insult, because I'm not here for that kind of disrespect." I waited for him to nod before continuing. "Second, sure, the Manfredis are probably involved in this, but that doesn't mean they're doing their own dirty work. Silvermane might be mostly metal at this point, but he still thinks like an old man. He doesn't want to have to go out of his way to get things done, which means hiring contractors. And anybody who contracts with the Maggia to do their dirty work is fair game for messing with, as far as I'm concerned."

"But where's the profit, boss?" Bruno asked, after swallowing a mouthful of bagel. "You never do a job without a profit."

I shrugged. "Maybe the FBI will pay a reward to get him back."

"Ha–"

"Or maybe I'll get to steal more from a potential kidnapper than just Dalton Beck. Either way, I want to lie low for a while after that mess yesterday."

Bruno and Boris looked at each other in perfect understanding. "Paps," they said.

"Yep. Those cretins will follow me everywhere if I go somewhere flashy right now, so it's better if I keep things chill for a bit."

"If you say so, boss." Bruno jerked his head toward Casey. "So, what's first? What's she doin', anyway?"

"She's currently figuring out the last known location of–"

"Here!" Casey called from the couch, standing up and waving the computer at me. "I think I found you!"

Boris's eyes narrowed. "Why is she looking for *you*, not for her father?"

I sighed. "Long story. Suffice it to say, five days ago I was one of the last people to see her father before he vanished."

"But how can she know–"

"McCarren Park!" Casey ran over and thrust the computer at me, already transferring her attention to her phone. "You were there with some old lady on a Wednesday–"

"That 'old lady' would be my mom, who loves that farmers' market, plus they were having an outdoor concert she wanted to go to."

"Right." She waved away my specificity. "The earliest concert picture I found you in was taken at around five, and the latest was at six-ten. Sometime in that hour, you must have seen my dad. I couldn't find any pictures of him there, but I *know* you saw him." Casey stared at me with an intensity that not even Doctor Strange could match. "You need to go back and look. See if anything jogs your memory. Right?"

Boris and Bruno both looked at me. How far are you willing to go to entertain this kid's ideas, boss?

I smiled. "Their next farmers' market is in two days. I could use some more bok choy."

Casey gaped at me. "But that's two days from now."

"Yes, thank you, I can in fact count."

"But we have to get to work looking for my father *now!* You need to go right now!"

I shook my head. "Nope. First off, I don't want to taint my memories of the day in question by seeing it drastically different than it was the day I saw your dad. Our best bet is to wait until the market is back, to up the chances of shaking something loose. Second, you're going to get a crash course in teamwork and our expectations before I let you help on a job. I won't have you screwing things up because you get impatient or pushy or scared and don't know what to do."

Her poisonous look could have taken out an elephant. "If something bad happens to my dad because you're wasting time–"

"Something bad has already happened to him," I pointed

out, standing up and brushing off my hands. "If he's not dead yet, then delaying our start by forty-eight hours probably isn't going to hurt him, whereas throwing you into the deep end with no training will *definitely* hurt all of us."

Casey switched gears. "If this is about running cons, then I already know how to do that. My dad showed me."

"Oh yeah? Great!" I beamed at her. "Then once I've had a little catnap, you can show me how good you are."

She firmed her jaw. "Fine. Who do you want me to go after?"

"Why, *me*, of course."

Of course I didn't throw her straight into an *actual* job. I was trying to assess her skills and build her confidence, not break her spirit completely. After my nap, we sat down together at the kitchen table and went over the most basic of basics: sleight of hand. Casey hated it. Yeah, I'd hated it too back in the days when Tamara and I were first learning from the Black Fox, but it was an inescapable part of the job.

"This isn't about doing card tricks and hiding balls under cups," I told her, after she sighed so loudly I was amazed there was any air left in her lungs to complain. "Misdirection is key in any con. On the best ones, you've got a crew to help you pull that part off." I nodded in the direction of the garage, where Bruno was forever tinkering with the cars. "Bruno and Boris are two of the best out there, but sometimes they're not with me, or sometimes they're working other parts of the job. That means the misdirect has to come from me."

I picked up the tube of lipstick I put on the kitchen table and took off the cap. In a few smooth moves, I'd painted my lips bright red. "Disguises are a classic choice," I said, smacking my lips together dramatically. Casey rolled her eyes. "But you've got to be ready to redo things on the fly." I twisted the lipstick down, then up, and this time when I used it, my lips became a deep, rich amethyst color.

"Wait. How did you–"

"Once might not be enough." I twisted the lipstick again, used it again. Black this time – always striking, I thought. Casey stared. I recapped the lipstick and put it back on the table, then blotted the makeup off on a napkin while Casey grabbed the tube and opened it up.

"How did you do that?" She twisted it down, then up again. The color stayed resolutely black. "I can't – how did you *do* that?"

"A thief never reveals all her secrets," I said primly, taking the tube away from her and tossing it toward my purse on the couch. It went right into the top pouch. *Score!* "The point isn't for you to do everything the way I do it," I told her. "And we don't have time for me to teach you how to pick pockets or palm IDs. The point is for you to think about ways you can utilize a misdirect that are within the skillsets you already have." I held her gaze for a moment, wondering if I should go there…

Oh heck, why not? "Your dad must have told you some of this," I said. "You said he talked with you about running cons."

"He did," she defended. "But it was different. There was more… you know." She mimed pulling a trigger.

Geez, what a story for a dad to share with his kid. "Your dad told you about all of that?"

"It's not like he could pretend the old stuff never happened!" Casey defended him. "He… really wasn't a very good actor. Mom worked with him on it, but I guess it never really took.

So yeah, I know about the guns and flamethrowers and bombs and stuff."

"Well, all of that's one way to do a job," I said, refocusing on the task at hand, "but not one we can pull off yet, and certainly not the safest. It's *definitely* not what your father would want you to do, either." She looked down, and now it was my turn to sigh. "Your dad wasn't actually telling you how to *do* anything, was he? He was just sharing war stories with you."

"That doesn't mean some of it wasn't useful," Casey said, but she sounded glum. "But… yeah, he wouldn't want me to get hurt. He was always really careful to tell me how dumb he had been, even when he was bragging. Mom always agreed with him."

Hmm. It was an avenue thus unexplored, and so I knew I had to go there. "What was your mom like?"

Casey perked up a little, brushing her shaggy brown bangs away from her face. She was cute, and that little snub nose and bow mouth had to have come from her mother. "She was an actress! Well, she taught acting," Casey amended, "at my high school. And she worked with the local theatre. She was a really good singer, too. She was rehearsing to be the evil mom in *Hairspray* before she got sick."

"Cancer, right?"

"Yeah." Casey looked away again, this time up toward the high ceiling, where the skylight let in just enough light to give her a bit of glow. "It was… pretty fast, once she was diagnosed. She died last year."

"That's how my dad died, too." We stared at each other in mutual commiseration for a moment before I cleared my throat and moved on.

"I bet you watched your mom practice for all kinds of shows, right?"

Casey nodded.

"Good! Then you've already got a foundation to build characters of your own off. Acting doesn't come into every job but, especially if you're running a con, you're going to need to make people think you're someone, or something, you're not." I sat back in my chair. "That means doing research, it means working up a backstory, it means memorization. It also means being able to pull every answer you need out of your hat at just the right moment. And *that* takes practice.

"Practice, practice, practice." I picked up the coin I'd set on the table and rolled it across my fingers. The metal gleamed as I moved it effortlessly across my hand, then rolled it along its edge up the length of my arm, then back down. "Is the job going to ask you to swipe a key card? Practice it. Is it going to demand that you say a phrase in German? Practice it. Is it going to require you to wear high heels? Better make sure you can pull it off."

Casey frowned. "But what if you don't know what the job is going to need?"

"You *ought* to know before you pull it off," I said. "Or at least have a good idea. But if you don't, and there's no way around that, then the next best thing you can do is fall back on a strength." I smirked. "I've got lots of those, because I've been practicing for a very long time. You have fewer."

"Hey, there's no need to be such a bi–"

"It's just fact," I said, interrupting what was sure to be a petulant teenage tirade. *Ugh*, how did people stand kids at this age? Had I been this bad? I owed my mother the biggest dang bouquet of flowers, or maybe another cruise. "I've been doing this for long enough to get good at most of the things my jobs require. I'm not saying you don't have skills, I'm just saying our skillsets are different. You're obviously a good climber," I offered as an olive branch.

"Thanks," she muttered. "My dad likes climbing too."

"And you're really good with navigating social media and computer programming."

"Yeah."

"And you're a great researcher."

Casey was starting to look a little smug. "Yeah I am. I found *you*, after all."

I rolled my eyes. "Yeah, yeah. The point is, think about your strengths. In fact, make a list of 'em." I pushed a handy pad of paper over to her. "Then plan your job around your strengths, and find ways to compensate for your weaknesses."

"And then?"

I grinned. "And then you give it a try. The worst that could happen is I laugh in your face when you screw up."

"I don't want you to laugh in my face!"

I spread my hands out. "Then you already know the solution!"

Casey frowned. "What kind of job am I supposed to pull?"

"Surprise me." I pushed back my chair and got up from the table. "Now excuse me, I've got another round of much belated self-care to handle. Skin doesn't stay this clear without plenty of rest, relaxation, and–"

"Botox?"

Now it was my turn to scowl at her. "Just for that, you're not invited to use any of my products. In fact, you can sleep out here." I pointed at the couch, then at the bathroom on the far side of the kitchen. "We'll make that your bathroom for the duration of your stay."

Casey gaped. "But there's no shower in there!"

"Hmm, true. Hope you like bucket baths."

I wasn't actually going to make her take bucket baths, of course, but I certainly wasn't going to give up my private space to someone who'd gone and interloped right into my life. She could sleep on the couch and like it. And there were separate bathrooms for each of the bedroom suites, because I wasn't a barbarian, so the one out here could definitely belong just to her. She'd be fine.

CHAPTER EIGHT

I gave Casey the rest of the day to plan, and full access to Boris and Bruno to pull off her "Black Cat con." They were alarmingly into it, which was a bit of a red flag, but not as much as it could have been. After all, they were an excellent resource, but one I was only letting Casey *borrow.* They knew who buttered their bread, so to speak, and so the next morning when I woke up, refreshed and rejuvenated after a night of perfect sleep, all it took was one look at Boris's face at the breakfast table to figure out what was going on. He'd tried to hide behind a newspaper, the search for New York City's golden apple splashed all over the front page, but when he peeped over the top of it at me, I knew.

I immediately turned around, caught my bedroom door before it closed and automatically locked, and looked for the attempt at infiltrating it. At first I couldn't see it, but then I noticed the seam in the concrete wall above the doorframe wavering a little bit. I looked up and there in the rafters was Casey, all in gray to make it harder to see her, concentrating on keeping the length of cable in her hands steady. When she saw that I'd noticed her, though, she groaned.

"Aw, nice first try. I see what you're after now." Access to my palatial suite, clearly. "But you're going to have to do better than that." I brushed her cable out of the way and closed my door, enjoying the audible *click* of my electronic lock.

"You said she wouldn't notice me!" Casey whined down at my crew.

"I said she wouldn't think to look up," Boris replied as he cut into his eggs. "I didn't say she wouldn't look at *us*."

"But you promised not to tell her where I was."

"I didn't say a word to her."

"This is one of the most important things a blossoming thief can learn," I told her while I headed for the coffee machine. *Cappuccino, here I come.* "Who to trust, and how far to trust them. Consider yourself schooled."

I knew this was only her first sally, so I didn't let my guard down. Casey spent the rest of the day sequestered in the garage with Bruno, who was still working on the cars. I didn't even see her for dinner – she was too busy working on whatever she expected to get her through the door next. That was fine. I didn't mind missing out on her scintillating conversation in order to catch up on my beauty sleep. I *did* disable the part of my lock that shocked anyone who wasn't me into unconsciousness when they grabbed the handle of my door.

"OW!"

Well, I turned the voltage down, at least. Usually I could barely hear anything through the soundproofing, so she must have shouted really loudly.

I got out of bed and opened my door. Casey was swearing and shaking out her hand, with a kludgey dinglehopper of some kind broken in several pieces on the floor. I recognized bits from an old com unit, one of the portable scanners, and some of the inert gel that Boris liked to use as a base when he was sticking a bomb together.

"I guess you saw me enter the code on the keypad, huh?" I asked.

"Checked the internal security footage from when you went to bed," she muttered. "Which you *gave* me access to."

"So I did. And yet, I didn't change the code, even though I knew you'd be able to find it like that." I snapped my fingers. "That didn't scream 'secondary security measures' to you?"

"I thought you didn't care all that much!"

"Are you kidding me? I'm not giving up my mattress without a fight. It's like sleeping on a cloud."

"Cold and wet?"

"*Delightful*," I told the little smarty-pants looking at me like she'd enjoy gouging my eyes out. "Oh stop it, your hand is fine."

"That hurt," she said petulantly.

"You're just annoyed that you didn't think this plan through. Do better next time, and have fun sleeping on the couch." I shut the door in her face and got back into bed without thinking twice about her. I was pretty sure I knew what her next move was going to be, so why waste the energy on it?

Turns out I was right.

It took Casey some time to work up to it. She was wary of letting Boris and Bruno know anything now, so when she locked herself in the bathroom off the kitchen right before lunchtime, I wasn't surprised. There was no surveillance in there, for one, and it gave her some space from the rest of us, for two. Space that none of us minded because she'd been behaving like a spoiled brat all morning.

"This kid is kind of a pill, boss," Bruno confided, as he made himself a triple-decker sandwich.

"She is," I agreed. I had my own thoughts on how genuine the act was – one way to get privacy was to ensure that no one wanted to be around you, after all.

"You sure you wanna work with her?"

I contemplated the question while I stared down at my questionable sushi. Mmm, breakfast sushi... but I wasn't sure how long this had been in the fridge, either. "I want to give her a chance," I said at last. "And I want to figure out what made her decide to look me up." I hated surveillance I wasn't in control of.

"If you say so."

"If she steals more gelignite from me, I won't be held responsible when she blows the place up!" Boris added from where he stood by the espresso machine. Bruno and I both turned to stare at him.

"Why did you leave *gelignite* in a place where she could get to it?" I demanded.

"Are you outta your gat-danged mind?" Bruno bellowed.

Boris just shrugged. "It's a very stable formula! It's not like she set it off."

"She shouldn't have had the opportunity to set it off! She–" Speaking of getting set off, one of the new motion detectors I'd had Boris install on the sides of the building began to ring an alarm. "Woops." I pulled up the video footage and, yep, there she was. She'd gone out the bathroom window – a pretty mean feat, considering the size of it, and she'd managed to keep the alarm from going off, so that was an improvement – and climbed around the edge of the building until she was nearly at my balcony.

I watched her hop up over the edge of it, nimble as a mouse. She didn't even try the door, still shy from her last run-in with my security, probably. Instead, she moved the fern I kept out there down from its metal table, picked the table up, and with all her might, threw it at the glass door.

Nothing happened. Not a scratch, not a crack, not even a nick. I could see her mouth something that rhymed with "brotherpucker," then pick up the table and try again, this time holding onto the legs so she could smash it into the glass multiple times. Still nothing.

Casey completely lost her cool. She stepped back and, mouth open in a scream I couldn't hear, hurled first the table, then the wooden lounge chair, then the decorative plinth covered in winding ivy after it. Nothing. There was no discernible impact on the glass at all, but Casey's temper was certainly getting the better of her. When she went for my fern, I booked it for the bedroom. I opened the door to the balcony just as she hurled the plant toward her reflection, catching it with my catlike reflexes – pun absolutely intended.

"I draw the line at you blatantly destroying a living thing to get in here," I told the girl, whose chest was heaving with anger and anxiety. "And so should you. This plant hasn't hurt anybody, after all." I set the fern down and stepped close to Casey, who was blinking back tears. "Another word of advice: never try to pull the same job twice, especially not on the same mark. You think I didn't realize you'd try to come at me the only way you'd been successful before? Think again. There are motion detectors outside my apartment now." I tapped the balcony wall. "Not that you'd have gotten in anyway, not with this glass, but still. Should have seen it coming."

"This is impossible," Casey said, her voice so tight I thought it might snap. "How am I supposed to do this when you've already thought of everything? You're the pro. I'm, I just want to get my dad back! You said you would help me! Why are we wasting time on these *stupid* tests?"

I shook my head. "If you think training is a waste, then you're not someone I want to work with." I gestured around the balcony. "Put my stuff back where you found it. The farmers' market starts at noon, so you've got—" I checked my non-existent watch "— about two hours to pull something together. I'm off to get some sushi." I turned around and headed for the door, leaving Casey in the care of my minions.

I did wonder a bit, as I took the elevator downstairs, whether I was really being fair to Casey. She might have a former crook for a dad, but she hadn't grown up in the lifestyle. She might be a precocious kid, but she was still just a kid. Teenagers *totally* counted as kids. I couldn't have come up with some of the things she'd tried when I was fifteen.

I hadn't had access to Boris and Bruno and some world-class equipment, either.

No, this was fair. After all, our lives could depend on her ability to do things right, to be reliable, to stay creative and motivated. If she couldn't handle that… welp. Then I'd be calling CPS to come and get her.

Then I'd go look for her father without her. I wasn't *totally* heartless, after all, and I was curious now.

My second-favorite sushi place was only a few blocks away. I went and ordered an early lunch – it was really too late to consider it breakfast now – and ate most of it sitting at their countertop, practicing my Japanese on the cute chef who gave me an extra serving of tekkamaki for my efforts. I decided to box that up and bring it home. Maybe Casey would like to try it.

Only when I got home, there was no sign of her. Not her backpack, not her shoes, not even her Browns hat. I turned a full circle, then looked at my crew. "Did she actually leave?" I demanded, setting my sushi on the kitchen table.

Bruno nodded glumly. "Took all her stuff with her. Told us that it was pointless to try working with you, that you didn't want her to be here and she was runnin' out of time."

"We tried to convince her otherwise," Boris said, poking at the bomb components on the table in front of him with sharp, snappish movements. "But she wouldn't hear it. She left right after you did."

"I…" I couldn't quite believe it. Casey had been so adamant about working with me to find her father. She'd been convinced I was the only one who could help her – heck, she'd convinced *me* that I was too, and that took some doing. And she'd given up, just like that? After only a few little failures?

She saved you the trouble of kicking her out, then, my brain tried to rationalize to me. You don't have any use for someone so fragile. Good riddance. But my heart wasn't having it.

"No," I said. "She didn't give up." I started to look around for a note, a scribble – anything that would function as a clue to where Casey had gone. Nothing on the table. "She wouldn't." Nothing on the fridge. "This is just her next move." Nothing on the couch or either of the end tables… I turned toward my bedroom. "She's trying to get me to chase her, that's all. She must have left some kind of message for me." Maybe she'd pushed it under the door? It was practically airtight, thanks to the soundproofing, but there was a tiny gap that she could have shoved a piece of paper through. I punched in my keycode, then pressed my thumb to the lock. After a second, it released.

"I'm telling you, boss, she didn't–"

I opened my door and froze. There, sitting on my bed cross-legged, her phone in her hand and her earphones on beneath her hoodie, was Casey. It took her a moment to notice me. "Oh, hey." She grinned widely. "Look where I am."

"You're... how did you..."

The boys joined me a second later, looks of identical confusion on their faces. It was kind of funny, but given that I'd been fooled too, I wasn't laughing. "How did you do it?"

"Shouldn't I make you figure that out on your own?" Casey asked, slightly heavy on the sarcasm. "Since that's what you've been having me do for the last two days?"

"Hmm." I stepped further into the room and looked around. The door to the balcony was closed – a quick glance told me that the lock was still in place, and the alarm hadn't been triggered. I already knew she didn't have the skills or the tech to get through those barriers herself, and besides that, none of my newly installed motion detectors had indicated someone was climbing the building. But she hadn't gotten through the main door either; I or the boys would have noticed if the biometric trigger had gone off, and Casey would have ended up, well... *stunned* was the nice way of putting it. And she hadn't succeeded in keeping it from locking in the first place, so...

Now that I looked more closely, the bed looked like it had been shifted about a foot closer to the bathroom. I flung up the bed skirt and looked under the bed. She hadn't gone through the floor – that was concrete, like all the floors – but the vent cover was slightly askew.

"Did you actually crawl through the *vents* to get in here?" Boris and Bruno were waiting with bated breath, Boris practically vibrating with his need to know.

Casey nodded. "Sure did."

Dang. I was reluctantly impressed. "OK, but how did you access the vents? My apartment is a closed system, and there are no blueprints out there."

Casey's mouth stretched in a smug smile. "Not of this building, but I found a copy of the blueprints of another building designed by the same architect as a starting point. I figured your system couldn't be completely closed, not if you want to be in the loop when it comes to the fire detection and sprinkler systems, so I based my route off that. I knew that climbing wasn't going to be the way in this time, but it wasn't hard to figure out who lives beneath you, either."

Oh my god. She'd pulled a con on my *neighbor.*

"Mrs Yu is a very nice woman," Casey went on. "When I met her downstairs this morning, she said I remind her of her granddaughter. I offered to help her set up her Wi-Fi, and she invited me into her place. She told me she's been planning to refurbish her son's old bedroom anyway, so when I offered to take down some of the wall for her, she was fine with it. She also had a really great set of tools."

Was I hearing this correctly? "You conned my neighbor into letting you drill into her A/C system and crawled up through it into my room?"

"Yep." Casey shrugged. "I also told her you'd pitch in some cash to help with the remodel. So." She stood up and brushed some dust – probably from the vent – off her shoulder. "I'm going to put my spare clothes away in here and shower, and then we can start looking for my dad. It's the farmers' market day, right?"

Laying claim to my room and telling me what to do at the same time. Well, dang. I put my hands on my hips and looked Casey square in the eyes. She didn't flinch, but there was a hint of uncertainty in the way she held her shoulders. "Yes, ma'am," I said, throwing her a little salute.

Casey grinned, then marched proudly into the bathroom. I turned back to my crew, who had gone from shocked to a mute state of dumbfounded.

"C'mon, gents. We've got a job to set up… and I've got to call Mrs Yu." Hopefully rebuilding her bedroom wouldn't cost *too* much.

CHAPTER NINE

McCarren Park, like so many of New York City's public parks, was in a constant state of renovation. Originally built over a hundred years ago, it had undergone a facelift in the eighties, then again in the early aughts. Now it was due, yet again, for more work – this time to the historic bathhouse, a big brick building with an open arch in the center of it that led to a huge outdoor pool. I wasn't entirely sure how it had partially crumbled this time, but my bet was on the Avengers not watching where they were throwing something.

In New York, you could count on people being really good at three things: paying their taxes, taking cover, and rebuilding. Construction was practically a cottage industry in this city, with every block having its own go-to guy for whenever the next disaster struck. This local approach to building had led to some… quirky architecture, here and there, but in my opinion that just made the city more interesting.

It also led to a plethora of hidden passageways, boltholes, and unexpected safe rooms. That was one of the reasons that finding people once they weren't in plain view any longer could be next to impossible – between the sewers and the secrets, a person could find a private place to stow themselves by going fifty feet in any direction.

"So," I said, slowly walking through the crowd and admiring the long tables of locally grown vegetables. Every word was picked up by my vintage platinum and diamond choker, and every response was transmitted via my emerald earrings. Was there anything better than jewelry that combined fashion and function? Honestly, I should go into design, I'd make a mint.

Nah. Too legal.

"I'm counting on you to help jog my memory of where I was," I said to Casey over the com, reaching out to sample a rye cracker dabbed with glistening golden honey. It smelled like sweet clover, and I had to close my eyes for a moment while I savored the mouthful. "Oh dang, that's good," I murmured. "My mom would love that." I grabbed a jar for her – paid for it, even, because my mother had a sixth sense when it came to me gifting her stuff and she would somehow *know* if I stole it. Also, I didn't care to steal from local farmers.

"Less shopping, more looking!" Boris prodded me. "You need to get to the same place you were for the concert."

"That's the football field." And it was currently full of people running over it, throwing frisbees across it, kicking balls around on it... nothing like the sweet-smelling and largely sedate farmers' market I was enjoying right now. "Five more minutes, Dad."

"That's *not* funny."

"Five more minutes, Mom."

"It's an *honor* to be compared to your mother," Boris said with a sniff, which – yep, he knew when he could be a jerk and when he'd better sing praises. "Now go mingle with more of the plebian masses so we can figure out this petty mystery and get on with our lives."

Bruno snorted a laugh over the line. He was sitting in one of our more sedate vehicles a few blocks away, close enough that I could sprint to him without breaking a sweat if things suddenly got dicey. "I never heard of a kidnapping get figured out in a single day, Doc."

"Most of them don't have someone of my elevated intellectual prowess working on–"

"I think I might finally see my dad," Casey interjected excitedly.

"What? Where?" Boris asked, sounding surprised.

I rolled my eyes behind my shades. "On the videos she dug up from the concert last week. Try to keep up."

Boris subsided with a huff, and I focused on Casey as my fingertips brushed across reusable cloth bags filled with bright red apples. "What was he wearing?"

"Blue jeans, a gray cargo jacket, and a Cleveland Browns hat." Casey paused, then added, "In maroon, in case you don't know who the best football team in the NFL is."

"Bah," Bruno said. "They got nothin' on the Jets."

"I'm sorry," Casey said heatedly, "who ended up in the playoffs last year while the Jets had, like, two wins? Oh yeah, the *Browns*."

"Who did the Jets have one of those wins against? Oh yeah, the *Browns*."

"That was a total fluke!"

"I'm going to totally fluke both of you if you don't quiet down," I warned. An older man walking nearby looked at me apprehensively. "Just telling the kids to be good for the babysitter," I told him with a smile, gesturing to my ear like I had a Bluetooth there.

He chuckled and nodded. "Little blessings, but boy, can they be scamps."

"Such scamps," I agreed.

"I'm not a scamp!" Casey snapped. "I'm the only one actually getting anything done right now, in case you didn't notice."

"Here's a good rule when it comes to working with a team – you don't single yourself out for credit," I said, walking briskly over to a stand selling tiny succulent gardens in animal-shaped pots. "Sure, you're doing something useful right now, but in five minutes it'll be Bruno, or Boris, or me who's putting in the time. When you brag, you're setting yourself up to be resented, and that leads to bad teamwork."

"Unless you're bragging to someone who's not on the team," Bruno added.

"Oh, absolutely, that's just good advertising," I agreed. "Especially if it's a super hero. There's nothing quite like rubbing your successes in some Daisy Do-Gooder's face, especially when they're trying to bump you off and steal your identity as part of the twisted fallout of a villain's madcap schemes."

Was I still a little salty about Queen Cat's attempts to do away with me? Yeah, I was, so sue me. Cats might forgive, but we never forget. I knew I was going to be in for a fun time with her, once she got her confidence back.

Maybe I should send her the succulent garden in the cat-shaped pot. I'd have to get some cacti put in there first, though. I didn't want her to think I was going soft.

"Time waits for no one, Black Cat."

I acknowledged the reminder with a sigh and walked on past the flowers and out of the farmers' market entirely, toward the football field. I let my eyes and my mind wander, thinking back to the concert. It had been pretty well attended, the press of the crowd getting harder to move through with every new step. Eventually my mom and I had set up chairs just outside the edge of the track closest to the pool, where we still had a view of the raised stage in the middle of the field but didn't have to defend our feet quite so closely.

I got there, then crouched down into about the same position I'd been in before and reviewed the scene, letting the present day wash away. Recall was an important skill for a thief, as my mentor had emphasized to me more than once.

I tried my best to conjure up the image of a man in a maroon ballcap, broad shoulders bumping people as he pushed through the crowd, but I got nothing. Either it had simply been too crowded, or I just didn't remember seeing him from this vantage point. "I'm not getting anything," I said quietly. "Are you sure that I saw him, Casey?"

"I'm absolutely, one hundred percent sure," she replied. I could tell from the way she'd slurred her "s's" a little that she was biting the inside of her cheek. "Keep looking around. You're bound to remember where you saw him at some point."

"This is a waste of time," Boris said, then yelped. "Ow! You vicious infant! That hurt!"

"Call my dad a waste of time again and it'll hurt worse next time," Casey threatened. Oh, fabulous. Brilliant idea, leaving those two together in the same room. I'd be lucky if no blood was shed by the time Bruno and I returned.

There had to be something more I could do. Casey's certainty was catching, and I never backed down from a challenge. So I didn't recall seeing Firestrike from this angle. From *this* angle... but I hadn't sat here the entire time. A breeze had blown my mom's straw boater hat off about forty minutes into the show, sending it straight backward. I'd gotten up to retrieve it... stood and turned like this, walked twenty paces back to grab the hat, bent over and grabbed it, and as I stood up someone threw a frisbee past me toward the building in the distance.

A dog ran after the frisbee, and leaning against the building watching the dog was a man with a soft smile on his face, maroon hat pulled low. I turned to watch the dog catch the frisbee, and when I glanced back at the building the man was gone. Gone in under two seconds.

"I remember now," I murmured. "He was leaning up against the side of the bathhouse. The left side as you enter, close to the far end."

"You really remember him?" Casey sounded somewhere between excited and scared. "You promise?"

"I really do." I started walking toward the building. "But there's no harm in verifying that. See if you can find some pictures while I take a closer look."

The bathhouse entrance was blocked off with temporary fencing right now, but I could still get right up next to the building on either side. I moved slowly, making sure I was going to just the right spot, and... here. Five feet from the far end of the building, a not-impossible distance to dart around in a very short period of time, but Firestrike had never had built-in superpowers. From what I'd read in the papers, Dalton Beck was just a regular guy whose ambitions of criminality had fallen apart in the face of protecting a woman he was in love with.

I examined the brickwork, looking for anything suspicious, any cracks that shouldn't be there or recent marks that seemed out of place. No luck with that, but then I paid better attention to what was beneath my feet.

"Uh-oh." We had a sewer grate. And not just any old sewer grate – this was a long, rectangular grate, the kind you might get in a storm drain or culvert to move large amounts of water faster. There was no good reason for a grate like this to be nestled up against the side of a building that was already on high ground.

"What uh-oh?" Casey asked apprehensively.

"Give me a second to verify something." There was one other place I'd seen grates like this recently – in the Maggia catacombs where they held their ceremonial weddings/mortal battles between young people, for the "benefit of the families." For the benefit of barbarism, more like. I'd seen what looked like a triggering method on a few of those… of course, I'd been looking *up* at them at the time, not down, but…

I pulled a glove out of my purse – never leave fingerprints if you don't have to – and felt around the back edge of the grate, finally catching my index finger on a lever. I reached around it, pulled firmly, and–

"Ah-*ha!*"

"What ah-ha?" Casey demanded. "Did you find my dad?"

"No, but I *have* figured out how whoever took him managed to get the drop on him. Literally, in this case." I stared down into the tunnel beneath the swinging grate, and – no. Nope. Not gonna happen. Nobody in their right mind went into the sewers of New York City without being crazy or in mortal danger, and I wasn't about to start. "Boris, find out who the last company to do repairs on this part of the building was."

I had my Silvermane-shaped suspicions, but I wanted them confirmed. Only a foolish thief went after a prize without getting a full picture of what they were up against.

I tilted the grate back up but left it unlocked, just in case I got really bad news that would require me to do something crazy, and thought the situation through for a moment. Dalton Beck, back in the city, incognito, about to be part of a major criminal trial and probably worrying about the child he'd left behind, had come to a park to listen to a concert. Of his own volition? Maybe, but if that was the case, what the heck were the FBI agents who were supposed to be keeping him safe doing? Why wasn't he given a plainclothes escort at least, or better yet, told "not a chance" when he brought the idea up in the first place?

Nah, I didn't buy it. "I think we're going to have to figure out who was Mr Beck's keeper among the feds," I said, far from relishing the prospect.

"Uh, boss." Bruno's voice was tentative. "You know they're kinda… um… well, their place is kinda–"

"Like a fortress, I know." Breaking into the city's enormous, well-staffed FBI field office probably wasn't going to be fun, but I had the feeling it would be necessary. And actually, it *might* be fun. I mean, how many people had done it and gotten away clean? None that I knew of.

Of course, I *wouldn't* know about the ones who got away clean if they were experts at the craft. I only heard about the ones who got caught, and when it came to federal buildings in the city, paranoia didn't begin to cover it. I suspected they had an illicit deal with a powerful psychic to keep an eye on the goings-and-comings of the staff. I'd have to–

"Here we are!" Boris announced. "Repairs were last

performed on the McCarren Park Bathhouse façade in 2017, by Helping Hands Construction."

I snorted. "Oh, that's a front name if ever I heard one."

"Agreed. It's just the sort of schmoopy, over-the-top friendly name that one would associate with a black-hearted evildoer. And… yes," he added, "it looks like the formal incorporation paperwork dead-ends in the Caymans."

"So the business was a Maggia front." I set my foot on top of the swiveling grate and wobbled it gently back and forth. "I doubt Firestrike had any idea of that, though. He's been gone for years. So whoever set him up probably didn't just suggest an outing to the park, they specifically told him to come to this location so the trap could be sprung."

"But my dad's not stupid!" Casey protested.

"That's up for debate," Boris muttered, then cried out, "Ouch! Hellion child!"

"He's *not* stupid! He wouldn't just walk into a trap like this! Someone must have forced him!"

"I don't think so," I said, thinking back on what I'd seen that day. "I think perhaps your father was given a suggestion by the agent in charge of him and felt… maybe he felt *pressured* to go along with it, let's say. I imagine the foremost thing on his mind was getting his testimony out of the way so he could come home to you. He wouldn't have wanted to ruffle any feathers in the FBI, so he did what they said." Like a meek little lamb to the slaughter. Boy, had he been tamed by his forced retirement.

"Why bother with the FBI at all?" Casey asked. "Why not just go directly after this Silvermane guy?"

Oof, this girl needed a lesson in proportional response.

"Because I don't want to bait the bear if I can get what I need by squeezing a rat. We're assuming right now that it was Silvermane who's behind your father's kidnapping, and that's a very reasonable assumption, but I doubt he did the actual legwork himself. In that case..."

I let my voice trail off as I heard the faint scuff of a sneaker on the concrete a few feet behind me. It was a slow scuff, the kind of noise that came when someone was creeping forward instead of walking at a steady pace. Someone was creeping up on me – not very skillfully either, not like I'd expect out of the Maggia. I was going to have to do something about that.

I waited for them to get closer, *felt* the distance closing between us. There was a quick intake of breath, then the pressure of a grubby hand on my shoulder. "Keep quiet or I'll–"

That was all my mugger had time to say before I pivoted, closing the distance between us as I secured his hand on my shoulder and wrapped my arm around his in a big circle that ended with his elbow jutting forward and his torso bent back at an acute angle. At the same time, I snapped my free hand out against the bottom of his opposite wrist, forcing him to drop the rusty box cutter he was holding.

"Oh hey!" I said brightly, jerking his elbow a little higher just for the pleasure of hearing him gurgle with pain. "You know, I'm glad you came along right now! There's this thing that I wasn't going to test out, but now as long as I've got *you* here, well..." I stabilized the grate with my foot and stood him on top of it. "You can take a look for me. Call up if you see something interesting, OK?"

"Lady, I don't know what you're talkin' about, but – *aaaahhh!*" I released the grate and his arm at the same time, and a second later my would-be attacker was falling into the stinky abyss below us.

"Boss? You OK?" Bruno asked, sounding a second away from getting out of the car and running over.

"I'm fine! It's all fine, I'll be leaving in a minute. I just have to have a little chat with some trash first. What's it look like down there?" I called into the darkness.

"You crazy b–"

"People who are *polite* get a hand up out of the sewers, while people who are *rude* get thoughts and prayers," I told him. "How far down did you fall?"

There was silence for a long moment, and then– "Shoot, I dunno. Ten feet, maybe? Twelve? Hard to tell in all the dark."

"Anything of note down there?"

"I don't know, I can barely see my hand in front of my own face down here! C'mon, lady, let me back up! You said you would."

"Mm, I said that I would help someone polite," I agreed. "Unfortunately, you fell out of that category the moment you started waving a box cutter around. So you can…" Uh-oh, more footsteps coming, only this time they weren't trying to be covert. I turned and looked at a couple of young women walking my way.

"Are you all right?" one of them called out.

I pasted on a smile. "Oh, I'm fine, but there's a gentleman over here who's taken a bad fall down into the sewers. No, don't bend over to look!" I cautioned the one in front as she leaned over the grate. "You never know if something will reach up and grab you, ha. If you'd call the cops for him, I'm sure he'd appreciate it. Be careful, though, he was armed when I met him."

"Are you sure you're OK?" the second girl asked, her auburn hair falling almost all the way down to her rear. "It sounds like he tried to attack you, and... huh." I didn't like the change of tone in her voice. "Oh my god. Are you *Felicia Hardy*?" she shrieked. "From the Gala? Omigosh! You were there when the golden apple showed up, weren't you?"

Great. Just great.

"Gotta go," I said, sliding by them and heading away from the bathhouse. Unfortunately, the crowd had heard her yell, and more than a few of them were headed my way, interest and avarice on their faces.

"Felicia, hi, I'm–"

"Miss Hardy, I'd like to chat about the–"

"Girl, I got money and I will give it all to you if you get me that apple!"

"I'll double whatever he offers you!"

"I'll triple it!"

"Felicia–"

"Miss Hardy–"

"Black Cat–"

They were all around me, buzzing around like a swarm of flies. I couldn't swat them, though, not unless I wanted to cause more trouble for myself than I cared for. "Are you seeing this?" I murmured over the line.

"Yes," Boris said, just as Casey said, "Yeah, and you're gonna want to go over the bathhouse and through the pool area if you want to avoid them all, because they're coming in on all sides."

"Thank you, that's helpful." I spun, ran a few steps, and then *leaped* up the side of the bathhouse wall. It wasn't very tall, hardly the kind of thing you needed to be Spider-Man to climb, but people watching me gasped like they'd never seen someone show off their moves before.

Quit acting like rubes. This is New York City, not Hick Town, Ohio. Heck, Casey was from Hick Town, Ohio and she'd already handled herself better than any of these guys. I dropped down to the interior of the swim park and ran for the far side before the people who'd been mobbing me could put it together that they could follow on the outside.

Ugh. I hadn't even touched that golden apple, but it was still determined to ruin my afternoon.

CHAPTER TEN

My evening wasn't shaping up to be so hot either, thanks to some unwanted suggestions from the peanut gallery about how to stay inconspicuous in the great melting pot out there.

Huh, food metaphors. I was probably getting hungry. I got up from the kitchen table where me and my crew were planning our next move and headed for the fridge. Leftover pad thai – score.

"You should consider dyeing your ostentatiously blonde hair."

I glared at Boris from across the kitchen as I grabbed a fork. "Absolutely not."

"A wig, then. Something to make it *slightly* harder to identify you on the street, at least."

I spent most of my working life in a disguise of one kind or another. I didn't like the idea of doing it in my rare personal hours either, but apparently a *lot* of people had seen the Met Gala reporting, and since there was still no sign of the golden apple having been used, I was a key "person of interest" for every Tom, Dick, and Mary who felt entitled to butt into my business.

"It's a moot point right now, since a disguise will absolutely be necessary for the next part anyway," I said, sitting back down and gathering up a bite of noodles.

"Which is… talking to the FBI?" Casey asked uncertainly, biting into one of my premium, small-batch, organic granola bars. She made a face at the taste. *No class.*

"Which is infiltrating the FBI and figuring out who the agent in charge of your father's movements was," I clarified. I stared at the live footage of their field office. "And that's going to be a challenge, given how it's buzzing right now." Not just from handling the Manfredi trial, but also from joining in the hunt for the golden apple, which had been labelled a "clear and present threat to public safety." Sheesh, were they ever right about that?

Agents were coming in and out of the tall Manhattan office building like it was a highway, which should have made my job easier. Find someone to imitate, steal a badge, slip into an unattractive pantsuit, and *voila*. But from the look of the surveillance, everybody going in and out of that building right now wasn't just showing off a badge – they were being verified by facial recognition software, fingerprinted, *and* in some cases, calls were being made at the security desk before they were allowed deeper into the building.

Still not undoable, but not ideal either. Speed was a factor now that Casey's intensive training was over – not just for the sake of Dalton Beck's welfare, but to stave off my crew's boredom. I didn't want Boris to get antsy and start tinkering with his latest malleable "I swear it won't blow up in my hands" explosive prototype, or for Bruno to get so deep into an upgrade on the cars that none of them were in a working state when I needed them. Heck, I didn't want Casey to get tired of hanging out here and start trying to find things out for herself, either.

Although, actually... that wasn't a *terrible* idea. In fact, the more I thought about it, the better I liked it. There were plenty of ways for *me* to get into that building, but there was also a decent way for her to do it, and it would function as both a teachable moment and a way of making her feel included.

Aw, go me.

"How would you like to be the one to infiltrate the FBI office, kid?"

Bruno choked on a mouthful of beer. Boris looked like he was about to have a heart attack.

Casey looked intrigued. *Good.*

"Boss, you can't be serious–"

"Do you really think it's wise to send a child into–"

"Gentlemen." I held up the hand not currently holding a fork. "I appreciate your concerns for Miss Beck's welfare, but I really do think the quickest way to get this done is by using the most inconspicuous member of our crew. Besides, it's not like the feds will shoot her if they realize she's up to something shady." Which was more than I could say for the rest of us. "At worst, she identifies herself as Firestrike's daughter and gets sent home or put into custody until the end of the trial."

Casey pushed her chair back and stood up. "I won't be sent home!"

I grinned at her. "Then you better not get caught, huh?"

It was strange being the backup instead of the headliner on a job, even a minor one like this. I wasn't used to being the voice in someone else's ear, yet here I was, dressed up like just another cog in the workings of bureaucracy and sipping my coffee at a café within eyesight of the FBI's Manhattan field office, looking at my phone like every other office worker taking a break. Except I was looking at a video feed sent to me straight from the cameras we'd attached to Casey's earbuds, which she'd left dangling over the neck of her hoodie. She had another, much lower profile earpiece in her right ear, covered by the wispy black wig we'd put on her, to hear me through.

"Remember," I told her as she walked slowly toward the door, "you're only fourteen, you're a tourist, and you don't know where your parents are." With her big eyes and pouty lower lip she could pull off a nervous kid no problem despite the fact that she was just a few inches shorter than me. It would help hide the regular "on the job" nerves I could see in her too, if the way her hands were shaking as they pushed through the revolving door was any indication.

Casey made it into the lobby and headed tentatively for the first line of defense: the front desk. A man in a generic black suit with a big earpiece and a bigger gun was sitting in front of a computer there, looking harried. "Um… excuse me?"

The man looked up so quickly his jowls jiggled. "What is it, kid?"

"Uh, I just – I–"

The stammering was good, but possibly a bit of an oversell. "Get to the point, he's getting impatient," I murmured.

"Let her act it out her own way," Boris chided.

"I'm only trying to–"

"I lost my parents," Casey said, getting firmly back on track. "I was with them an hour ago, but then we got separated on the subway and now I don't know where they are, and my phone doesn't get service here like it does back home, and I really need some help, please."

The man heaved a sigh. "Are you kidding me? We're the FBI, miss, do you know what that means? It means we don't waste our time on kids whose parents can't keep their eyes open on the subway." He got up and came around the desk. "You need to go to the regular police," he said, setting a hand on her shoulder and turning her back toward the door. "There's a station just a few blocks away. C'mon."

Oh dang. She was going to get booted out the door before she even got into the building proper, much less an office where she'd have access to a computer. "Don't let him walk you out of there," I urged. "Once you're out, you won't get back in so easily."

"I... I..."

Just as I thought I'd have to trigger my distraction early, Casey found her voice.

"Don't throw me out!" she wailed, bursting into what sounded like very genuine tears. "I just want someone to help me find my parents, because what if they're dead already, or what if you send me out there and I get lost, or someone kidnaps me? I – just – want – my – Daddy!"

"Jesus, don't throw the kid out like that," one of the other agents just walking in hissed at the man holding Casey's shoulder. "Someone will film her having a fit and post it to social media, and then we'll be in an even bigger crapstorm than we already are."

"We're not in the business of finding lost parents!" the desk agent replied, but he didn't sound as assured now.

"Looks like we are today. Heyyy, little girl." The new guy had doubled down hard in the opposite direction from his fellow agent, acting schmoopy with a dollop of extra schmoop on top. His smile was so sweet, saccharine would hang its head in shame. "Did you say you're looking for your parents?"

"Yuh... yes." Casey sniffed dramatically. "Please, can't you help me? Don't send me out there on my own again, I don't want to be alone in this big city."

"Of course not, of course not. Can you give me a number for them?"

"Tell them this," I said quickly, then rattled off one of our burners. "Bruno, you're on dad duty. Try to be super incompetent, OK? Throw in some bad reception, maybe a dropped call. We need them to take her to an office."

"You got it, boss."

Bruno actually played the country bumpkin better than I'd imagined. He got the agent on the other end of the phone to give him the address of their building three times, then asked for landmarks, then commented on how "then again, all them big buildings look the same to me, heh." By the time they reached the ten-minute mark, the man who'd initially been supportive looked like he was going to have a stroke.

"Look sir, just get on the C – that's one of the lines in the subway – and you can be here from where you are in less than thirty minutes. It's stop – hello? Hello?" He stared at his phone like he wanted to crush it. "The call dropped. That or the son of a–"

"Lou," the first agent snapped, with a meaningful glance at Casey, and they both shut up for a second.

"Look, put her in a conference room while I get this straightened out," he muttered before heading outside.

"C'mon, kid."

"Conference rooms probably won't have the computer connections we need," I said quickly. "Ask if you can sit at the front desk."

"Can't I just stay up here?" Casey asked, a whine building in her voice. "I'll sit really quietly behind the desk, I promise, I just want to be able to see my parents when they come in. Please? Please?" She sounded like she was about to start hyperventilating. "Sorry, I get anxious sometimes and usually I have a rescue inhaler for if it gets really bad but my mom put it in her fanny pack this morning and–"

"Geez, all right!" The jowly man led Casey back to the desk and sat her down immediately. "Put your head down between your knees. Do you need water?"

"No, thank you," she said in a small, wheezy voice.

"OK then, I… um…" Just then a big group of people came in through the door, and the security officer in front of the elevators waved the agent over to help scan the crowd through. "You just sit here, I'll be back in a few minutes, all right?"

"OK," she sniffled. The agent hurried off, and a second later Casey popped back upright in her chair.

"Don't look too eager all of a sudden," I said. "They still have you on camera, you know."

"Duh."

Don't you "duh" me! I didn't say it, but I wanted to. Oh, I wanted to. "You'll have to plug the dongle in to the computer right there." Hopefully that would be enough time for this particular piece of tech to access the information we needed. If it couldn't go deep and specific, it would go broad, and grab everything it could reach – all hopefully without setting off the FBI's firewalls. I'd paid a mint for this thing – well, more like traded a shipment of rhodium I'd picked up to an engineer who desperately needed it in exchange for this – and if it didn't work, we'd have to go back to Plan A.

"Got it." Casey opened her backpack and began to rummage through it, tossing wrappers and spare clothes and at least two hardback books onto the desktop, like she was searching for something. It provided a decent cover for her to plug the dongle into the computer. *That* part took her three fumbling tries.

"This is why we *practice*," I sing-songed as I took a final sip of my drink and got to my feet. "Bet you wish you'd spent more time working on this move, huh?"

"I got it in the end," she said.

"Data is transferring," Boris announced. "But – hmm. Everything is encrypted."

"Of course it is. What about the decryption software on our device?"

"Unresponsive. This is too much for it."

Crap. That was the best stuff I had, made by the best hacker I personally knew. The FBI had been making some improvements, it seemed.

"How long on the data?"

"At least another three minutes to get through the bulk of it. We need to–"

An alarm began to go off in the building, complete with revolving yellow and red lights and a siren. "We are experiencing a security breach," a mechanical voice said over the intercom system. "Please remain calm. Investigation is currently underway. Stand by for action plan."

Action plan, good grief. Who wrote this thing's script? Still, cheesy or not, now was the time to get Casey out of there. "Grab the dongle and head for the door," I told her, leaving the coffee shop and crossing the road toward the building. FBI agents who had been out on breaks were running back toward the building, some of them with guns in hand.

"Doesn't it need more time to work?"

"We're out of time, Casey." I slipped the tiny rectangular canister I'd taken from my purse into the jacket pocket of one of the rushing agents, then walked away, pulling my phone out again so I could see what happened next. "There's no sense in pushing our luck any further. Get out of there."

"But–"

"Hey!" It was the desk agent she'd first met, now back beside her and staring at the mess she'd made. "What do you think you're doing, huh?"

"I… um…"

"And why are you touching my computer?"

"Pull it and go!" I shouted, then activated the canister a second later. The man carrying it, who was about twenty feet away from the front desk, began to smoke. Literally, smoke poured out of his pocket, a flood of it, spreading through the lobby.

"That guy's on fire!" Casey shrieked, pointing. The desk agent glanced away, then swore and ran for the other agent, tackling him to the ground and rolling them both across the polished concrete floor.

"Now go, go!" Casey listened to me this time, grabbing the dongle and shoving it, and as much of her stuff as she could grab fast, into her pack before rushing out the door. I timed my stride to intercept her mad dash, and a minute's brisk walk later we were out of sight of the FBI office, and Casey was shaking like a Category 7 earthquake – so hard she was close to cracking.

"OK." I led her in between two buildings and put her back to one of the walls, trying to ignore the trash at our feet as she hyperventilated. "It's OK, deep breaths. C'mon, you can do better than that." I tilted her chin up so we could see eye to eye. "Look at me. Focus on me, OK? You're safe. Breathe." I inhaled extra dramatically, then gusted out an exhale. "Like that. Good, again. You can do it."

It didn't take very long for her to get control of her body again. As soon as she was breathing normally, though, she broke eye contact and looked straight down at the ground, her cheeks and neck going red. "Hey, none of that," I said. "You did fine. You got in, got out, and didn't get caught. That's a win."

"He saw me," she said in a small voice. "I should have done a better job covering my stuff up. I should have put the dongle in faster. I should have–"

I moved immediately to head that off. "*Should* is a poisonous word that doesn't do anyone any good. There's no such thing as *should* on a job. There's what you do, and that's all. Everything else is just wishful thinking."

"But what if we didn't get the information we need because I screwed up?"

I scoffed at her. "I'm sorry, who planned this job? Was it you?" Casey paused, then shook her head. "No, it was me. I'm the boss; it's my job to assess what my crew can and can't do, and to plan accordingly. Do you think I'd send Boris in to schmooze people at a ritzy museum?"

Casey sighed. "No."

"Impugning my honor," Boris muttered over the com, but he didn't sound too offended.

"Do you think I'd ask Bruno to crawl into a building through the ventilation system?"

Ah – now she'd cracked a little smile. "No."

"Have to be the world's biggest building," Bruno commented lightly.

"Exactly, buildings like that aren't even made. But are you taking my point?"

"I asked you to let me do it," Casey insisted.

"And I *did* let you do it, because I weighed the odds and thought for a first salvo, it was worth a try. And look, here we are!" I stepped back and turned a pirouette. "Free as birds!"

"Rats, more like," Boris murmured. "How does that filthy alley smell?"

"Boris, let the ladies have a moment, for Pete's sake."

Casey started to laugh. I took it as a good sign and gently eased the dongle out of her grasp, then put it into my purse. "Any luck on the decryption, guys?"

"Nada, boss," Bruno said. "Our program is pretty heavy duty, but it can't crack this code."

"Dang it." I was going to have to do something I really, really disliked. "Are you sure?"

"Give it another five years and we might get lucky," Boris said, in a rare moment of optimism – for him, at least. "But I doubt we have that kind of time."

"Yeah, no."

Casey looked up at me, hazel eyes brimming with tears. If it was an act, and I was fifty percent sure that it was at this point, then it was a good one. "You're not giving up, right?"

"No." I wasn't giving up, but I *was* giving in. *Shoot.*
I was going to have to talk to Tony Stark.

CHAPTER ELEVEN

We opted to meet that afternoon in Central Park. I could have gone to Stark Unlimited headquarters, but Tony had mostly divested himself of that particular brand these days, and I wasn't about to invite him to my place. I'd never be able to shut Boris up long enough to talk to Tony myself if I did – the man had *reams* of articles cued up in a folder he titled "Arguments Against Stupidity." Yeah, I'd be asking for trouble with that.

So, Central Park it was. Casey came with me, and together we ambled over to the Ramble, one of the prettier, wilder parts of the park. She was wide-eyed, looking like she'd fallen into a perpetual state of surprise. "I didn't know this place was so big," she said once we finally got to the designated 'meeting bench.' "It's like a real forest."

"It *is* a real forest," I said. She rolled her eyes. "Seriously, just because it's not out in the middle of nowhere doesn't mean it's any less real than any other forest. What have you got against New York City anyway?"

"Other than the fact that someone in it kidnapped my dad?"

"Other than that, yeah." She scowled. "Oh come on, that

can't be enough to spoil the whole city for you. You might be a girl on a mission, but you're also allowed to be a tourist. Look." I pointed down the trail. "The lake is just a few minutes' walk that way, and it's gorgeous. Go, take some pictures, give your dad something to feel good about when we find him instead of lamenting the fact that his daughter came to the greatest city in the world and didn't even stop to smell the roses."

"I want to meet Iron Man!" she protested.

"But this meeting isn't with Iron Man," I pointed out. "It's with Tony Stark. They're not always interchangeable these days, and anyway, you can still listen in." I indicated her com.

"But–"

"Seriously, go. While you're there, find someone selling a decent hot dog and bring me back one, OK? I'm starving." I tossed her a fifty, and she managed to grab it out of the air. She looked like she wanted to argue, but then her stomach rumbled. Hunger won out.

Not a minute after Casey disappeared down the path, Tony Stark sat down beside me. He was looking as sharp as ever – honestly, did the man ever wear anything *but* a suit of some kind? This one was blue, and the fabric had a slightly metallic sheen. Toss a few nuts and bolts in there and he could double as his own armor right now. "Cute kid. Yours?"

I rolled my eyes. "I'll pretend I didn't hear that." I smiled the kind of smile I reserved for the whales – the biggest marks – in every con. "Thanks so much for meeting me, Mr Stark."

"Oh, when you get an invitation from an old adversary with that many emojis in it, you've just got to respond," he replied lightly, giving me the exact same kind of smile.

Hot dang. It was too bad neither of us was the other's type, because otherwise we could have stolen the entire world together.

"So, Ms Gros. *Ah.*" He shook his head. "I'm sorry, Ms Hardy. What is it you want from me?"

Well, I couldn't let him start things off on *that* foot. "Aw, c'mon," I said. "You're not still holding that little visit I paid you against me, are you?"

"Oh, that little visit in which you conned your way into my building, architected an emergency, broke into my fabrication facilities, and proceeded to waste millions of dollars in tech?" He raised his sunglasses and looked straight at me. "That visit?"

"Oh, pish." I waved a hand. "It wasn't that bad. Think of me like a surprise security contractor. I identified your facility's weak points while *not* exposing you to huge levels of liability, if you don't count the aerial combat, and I–"

"Odessa Drake sued me."

I snorted a laugh. I couldn't help it. "She *what?*"

"She sued me. For 'failing to secure my technology against known threats' and 'invading private property' and half a dozen other things that I got my lawyers to toss out, but I had to devote an hour of my precious time to putting up with her face-to-face." He sighed a put-upon sigh. "That's an hour of my life I can never get back."

"Welcome to my world," I said. Odessa was like a cockroach – you stomped her flat over and over again, but she popped right back up with no more trouble than a bent antenna. "Sorry about that," I offered as an afterthought. "But honestly, the flight was more fun than annoying, wasn't it? And it was a neat little puzzle for you to figure out how I was pulling all those G-forces, right?"

"I'm not going to congratulate you for breaking into my lab," he said sternly, then added, "Legally I'm not allowed to. But that *was* pretty cool, which is why you have–" he glanced with exaggerated patience toward the limited-edition Patek Philippe watch on his wrist, which he definitely didn't need to tell the time "–one minute to tell me what this is about before I go and get lunch. I'm craving nachos, for some reason."

Touché, Stark. "It's really a very small thing, hardly worth your time, but..." I leaned a little closer, lowering my voice to add an air of intimacy. "I need some information decrypted."

"Oh, really?" he replied, equally quietly. "Is this about your breaking into the FBI office this morning? Because I've gotta say, I'm not thrilled at the idea of aiding a federal fugitive."

I frowned. "How did you know about that?"

"The same way I know everything – technology, baby." He leaned back and shrugged. "I know it's not publicized very well, but my company does have some of the most sophisticated facial recognition software in the world. I put a lot of R&D into it after the last time Stark Unlimited was infiltrated by a pretty redhead. I prefer the blonde on you, by the way," he added.

"Gee, I'll sleep better at night knowing that."

"It's none of my business what helps you rest your felonious little head."

Do not punch the mouthy billionaire, do not punch the mouthy billionaire... "Yes, I did get some information from the FBI this morning," I said at last. "But I'm not at all interested in compromising national security. This is a very personal matter for a friend of mine, and there's a lot at stake."

"I didn't know you were friends with Firestrike." His smirk

was back, full force. "Or his daughter, Casey. I learn something new every day."

I threw up my hands. "Anything else you want to lay out on the table while you're being a secretive, overly superior, supercilious di–"

"Careful there, boss," Bruno warned me. I sighed.

"Look, I wouldn't be talking to you about this if I didn't have to," I said. "Believe me. I have no interest in involving you in anything shady." Someone like Stark wouldn't be able to pull off shady if his life depended on it – he was turned up to ten thousand lumens all the time. "I just need you to point the way toward someone who can decrypt this for me. None of my contacts are up to it, not since the FBI upgraded their systems."

Stark raised a wry eyebrow. "They actually did a good job, huh?"

"Crazy good," I acknowledged. "So really, all I need is a name, maybe an introduction, and you'll have the satisfaction of helping a girl find her beloved father without compromising your delicate moral sensibilities."

"Well, when you put it like that... but no."

No? Crap. Except he wasn't standing up and walking off, so I was encouraged that "no" in this case probably meant "let's negotiate."

"Not for nothing," he went on.

Ha, I knew it!

"Before I help you, I want you to get the golden apple for me."

Dang it! "Stark–" I began warningly, but he cut me off.

"It's not because I want to use it," he explained. "It's because

I don't want it being used at all." The mirth was gone from his face like it had never been there, leaving something stern and slightly sad behind. "I know the draw of temptation like that," he said. "I know how badly it can mess things up for you, and all the people around you. I have no intention of letting that kind of power loose in my city, and I think you're smart enough to agree with me on this one." He arched an eyebrow. "Or *didn't* you have the opportunity to grab the apple for yourself and hesitate?"

"Hail the all-knowing Tony Stark," I said, without nearly the amount of venom I could have put into it. "Do you actually have a way of containing it, or – no, nope, never mind, I don't want to know." I sat back and considered the problem for a moment.

I could find another hacker, someone outside of my usual circles. It would take me a while, but I was sure I could do it. The FBI was a government agency, for heaven's sake, how good could their encryption be?

Good enough that Dr Steve's program couldn't crack it. Good enough that I'd probably be paying through the nose for anything that *could* get into it, and that went against my principles. I didn't pay for things like this – I stole them. Traded, worst came to worst. And, not insignificantly, we were working on a timetable and I couldn't even see the clock. Without knowing if Dalton Beck was even still alive…

But no, we were operating on the assumption that he was, thanks to the puzzle pieces that Casey was letting me catch a glimpse of.

"Are you waiting for the mood to be right, or…"

"Don't rush me," I chided Stark. "Geez, so impatient."

"It's kind of a time-critical operation."

"No kidding. If you're in such a rush, though, maybe you should hire some mercenaries to go after it for you." I tapped my chin with the nail of one manicured finger. "Didn't I hear you hired Domino and her crew to–"

"Always find the right person for the job," he said quickly. "In this case, that's you."

Hmm, to be acknowledged as the best was always a little flattering, even when it was coming from Tony Stark. I faced him more directly. "Who has the apple, then? Why are you so sure it hadn't been used already?"

"I'll tell you once you agree to get it for me."

Ooh, now there was a term I couldn't accept. "I won't agree to anything until you tell me who's got it." I wasn't even bluffing – there was no way I'd bind myself to doing something blind, and no way in *heck* that I'd tie my crew down that way either.

"Fine." Stark sighed and pulled his sunglasses off, rubbing the bridge of his nose. "The apple is in the possession of Sasha Hammer."

"Sasha... Hammer." I started to chuckle, then broke into a belly laugh. "The granddaughter of Justin Hammer? Whose company you keep crushing in the stock market? No wonder..." I tried to speak through my wheezes. "No wonder you're... in such a hurry!"

He frowned at me, but nodded. "Yeah. She's desperate for revenge, and she's not the type to waste a chance at taking me and my company out."

"And yet, you're still unscathed." I nodded. It was as good a guarantee as any that Miss Hammer hadn't used the apple yet. Surprising, given that she wasn't known for her restraint. If she'd had it since the Gala, then I'd underestimated her patience. "What do you think she's waiting for?"

Stark shrugged. "She's probably doing research on the best angle to take, maybe waiting to confer with her mother, Justine, before making her final decision. Does it matter?"

"Not really." Not that I was looking forward to going up against the power-hungry, tech-augmented wild child that was Sasha Hammer, but I could handle her. "Where is she?"

"In her family mansion on Long Island. Which," he continued with a sigh, "is filled with tech designed to detect, identify, and destroy any intruders, particularly those carrying Stark technology."

"Ah." I saw it now – the reason Stark wasn't going in himself. "You'd be fried, huh?"

"It's a problem I don't want to waste time solving, not when there are other options open to me," he said. "So. Will you do it?"

Out of the corner of my eye, I could see Casey was on her way back. I needed to wrap this up fast. "On the condition that you help me out whether I get the apple or not. Ah-ah!" I raised a finger and shook it in his direction as he opened his mouth. "Sasha Hammer might use it in the next five seconds. She might give it to someone else. Someone else might steal it before I get there. I'm not sticking my neck out for you without a guarantee, Stark."

"Isn't my word enough of a guarantee?" he asked.

"I wish it was," I said honestly, because I could see that he meant it. But I didn't trust easily, and I certainly wasn't about to trust a guy I'd ripped off not so long ago. "But no. I want the name of the person who can help us, as well as whatever their fee is going to be, uploaded to a secure server that you'll share the link for within the next hour."

"Hey," Stark began to protest. "We didn't make any sort of deal about payment–"

"It's not for *me*," I interjected. "Try to keep that in mind, huh? It's for her." I pointed at Casey, who had huge, messy hot dogs in both hands. "A motherless child who we're trying to keep from becoming an orphan. C'mon, listen to your heartstrings, Stark! You know you want to."

He pursed his lips for a second, then sighed and stood up. "Fine. But it has to be done today. The longer you wait–"

"I won't." I smiled winsomely at him. "Cross my heart."

"I must be insane," he muttered. "Trusting the Black Cat not to run off with the golden apple as soon as she gets her claws on it."

"I'll try to get footage of the entire heist," I promised him. "So you can verify for yourself I'm not ripping you off. Seriously, Tony, I have no personal interest in this apple, and I'll prove it."

"You'd better."

Casey joined us then. One corner of her mouth was stained with mustard – clearly she'd already indulged. "Um." She looked between us, then held a hot dog out to Stark. "Lunch?"

He looked at the dripping hot dog, then at her, then at me. All of a sudden, his stiff, square shoulders relaxed, and he settled back on the bench with a chuckle. "Eh, why not?" He took the hot dog in both hands. "Thanks, kid," he said before taking a huge bite.

Hmm, winning friends and influencing people one hot dog at a time. Casey was a natural at this.

After I finished my own lunch, I put Stark in contact with Boris to work out the details of the transfer – no doubt they'd have a *screaming* good time – before whisking Casey back to where I'd asked Bruno to wait for us. I had a job to plan, and no time to waste on the subway.

CHAPTER TWELVE

Some jobs called for the upfront approach, like the one Casey had pulled in the FBI field office that morning. Sure, she hadn't outright said she was there to steal from them, but she'd hardly hidden it either.

Other jobs called for being covert, which was why I'd left my loudly complaining, teenage sidekick-wannabe at the apartment and headed out to Long Island with only Bruno on standby as my driver.

"Don't seem like enough firepower, boss," he said, a little worriedly as he watched me doublecheck my gear. "You sure you don't want to take at least one more gun in with ya?"

"I'm good," I said, checking to make sure my earrings were securely fastened. To be honest, I was a little nervous about breaking into a mansion whose security system was designed to detect subdermal, integrated Iron Man technology. My suit, fetchingly skin-tight though it was, was actually full of micro-servos and other implants that increased my speed, strength, and agility. My earrings, my gloves – heck, my contact lenses –

all had implements in them that were vital to giving me the high-level performance I relied on during a job. If my hardware was detected and my cover was blown, well, having an extra gun wasn't likely to help me all that much.

I had a feeling I'd be relying an awful lot on my quantum probability pulsator tonight.

At least Stark had been good for getting me a basic blueprint of the place. Even Sasha Hammer's home wasn't immune to a satellite flyby. "There are only three guards in there with her right now," I said, mentally reviewing their potential routes. "The rest of her security detail is traveling with her mother. Sasha's personal rooms are on the west side of the mansion, and the guards aren't allowed in there. It's the likeliest place for her to have the apple."

"Then why not just hop the wall over there and go in close?"

"Because the security system is most densely distributed over there too," I said. "I'd rather get a handle on it somewhere I don't have to dodge bullets."

"Oh, now you're just being dramatic," Boris said over the line. "Get in there and start spreading the bad luck around and you'll be fine."

"Maybe one of them will trip," Casey suggested.

"Oh, they'll do much more than trip," Boris replied with an evil laugh. "She once made a man lose his entire–"

"Quiet, please. I need to focus." And I didn't want Casey barfing up her lunch when Boris got too caught up in relating the gory details. Nobody needed to know that much about another person's bodily functions.

I got out of the car and Bruno drove off, just the way he was supposed to, to start his fifteen-minute round trip of this part of town. It was safer than him idling and hoping security didn't notice him.

All right. Fifteen minutes to get in, get the apple, and get out. Piece of cake.

First things first – the outer wall. This mansion really was built like a fortress, but no wall could withstand the steel micro-filaments that made up my claws. Climbing the wall was easier than climbing a set of stairs, and I barely left a scratch on it. At the top, I carefully cut through the layers of barbed wire and pushed them back to slink through the gap. After a twenty-foot drop, I was inside the compound. I could practically feel the electronic eyes turning my way.

I also saw the enormous Irish wolfhound coming my way. The dog was running straight at me, teeth bared but not barking, a long line of drool dangling from its lower jaws. It looked like an absolute killer.

Good thing I kept the equivalent of catnip for dogs in the top of one of my gloves. Casey, who followed an unnerving number of super hero social media accounts, told me that Squirrel Girl swore by it. I hoped so. When the dog was within ten feet, I fired an irresistibly noxious concoction of creamy peanut butter and anchovy paste toward the closest wall of the mansion.

The dog immediately turned, following the spattered trail of treats, and I ran with it, getting as close to the enormous beast's body as I could to help hide my biosignature. By the time the pup had inhaled the treat and remembered I existed, I was already perched outside the nearest second-story window, triggering my pulsator. *C'mon, gimme something good.*

Suddenly, down on the lawn all the sprinklers went off. The

dog, who had been starting to growl, whined instead, running and barking as it tried to escape the water.

The nearest guard, who just so happened to be passing by the room whose ledge I was clinging to when the sprinklers went off, ran into the room and, after a moment of undoing probably five complicated locks, opened the window up. "Aw, for the love of–" He got on his walkie-talkie. "Andy, what's going on with the sprinklers? They're not supposed to go off for another three hours!"

Focusing on him, I triggered my pulsator again.

"Yeah, well I don't care whose fault it is, figure out a way to – *whoa!*" He fumbled the walkie-talkie, then swore as it fell into the shrubbery below. "You've got to be kiddin' me," he muttered as he ran out of the room… leaving the window conveniently open.

I did a muscle-up into a forward roll and landed in a crouch on the floor before he was all the way down the hall. "New lifeform detected," a mechanical voice announced. "Identify yourself or be destroyed."

Uh-oh, not good.

"What the–"

And the guard was coming back.

"Identify yourself or be destroyed in five… four… three…"

I leapt across the room to the top of the wall right above the doorframe and held on tight. "Two." I triggered my pulsator one more time.

"One." A crackle of light flared across the room from an array set into the wall just above the huge flatscreen TV, which had been muted so that I couldn't hear what the beautiful, dark-haired woman whose face filled the wall was saying. On the other side of the room, right down by the floorboard, a cockroach suddenly died a quick and very smoky death.

The guard who'd gone running to retrieve his walkie-talkie ran into the room, stopping just in front of the door to wave a hand in front of his face in an effort to clear the smoke. "What the..." He was coughing so hard he didn't even feel me detach the shielding device from his lapel.

His DNA was input into the computer system already, I figured – the secondary device was just a backup, the sort of thing you'd hand a visitor whom you didn't want to give free rein in your personal monument to paranoia. I figured I qualified as a visitor, and I didn't want to roast any more bugs if I could help it while I was here.

While the guard hacked and coughed, I crawled out into the hallway, clinging to the plaster and brick fifteen feet off the floor. The Hammers had a decent set of security cameras, but as long as I stayed right in the center of the vaulted ceiling, I'd be hard to see. Now, to crawl to Sasha's rooms.

It was slow going, and I had to stop several times to catch my breath while resting against a gaudy crystal chandelier. *Spider-Man I am not.* My claws were meant more for cutting than clinging, so I had to take it slow to keep from crumbling my handholds. *This is my ab workout for the next week... maybe two.* I was getting close, though – close enough by now that I could hear Sasha yelling at her mother over the phone, which was evidently on speaker.

"–don't see why I can't use it now! I know *exactly* how to take Stark down!"

"This isn't a discussion," her mother, Justine Hammer, said crisply. Her voice had the authoritative sound of a woman used to ruling whatever sphere she was dealing with, whether it was her company boardroom or her family. "You will wait for me to return from Shanghai before you do anything with that apple, do you understand?"

"But it's dangerous to have it around and not use it!"

"Pfft, how dangerous could it be? It's not as though you let anyone know you have it, right?"

There was a moment of profound silence, then a shrill grunt of inarticulate rage. "*Sasha*, tell me you didn't!"

"He's supposed to feel menaced," Sasha practically shrieked. "How is he going to feel menaced if I don't let him know I'm coming for him?"

"Are you a complete idiot? The fox doesn't send snarky DMs to the hens in the henhouse letting them know it's coming to dine." Justine sounded like her daughter had just stomped on her last nerve. "I should have known better than to trust you with something like this. This kind of behavior is why you couldn't cut it as Detroit Steel. This is why you'll never amount to anything more than – what's that sound?"

"What sound?" Sasha asked in a small voice. "I don't…"

I could tell the moment she started to hear it, because I did as well. A low hum, quickly becoming more high-pitched, and then–

CRASH! The sound of glass shattering pierced the air, and Sasha screamed. I dropped to the ground and ran for her rooms, caution thrown to the wind. Someone had gotten here before me – but who?

Or rather – *hoot*. The party crasher's head turned a hundred and eighty degrees to face me as I ran into Sasha's suite, and snapped his fanglike teeth at me. "Stay back, Cat," Leland

Owlsley, also known as the Owl, grunted as he snatched the golden apple up from the literal pedestal Sasha had put it on. He had a gun in the other hand, which was trained right at my head. *Ugh. Rude as ever.* Sasha's security system blared in the background, but I could already tell that the Owl wasn't going to be around long enough for it to make a difference.

"You too?" I demanded. Seriously, was *everybody* interested in this thing?

Leland smirked. "Kingpin's paying me a fortune for it, money I don't have to mess up my karma to get. I'll mess you up plenty if you come after me, though."

He tucked it into his voluminous black cape and darted for the broken window. I ran after him, claws extended because screw his threats, but he leapt just before I could grab him, firing a few rounds at me for good measure as he went, making the wooden window frame spit splinters. He glided across the lawn and over the wall.

No, I could still get him. I pulled out one of my grappling hooks and readied it to fire, aiming right for the spot where his cape looped around the back of his neck. If I could grab him –

A hand grabbed me first and spun me around. I wrenched myself free and dropped just as Sasha let loose with a blast from the repulsor tech in her fingertips. The power was immense, enough to blow out the remnants of the window as well as blowing off the hood I'd covered up my hair with.

"Got you now, you *bi–*"

I spun around and swept Sasha's legs out from under her right before she fired at me again. She ended up blasting the floor while she was just a few inches above it, sending herself into a whirling, chaotic backflip that ended with her crashing face-first into the TV on the wall. It shattered and followed her to the ground with a resounding *smash*.

Ha. I didn't even have to use my quantum probability rig to pull it off, either! I patted myself on the back even as I prepared my own exit. Sasha might be down, but I knew she wasn't out. I heard her power up her tech again, about to put the "lash" in "flashy" with her built-in energy whips, and knew it was time to get out.

Without the apple. *Dang it.*

Oh well. At least *I* didn't have Justine Hammer to explain myself to. Tony Stark would make good on our deal one way or another, and at least he couldn't take away my allowance.

CHAPTER THIRTEEN

"Is he here yet?"

"Stop craning your neck like that, you're going to get a crick in it," I scolded Casey for the tenth time in as many minutes. "Not to mention make people notice you. We're not here to get noticed."

"You're wearing a snakeskin mini-dress," she said, completely deadpan. "There's no way at least half the people coming into the museum aren't noticing you."

"Aw, that's sweet, but it's a different kind of notice and you know it," I replied. "Look at us. Look at the picture we make." I indicated myself where I was sitting one leg crossed over the other in the uncomfortable plastic chair, then her across from me at the small table. "What do we look like?"

"*I* look like a normal kid," Casey said, hunching her shoulders in the depths of her hoodie. "*You* look like a Barbie doll."

Ha, a Barbie doll covering up a multitude of bruises. I was lucky that sheer stockings were back in style, because going bare-legged wasn't an option for me today. I'd passed on the name of the apple's new owner to Stark, who'd sworn and admitted the chase was over after that.

Why? Because the man paying the Owl to do his dirty work was none other than our fine city's mayor, Wilson Fisk, also known as the Kingpin. He'd gone from a hard target to a near-impossible one once he became mayor, and I wasn't going to tangle with that unless I had no choice. Which I did, so...

"Hell*oooo*?"

Oh right, I'd been having a moment with my annoying sidekick. "Everything about my appearance is deliberate. Remember why?"

She heaved the sigh of the put-upon teenager, but the quickness with which she answered let me know that she was more interested than she was letting on. "Because we're trying to make this guy let his guard down around us."

"Exactly. If I came to him dressed like the competent criminal mastermind I am, he'd worry he was about to get taken advantage of."

Casey raised one eyebrow. "You're, like, a super narcissist, aren't you?"

"It's not narcissism if it's true," I said, leaning in. We had a few minutes before Special Agent Jacobs, the name our hacker had wrangled from the FBI's data, was supposed to show up, so it was as good a teachable moment as ever. "Look. Confidence is important in any line of work, but if you're going to be successful as a thief, you've got to have it in spades. Sure, there's your crew for backup, but often the act itself is going to come down to you conning the right person at the right time, or breaking through the door at just the right moment, or getting people to look at your right hand while you steal from them with your left. You follow?"

"But… I'm not trying to be a successful thief," Casey said slowly.

"Oh, no? Then we shouldn't be trying to steal your father back from the Maggia?"

"No, we should!" Her hazel eyes went wide with alarm, and her hood fell off as she abruptly leaned forward. "We should! I'm not saying we shouldn't."

"Then you need to treat this seriously," I said. "Now. What's the show we're putting on right now?"

"Um… well, we're in the Guggenheim Museum."

"One of the greatest art museums in the world," I agreed. "And what are we doing here?"

"Sitting in the cafeteria."

"Why?"

"Because…" She looked between us. "Because neither of us is interested in the art. You're, like, interested in looking good, and I'm just into playing on my phone and stuff. Maybe we're waiting for someone, or maybe we're just killing some time, but we're not here to look at pictures."

"Exactly. Because we're shallow. And why do we want to appear shallow to an FBI agent?"

"So he'll underestimate us," Casey said firmly.

"Got it." I winked at her, then glanced at the door. "And if I'm not mistaken, our mark has made us. Remember – you're a surly teenager who's too cool for everything, and I'm a dumb bunny who lucked into the right bit of information. Nothing about the infiltration, nothing about Stark, nothing that could get us in trouble. OK? We're talking pure bribery here."

"I *got* it, geez."

"Good." I sat back and watched our contact swerve around random groups of people as he headed our way, as focused as a laser.

Agent Gregory "Don't call me Greg" Jacobs was the perfect picture of a model FBI agent. He had the sharp jaw, the upright carriage, the alert eyes. He even made their off-the-rack suits look good. What he *didn't* have was a sense of morals, since according to the data Boris had mined out of our decrypted thumb drive yesterday, Jacobs had been Dalton Beck's direct minder while he was here, in charge of his personal security and all his movements. Beck getting kidnapped on his watch was a huge black mark on his record, for sure... which was undoubtedly assuaged by the covert half-a-million-dollar deposit delivered to his ailing grandmother's bank account the same hour Beck went missing. Apparently, he'd already put in for early retirement from the feds.

I got that I didn't have a leg to stand on when it came to moral high ground in most situations, but you could bet I wouldn't be selling out the people who depended on me, not for art, gold, money, or magic. Once you did that, once you'd rotted away to the extent that everyone under your care became nothing but an equation with a solid "sell-out" figure at the end of it, you were done. That kind of reputation would ruin you in the field. Special Agent Jacobs had *better* retire, after what he did. His fellow agents knew they had a snake among them now, no matter how he'd spun it to them.

Right now, I was counting on that snake to have a little more left to sell.

He was almost at our table. I stood up, silently congratulating myself on my choice of shoes – so many people loved long legs but didn't care for the company of women who were taller than them, and getting to just the right height in your heels could be a real pain – and offered the back of my hand. "Mr Jacobs," I simpered, then batted my eyelashes. "Or is it Agent?"

"Special Agent Jacobs," he said, with full-strength pomposity, shaking my hand instead of taking the kiss bait. All-righty, then. "My mysterious contact, I presume?"

"In the flesh." I could see his eyes linger on it, too – which they should, after all the trouble I'd gone to put it on display. "Won't you sit with us?"

He glanced down at Casey. "Who's this?"

"An interested party."

I thought it was going to go over his head for a minute, but then the frown of confusion cleared. There wasn't a hint of guilt in his face, though. He might have been sitting next to some random kid at a bus stop instead of the daughter of a man he'd sold to the Maggia.

A sociopath, great. Just who I wanted to deal with today.

Jacobs sat down, ignoring Casey completely so he could focus on me. "Your request to meet was very vague," he said. "I'm not sure what you're hoping to get from this. I can't talk about any of our active investigations. If you have information about a missing person and are interested in claiming a reward, then–"

"Oh, Special Agent Jacobs, there's no need to be coy," I said with a smile. "We're both in the business of… information gathering, after all. There's no need to pretend you weren't handling Mr Beck's affairs while he was here in New York."

Jacobs' vaguely superior expression turned flinty. "How did you learn that?"

No denial. This guy really wasn't used to being on the other side of an interrogation. Maybe it was just because he hadn't figured out that this was one yet, but probably because he wasn't nearly as smart as he thought. "I have my ways."

"Ways like breaking into our Manhattan office?" He leaned in and folded his arms across the table. "You realize I could arrest you for that, right?"

"You realize if the FBI had any conclusive evidence that I was behind it, they already would have, right?" I replied, still keeping it cool. Casey stared between both of us, the line between her eyebrows getting deeper and deeper. *Calm down, kid.*

Jacobs shifted like he was about to stand up. I spoke quickly. "I don't care about the past," I said. "What's done is done. All I care about is finding Mr Beck before something unfortunate happens to him. There never needs to be any mention of you at all, and as I understand it, you're leaving the FBI soon anyway, right?"

The look on his face got even darker. Shoot, I was losing him. "That's none of your business," he snapped, and pushed the chair back. "I'm not going to sit here and–"

"There's a bomb under your chair."

Jacobs and I both turned to look at Casey with incredulous eyes. "What are you talking about?" our very special agent demanded.

"A bomb," Casey repeated slowly, like she was talking to a child – or an idiot. "Under your chair. Triggered by a change in pressure. If you stand up now – *boom*." She mimed a mushroom cloud expanding with her hands.

"You're lying," Jacobs scoffed, but his face was covered in sweat. "You're just a kid. You don't know how to–"

"My father is Firestrike," Casey said, mean and condescending and so much like an angsty teenager I would have laughed, if I wasn't worried she was serious. "You think he didn't tell me how to make a basic bomb with a pressure switch? My dad could make flames *dance*. A bomb like this is child's play. The fire probably won't even spread beyond your chair."

"I – you can't–"

"Try standing up and find out." Casey sneered. "Go on. I dare you."

Jacobs glared at me. "How could you let her do such a thing?"

"You must not hang out around many kids," I replied, letting my exasperation show. I was almost certain Casey hadn't put a bomb under that chair, but I couldn't be entirely sure. I hated being out of control, but now wasn't the time for a scolding. "It's not a question of *letting* them do things, most of the time. Look." I smiled as placatingly as I knew how. "All you have to do is tell us who kidnapped Dalton Beck, and we'll get out of your hair. Who were you in communication with? How did they arrange the details of what they wanted you to do?"

"Talk or get crispy," Casey added. "It's your choice."

Oh my god, shut up. I kept my placid smile on my face, completely ignoring the teenage menace sitting next to me. I watched Jacobs weigh his options in his mind, the urge to stand up and walk out of here fighting against the idea that maybe, just possibly, Casey was telling the truth. "I strongly suggest cooperating with us," I said as his legs twitched. "After all, I do have quite a bit of evidence about your personal affairs that I'd hate to bring to the attention of your colleagues."

"You–" He clamped his mouth shut for a second, then glanced at Casey again. "Fine," he snapped after a few more sweaty seconds. "Two weeks ago, I received an anonymous phone call about Mr Beck, and decided it was in my best interests to comply with the demands the caller made. I want to make it clear, this was a matter of life and death for me–"

"My *father's* life and death," Casey almost shouted. I grabbed her wrist warningly.

"Please go on," I said.

"I was told where and when to make Mr Beck available," Jacobs continued, now focused on me like his life depended on it. Which – honestly, perhaps it did. "And I was told that … that if I happened to see the criminal known as Mr H in the vicinity, that I should do nothing to interfere with him."

"Hammerhead," I muttered. *Great.* Ugh, I had a history with that guy that didn't bear dwelling on. There was no escaping it now, though. I sat back. "Thank you for sharing this information, it's very helpful to us."

"Screw you," Jacobs said. His hands were so slippery with sweat that they squeaked as he laid them on the tabletop. "Now deactivate the bomb."

"Nah," Casey replied before I could speak. "I'd rather do this." She swiped a few times on her phone, then showed Jacobs the screen. On it was a big red button that read BOOM!

"No!" Jacobs shouted, reaching desperately for the phone. "You can't–"

"Boom!" Casey pushed the button before I could get the phone away from her.

There was a sudden loud *crack-crack-crack* like someone had just popped a whole roll of bubble wrap at once, and the air was quickly filled with smoke. People all around us began to panic, running for the exits. And me?

I was furious. I grabbed Casey's phone out of her hands, turning her vindictive laughter into an affronted "Hey!" as I shut down the audio file she was running. The cracking noise stopped. I put her phone in my bag, then got up and walked around the table to where Special Agent Jacobs was still sitting, completely un-scorched and all right, on his chair.

Well, not *totally* all right. "I'm so sorry about this," I said, but he was already getting up and stumbling away from us, his white face rapidly turning red as he realized Casey had pranked him. He didn't say another word, only straightened his back and walked out of the Guggenheim like he hadn't just been publicly humiliated.

I turned to Casey, who was back to snickering, and grabbed her by the arm. She tried to pull away, but I didn't let go, marching her toward the exit.

"What?" she demanded, still tugging fruitlessly as we entered the relatively fresh air outside. I could hear sirens approaching – this place would be a mess of police soon. Fortunately, Bruno was standing by not far away, and had the car over to pick us up before the cops got here.

He didn't say a thing as I pushed Casey into the backseat and followed her in, just gave me a meaningful look. Boris was uncharacteristically silent too. Yep, they knew what had gone down, and they expected me to do something about it.

Ugh. I hated being the disciplinarian, but I hated being endangered by someone else's theatrics more.

"What is *wrong* with you?" Casey was saying as we pulled out from the curb. "That was funny, admit it! And he deserved it, too! He sold my father to the *Maggia*, I think that means I get to take revenge and–"

"Is that what you think it means?" I snapped. "That you get to steal one of my smoke grenades – and don't lie to me about that, I know that smell, it's a Boris special – and set up a trap for someone in a public place, where we're supposed to be keeping a low profile, just so you can have the satisfaction of scaring a contact?"

"He's not a contact," Casey said. "He's no better than a murderer!"

"Maybe that's true, but he's a murderer we needed information from," I replied frostily. "We might *still* need information from him if the little bit we got from him doesn't pan out. I didn't get a chance to ask him more questions, because I had an angry child with a grudge with me who was waiting to make a stupid move for the sake of her own personal satisfaction."

"Why wouldn't his information pan out?" Casey asked, some of her viciousness gone as uncertainty began to set in. "He said Mr H, and you sounded like you knew the guy, so I figured…"

"That that was it? In the worlds of both crime and chess, Hammerhead is a pawn," I told her. "Maybe he knows something, maybe he doesn't, but it sure would've been nice to have an FBI agent willing to talk to me about what *else* he might know about your father's disappearance, just in case."

"But… I don't…"

"And worse than that," I went on, getting to the heart of my discontent, "because I really don't care that you humiliated a corrupt man, is the fact that you didn't bring any of this up with me before you did it. You acted on your own, in secrecy, on a job we're all working together on. A job meant to benefit *you*, and your dad. And let me tell you, you couldn't find a more sympathetic ear to listen to when it comes to dad troubles, but if you just spiked the wheel for us? I'm not going to feel bad when we come up empty."

That was a total lie, I'd feel like crap if we never found her dad, but I couldn't let Casey know that right now. This was a teachable moment, something she desperately needed to understand if she wasn't going to screw things up for all of us in the future. Black Fox had done the same thing for me when I'd let my emotions get the better of me.

"Tell me you're getting this," I said, watching her desperately try to keep her face from crumbling. "Tell me this is sinking in. Because if it's not, and you're planning to keep going rogue, then I'll cut you loose right now. And if you try to come back at me or my crew for that, or think you can play me right now–"

"I'm sorry!" Casey cried. Literally cried – tears were rolling down her cheeks, her thick black mascara creating rivers of regret. Poor thing, had she never thought to buy the waterproof version? "I didn't think it would be such a big deal, and I was so angry at him, and then when you got up and I saw my chance, I…"

"Used the grenade you'd stolen and the program you'd prewritten to screw with my plans." Actions spoke louder than words. "Forgive me if I'm having trouble believing your change of heart, given your preparations."

"I wrote that program when I was thirteen," Casey protested. "And the grenade… OK, I took that last night. I thought, after what happened at the FBI office, something like that might come in handy if I had to escape from a place again."

Well, she had a point there. "If you need specific things on you in order to feel safe, talk to me about them," I said. "I don't care if it's a grenade or a gun or a stuffy, I'll make sure you have it, I just need to know about it. OK? The more I know, the better my plans will be. We could have *totally* made that guy wet himself without causing a panic in the Guggenheim."

Casey sniffed. "Really?"

"Really really."

"OK." She wiped her face on one of her long sleeves, then looked in distaste at the black marks left behind. "Oh, gross."

"Here." I pulled a tissue out of my bag and handed it to her. From up front, Bruno chuckled. "What's so funny?"

"Nothin', boss. Just… I never figured you for the kind of person who'd end up carrying a 'mom' purse around." He caught my blank look in the rearview mirror. "You know, a purse that's got something for everything – tissues, water, breath mints, band-aids…"

"I'm not carrying that stuff around for her," I objected. "It's all useful!"

"Grenades are useful," Boris said over the line, finally putting his two cents in. "Breath mints are pure vanity. If someone is close enough to you to dislike how your breath smells, they're too close."

"Spoken like a guy who never gets laid."

"Bruno, I swear to heaven I will–"

I let the bickering go, sitting back in my seat and only occasionally looking at Casey out of the corner of my eye. After a bit of thinking, I pulled out my phone and shot off a text to "Spider": *Care to go for a stroll in the moonlight?*

I got a reply gratifyingly fast. *Who would we be strolling for?*

Can't it just be about enjoying your company?

It's like you think I don't know you at all. Come on, who is it?

Hammerhead. I've got some questions that only he can answer.

There was a pause, and then – *I think I know where he's been hanging out lately. He's not alone, though.*

I smiled. So much the better.

Meet you on your roof at eight.

Make it nine. It was going to take me a while to scrub the smell of smoke off myself.

You got it. He put a little spider emoji at the end of his text. I rolled my eyes – what a dork – but my smile was so wide it hurt my cheeks.

This afternoon might not have gone so well, but tonight I had a date with Spider-Man, so things were looking up.

CHAPTER FOURTEEN

"So why are you after Hammerhead?" a familiar voice asked me, as I climbed over the edge of my building's roof. "I thought you guys were buds."

"We've worked together in the past," I clarified, coming over to stand next to Spider-Man, aka Peter Parker. "We're not 'buds' though. He's a little too demented to be reliable."

"And that's saying something," Peter said. This close, I could tell he was smiling beneath his mask, that brat. How a man could keep such a childlike sense of humor into his late twenties was beyond me.

Then again, I lived with two man-children who were in their forties, so maybe the issue was my expectations.

"Yes, it is," I replied, nose in the air. "I only associate with very sane and competent people, thank you very much."

"What about the time you decided to date Flash Thompson as part of your harassment campaign against me?"

"I was emotionally distraught."

"Or the time you faked your own death?"

"Nobody was acting sane or competent during that time."

"Or when you decided to become the crime boss of New York City?"

I crossed my arms. "Well, *that* time I was recovering from having the tar beaten out of me by Dr Octopus, who was wearing your body when he did it, so I think you of all people don't have a leg to stand on when it comes to that."

"Yeah, you're right. Sorry," Peter said, the teasing edge fading from his voice. I didn't care for that – we'd said our sorrys a long time ago. There was no looking back now, only forward.

"Anyway, I need Hammerhead because he might have abducted someone I'm on the hook to find. Talk to me about him," I said. "Where is he hiding these days?"

"In an abandoned movie theater in Queens."

Oh, my. How very unsurprising. "The RKO?"

"That's the one."

The place was a relic of the Roaring Twenties and perfectly fit with Hammerhead's aesthetics – no wonder he'd settled into that derelict old monument. "Well then, I guess I'm going to Queens." I inspected my grappling hooks, then glanced at Spidey. "How about a lift?"

"Aw, I thought we'd get to take one of your fancy cars," Peter said. "Don't you have a new Ferrari? I'm sure that's what I saw you driving in the pictures from the Gala."

"That's not mine, it's Danny Rand's." And sheesh, I needed to get it and his other stuff back to him. I'd have to remind the guys about it tomorrow. For now, Danny hadn't said anything, and I had other priorities. "And what would MJ say about you being so ungallant toward me, huh?"

"She'd probably say 'good job.'"

She probably would, but only because she liked to tease me

almost as much as Peter did. Our truce was hard-fought but quite solid these days. "Well, if you're really going to be that way about it..." I fired my grappling hook at the building next door, then smirked at Peter. "Try to keep up." I jumped off the roof and straight into a long, swinging arc that gave me plenty of time to deploy my next hook.

The wind in my face, the swooshing sensation in my stomach as I fell, the people and traffic all bustling below me, and the comforting presence – not that I'd ever say it out loud – of Peter at my side... it was everything a girl could ask for. Better than diamonds, better than gold, better than all the treasure the world had to offer. I was strong, I was happy, and I was free. Nothing could beat that.

Although big, beautiful diamonds came pretty darn close.

My whole body was thrumming with energy by the time we reached our destination, landing on its front wall just above where the dilapidated "RKO THEATRE" sign was half falling off. The building looked completely dark from the outside, but Peter was tilting his head in that way that meant his enhanced senses were at work.

"I can hear five people," he said after a moment. "I think. It's a little hard to pick them all out thanks to the echoes in there. Lots of plaster, really tall ceilings, and most of the seats have been torn out of the floor at this point."

"Five is doable."

"Black Cat." I couldn't see his eyes behind the mask he was wearing, but he sounded concerned. "Hammerhead is tougher than he looks."

"I've worked with him before," I reminded Peter. "I know what he's capable of."

"Do you really?"

I sighed. "Spider-Man. Come on. Do I look like the kind of girl who underestimates her opponents?"

"No... but just, tell me this: is it seriously important that you talk to him? Like, life and death important?" His voice was low and intense, enough to send an appreciative shiver down my spine. "Because if it isn't, it's not worth it."

"It really is life and death," I said, perfectly genuine.

Peter sighed. "There's no need to make fun of me, I'm just trying to be nice."

"I'm not making fun of you! Who said anything about making fun?" I demanded, putting my hands on my hips. "I'm being *earnest*."

"No wonder I didn't get it."

"Oh, ha-ha." I readied myself to jump down to the ground, but Peter caught my wrist before I could go over.

"Don't let him grab you. OK?"

"I won't," I promised. He let go, and we both hit the ground in almost perfect silence a second later. From there, we crept in through the front entrance of the building – there was no door, thankfully, because it would surely creak – and headed through the lobby for the main theater.

Posters of golden-era movie stars lined the walls, their colors impossible to make out in the darkness. All the glass was broken, scattered across the floor and stepped on so many times it had been ground back into sand in some places. The architecture was done in a Spanish Baroque style, gilt and curlicues and twisted carvings along the ceiling and doorways. It was quite lovely, in an eerie, desolated kind of way.

The closer we got to the theater, the easier it was to hear

our targets. Low voices laughed raucously, and the clink of bottles hitting cement was a welcome counterpoint. They were drinking. That would make this easier.

Honestly, I was kind of hoping for hard though. I still had energy to burn after my doozy of a day.

"Don't forget to try out your new toy," Boris said over our com.

"Oh, I won't."

Peter perked up. "Is that Boris? Tell him hi for me."

"Spider-Man says hi," I said.

"Tell him he's a wretch who owes me twenty dollars."

"He says you owe him money," I passed on.

"No, he's completely wrong about that bet, and by the way if MJ ever asks, I absolutely do not bet on which super hero's costume is going to rip first in a fight."

"He says you're wrong," I told Boris. "And I'm done playing telephone, so if you want to make silly bets together, you can do it on your off hours. Capische?"

Bruno started to laugh. "Gettin' real into the mood of the job, huh boss?"

"Shaddup, ya mook." We paused at the center entrance to the theater, crouching behind leprous-looking colonnades to glance down at the stage below. The immense, elaborate backdrop of this once-glorious theater was marred by the cheap folding chairs laid out on the raised cement platform, where five men were gathered around a folding aluminum metal table playing poker. Hammerhead was the biggest goon by far, and the only super powered one as far as I could tell. He was in his classic pinstripe suit, his Frankenstein monster's-noggin taking up more airspace than his intellect warranted.

"I'll handle Hammerhead, you take the other four," I whispered.

"Black Cat, seriously, I think it would be better if we worked together on–"

"Ah-ah." I put one of my fingers against Peter's mouth, claw extended. He shut up. Smart guy. "This is my job, and my call. I'll ask for help if I need it, promise, but I can do this."

Peter nodded. "OK."

"Good. Now." I grinned, adrenaline amping up in my veins. "Shall we crawl in, or would you like me to make a scene first?"

"Whatever won't get you shot," he said.

"Scene it is! You get one minute to get set up, use it wisely." I waited for Peter to disappear over the edge of the door, then started counting down in my head from sixty, plotting my attack.

Hammerhead had a head that was, unsurprisingly, harder than a hammer. His skull was enhanced – heck, every bone in his upper body was harder than adamantium, and his muscles were enhanced as well. He was strong enough to crush a person with his bare hands, tough enough to get thrown through a wall and come back swinging, and dangerous enough that the Thompson sub-machine gun by his feet seemed entirely unnecessary.

In other words, he was going to be fun.

Three... two... one... I stepped out from behind the wall and posed for a moment in the shell of the door. They probably couldn't see much more than my silhouette from down there, given the scarcity of light, but that was fine.

"Having a party without me, boys?" I called out. "How rude."

CHAPTER FIFTEEN

All five men swiveled around in their seats. The four helper-goons stood up, groping for their weapons and hastily pointing them at me. Only Hammerhead remained seated. "Black Cat," he said, his voice faintly tinged with a Russian accent. I knew he'd overcome the brain damage that had made him think he was an old-school gangster, but I didn't know his original accent had come back with it. "What are you doing here?"

"Oh, I was in the neighborhood and thought I'd drop by and say hi to my favorite semi-cyborg," I replied, sauntering a few more steps down. I couldn't see Peter, but I knew he was out there, putting his plan into place. I just needed to give him time to enact it. "I like the new digs. They're so..." I smiled. "You."

He didn't care for my little quip. I watched the edge of the metal table he was holding onto crumple in his grasp. "I will ask you again, Cat, one last time. What are you doing here?"

"I'm looking for answers," I said. Huh, maybe this would work out; maybe we wouldn't have to fight about it. "About a possible kidnapping you and your guys pulled off a little while back."

Hammerhead laughed. "And you think I'm just going to tell you about my business? How do I know you're not wearing a wire? How do I know you won't bring the police down on my head?"

I rolled my eyes. "I could bring this entire *building* down on your head and it wouldn't even faze you. And honestly, you think I would work with the cops? To grab *you*? C'mon, Mr H, we've worked together before. Have you finally been hit in the head too many times to remember that little detail? Honestly, what kind of low-rent stooge do you take me for?" I waved a hand at his crew, all jutted jaws and wavering gun hands. "*I* have quality standards, OK? If you're worried about the cops, look to your own flock first, that's all I'm saying."

"You callin' us low-rent stooges?" one of the guys shouted.

"Shut up," Hammerhead snapped at him, not breaking eye contact with me. He folded his massive arms. "I think you'd better leave, little kitty. Before I decide you need to be collared."

Oh, better men than you have tried. I knew Peter had to be ready by now, and I was also positive that there was nothing more to be gained from my attempts at friendly conversation. Hammerhead didn't want to play nice? Then it was time to get rough.

"I think I'm gonna go with 'no' on that offer," I said, watching his twitchy crew get even twitchier. The one on the right was about to fire, I could tell from his stance. I focused hard on him, then triggered my internal probability pulsator. This guy was about to get unlucky. "But you're going to answer me either way."

"Answer this!" the guy shouted, stepping boldly forward as he fired his first shot… which went straight up toward the ceiling as he fell toward the ground, since he'd just strode right off the edge of the stage.

The shot hit the chain holding up the heavy metal chandelier that had once been the pride and joy of this theater. It fell to the stage with a clatter and a crash, right in the middle of their cheap aluminum table. Cards and bottles went flying, and a second later, so did Hammerhead's men, courtesy of Spider-Man's webslingers. Two of them were plastered to the walls in seconds, while the third one fired blindly at a whole lot of nothing before Spidey took his gun away.

That was some pretty nice return for one little change in probability. I'd better capitalize on it while I could.

I sprinted down the aisle, leapt over the final row of chairs and onto the stage, and got to Hammerhead just as he began to turn from the mess to face me, arms outstretched, fingers ready to grip and grind. There was no doubt I'd be in for more than I could handle if I let him get those massive mitts on me.

I wasn't interested in dancing with the guy, though. I knew my limits as a combatant, and while I was a bonafide badass, sometimes you just wanted to *win* already. Rather than closing the distance, I stayed just outside of reach, grabbed the new, wonderfully whippy extendable baton at my hip, and swung that puppy toward his right kneecap like I was trying to get my golf ball from the tee-box to the green in one long drive.

Hammerhead managed to block it, the big jerk, but just barely. "Not gonna get through, Cat," he ground out between gritted teeth. "Just give it up, pretty kitty. I promise not to hurt you *too* bad."

"No deal!" I said in the perky tones I knew annoyed the heck out of him as I swung again. This time I got him right on the temple, but that didn't do anything for either of us. He shook it off like his head hadn't just rung like a literal bell, and I knew I needed to do better. I went low again, trying for his sciatic nerve.

He grabbed the very tip of the baton right before it hit his leg, ripping it out of my grip and crushing it in his ginormous hand, grinning like the Cheshire cat. He opened his mouth, no doubt to taunt me for a second before trying to make mincemeat out of me.

Too bad for him he wasn't focusing on the *second* baton I pulled out, twisting and swinging it with perfect form right up the middle of his legs before it impacted with an arm-jarring *thud* against his groin.

It was the groan heard round the world. I didn't know if most male super heroes and villains didn't go for the groin out of courtesy when it came to fighting, or if they simply didn't think about it because it was so… well, unthinkable. Me though, I'd learned in juvie that the best way to end a fight quickly was to concentrate your force in a spot that couldn't be strengthened with working out, steroids, or in most cases, enhancements. Hammerhead's upper half was super strong, super durable, and super dangerous.

His lower half? All I could think as he hit the grimy stage floor, his dangerous hands now cupped protectively in front of his crotch, was: *paydirt.*

Spider-Man was by my side in an instant, and covered Hammerhead with enough webbing that even if he suddenly felt a hundred percent better – which he wouldn't – it would still take him a few seconds to tear his way free. That would be more than enough time for us to back out of the danger zone. For now, I knelt down next to him and clonked the baton on his forehead.

"Let's try this again. I'm interested in a guy you kidnapped a week and a half ago, a guy in federal custody. His name is Dalton Beck. Ringing any bells?" I clonked him again. "Or would you like me to ring yours a little harder?"

Hammerhead bared his teeth at me, wheezing like an old man. "You... vile, two-faced... coming in here... *Spider-Man*..."

"Don't get mad just because I've got better taste in backup than you do."

"Speaking of," Peter said, and a second later he whirled around, web spraying right in the face of the guy who'd just picked himself up from falling over the edge of the stage, gun still in hand.

"Nice," I congratulated him before turning back to Hammerhead. *Clonk.* "So." *Clonk.* "Tell me." *Clonk.* "What did you do with Dalton Beck?" *Clonk.* "Who hired you?" *Clonk.* "Where did you deliver him?" *Clonk clonk clonk.*

"You're working with Spider-Man? *You?* I'm going to rip your face off," Hammerhead managed to gasp. "Then I'm going to feed it to you, you filthy piece of–"

Smash! I whacked my baton into his mouth. His skull was harder than rock, but his teeth? Not quite as tough. Despite how tightly he clenched his jaw, it only took a few hits for me to make a gap big enough to shove my baton through.

"Black Cat," Peter began worriedly, but I ignored him and focused on my downed opponent. This was a dangerous moment, one that might come back to haunt me if I didn't play it just right. I already knew I wouldn't get to kill this guy, not with Spider-Man around, no matter how much he might deserve it.

But I doubted Hammerhead knew that.

"I tried to be reasonable. I gave you a chance to help me, would have bargained with you if you'd bothered to try," I said as nonchalantly as I could manage while shoving my baton to the back of his throat. I scraped my claws across his lips, leaving thin red trails behind. "But you had to go and be a tough guy. You're the one who made this into a fight, Mr H. Not me. But I'll make it into a funeral if you don't tell me what I need to know."

"So cool," Casey whispered over the com. Spider-Man huffed in exasperation. I ignored them both, keeping my eyes on Hammerhead. I could see him doing the classic mental arithmetic of the criminal – what did he stand to gain by refusing my request? And what did he stand to lose if he held firm? I wanted to make sure he knew he could lose a whole lot more than his two front teeth.

He opened his mouth and garbled, "Dunno who paid for it," around the metal rod pressed against his tongue. I obligingly pulled it out, and he coughed a few times, then continued. "Got an anonymous offer via one of the brokers."

"In person?" I asked.

He shook his head. "Site on the dark web. Let me know they'd pay me twenty grand to grab this guy on this day, then leave him in an abandoned warehouse in Queens. Did it. Got the money. Been drinkin' on their dime ever since."

Twenty grand was a heck of a lot of money for that amount of work. "Did they tell you how to do it?"

"You mean did they tell us about the sewer grate?" He smiled, blood trickling out of the corner of his mouth and running down his craggy cheek. "Yeah, but we already knew about that. Everybody who works for the Maggia these days knows the best boltholes. You're wasting your time with me, sweetheart. There's only one person who's got reason to want Firestrike out of the picture. Why don't you go talk to him instead?"

Ugh. I was still hoping to avoid an actual confrontation with the Maggia, and Silvermane in particular, but it was looking less and less likely that I'd pull it off. Still, there were a few other things I could try before I committed to that path. I leaned back, stood up, and retracted my baton. "You've been super-duper helpful, Hammerhead. I wish we could have gotten this far without the drama, but it is what it is."

"Yeah," he said, voice low and menacing. "It sure is. And I know where you live. *Boss.*"

Oh, honey. Bad call.

I bent back down and stared him right in his bloodshot eyes. "And I," I said calmly, "know where *you* live. And I know where your people live, and where their families live. I know where your mother lives, in Italy. I know where your grandmother lives, back in Mother Russia." I didn't actually know *all* of this, not the stuff about his current gang, but him? I'd done my due diligence prior to deciding to work with him before. "And you might not care about them anymore, that's not my business, but I guarantee it'll turn a few heads in the wrong direction when word gets out that you let your momma take the fall for your bad decisions." Gangsters might be gangsters, but most of them still loved their mothers.

"And then I'll dislocate both your hips, tie some concrete blocks to your feet, and have you thrown into the Hudson!" I added cheerfully, standing up again. "*Or* we can just call this what it is, business, and leave it at that. It's not like I really want to travel to Minsk anytime soon – I hear it's absolutely miserable in the summertime."

Hammerhead's glare faded into a tired sag as my threat sank in. "You're harder than any of your jewels, Cat," he said to me, grudging respect in his tone. "Fair enough. We leave each other alone for now. But you mess with me again, I won't be so nice next time."

I winked at him, letting him have the obvious lie as a little personal balm for the sting of getting his butt kicked. "Got it, Hammerhead. You take care now." I walked away feeling confident that he'd keep our deal, but still… "Let's make sure we know Hammerhead's whereabouts at all times for the next couple of months," I said over my com. "Same for my mom."

"Your mother isn't going to like that," Boris said with a sigh. "And while what other people like normally doesn't concern me, in the case of Lydia…"

Everybody on my crew had a soft spot for my mother, as they should.

"Hire someone new to do the tailing. Someone more discreet than the last one. Geez, my mom made that guy *cookies* before she sent him packing. She doesn't even make me cookies anymore if it's not a holiday!"

"Got it, boss." That was Bruno, reliable as ever. "Nice job in there. You need a pickup?"

"Nah." I glanced over at Peter, who was being suspiciously

quiet. Probably listening to every word, the little eavesdropper. "I'll take the high road home."

When I asked for a lift this time around, Peter was nice enough to lend an arm. It was soothing, being carried across the city like this and feeling certain that I wouldn't fall. I kind of hoped someone caught a picture of us together and posted it somewhere MJ could see – but that was petty, and I thought better of it almost as soon as I considered it. What the two of them had might be complicated, but it was also strong. Certainly strong enough to withstand most of the blows I'd leveled at it so far, and I didn't care to keep throwing myself against something that wasn't going to give. A girl had to have self-respect, after all.

Still, it was nice. There was a part of me that would always love Spider-Man, even if I didn't like Peter Parker himself quite as much. Nice guys were just so… predictable.

He set me down on my rooftop a little while later. The moon was full, making his costume look washed out, like he could have been a figment of my memory instead of the real thing. Then he took off his mask and smiled, and I couldn't help but smile back.

"Is everything going to be all right with this job?" he asked.

"Oh, it'll be fine," I said airily, sitting on the edge of the rooftop and leaning back on my hands. "I just have to squeeze a certain FBI agent a little harder and see what falls out of him." Jacobs might have made a bad deal, but he wasn't a moron. He had to have some failsafes in place, information he'd held back that would give me another good lead.

"Why not go straight to the Maggia? If you're so sure they're the ones responsible for taking this guy?"

I made a face. "I prefer not to get dragged any deeper into that organization than I have to. If I can get what I need without having to come face to face with that disgusting old head in a jar, so much the better."

Peter chuckled. "Yeah, I get that. I hope you get to the guy in time."

"Me too." Not that I really cared all that much about Firestrike, honestly. He'd done plenty of shady things in his day, and the fact that he'd turned state's evidence and gone into hiding afterward, well... that didn't make him a good person, just a calculating one. But Casey... she was different. "His kid really misses him."

"Oh, no." Peter actually put a hand over his heart. Could he get any more disgustingly cute? "Is she OK?"

"She's fine," I said, gesturing to my ear to give him the message that she was probably listening in right now. "She's very eager to get him back, though."

"I bet." He sat down beside me, and I savored the quiet togetherness for a moment.

It didn't last long, of course.

"Want me to play some romantic music, boss?" Bruno asked.

"Please, your idea of romance is saccharine and clichéd," Boris cut in. "What this requires is nothing less than a sonnet! He seems like the kind of man who would appreciate the Bard, perhaps number eighteen... or honestly, perhaps number one hundred and thirty, given the way you always seem to strike out with Spider-Man..."

"OK, that's enough of that," I said, rising to my feet and resisting the urge to shout into my communicator. It wouldn't increase the volume on their end, just make me look a little more ridiculous than I already did. "It's bedtime for all good little sidekicks, and that means all three of you."

"But, boss–"

"I'm not done–"

"But I wanna–"

"At the very least, you all need to stop listening in on me. I'll be in in a second." I took my own com out of my ear and stuck it in a handy little pocket – couldn't wear a super hero suit without pockets, no matter how much The Tinkerer moaned about it potentially throwing off the microservos – then turned to Peter.

"Thanks for the assist," I said. "I appreciate it. Tell MJ hi for me, OK?"

"Yeah, I will. And you're welcome," he added. "Anytime."

"Hmm…" I tapped my chin thoughtfully. "So if I need to stage another wedding for a job–"

"Find somebody else," he said immediately. "Seriously, I thought I might lose my head over that when I told MJ about it."

"Got it. No wedding-related shenanigans for you. But the next time there's a gala in town and I need a date, I'm calling in a favor."

"Yeah, I could do a gala." He leaned toward me for a moment, almost like he was going to hug me… or something. But of course he didn't, and I didn't push it, not tonight. He put his mask back on and leapt off the side of the building. I stood there and watched him swing away until he'd completely vanished into the night. Part of me would always hate to see him go… but boy, did I ever love to watch him leave.

Catch ya later, Spidey. I headed down into my apartment,

ready for a good night's sleep followed by a morning of productive butt-kicking.

Special Agent Jacobs thought he had it bad the first time around? He wasn't going to know what hit him.

CHAPTER SIXTEEN

I'd spoken too soon.

It turned out nothing was going to be hitting Special Agent Jacobs hard today, because he was dead. Just my freaking luck, the guy I was counting on squeezing hard enough to spill some more beans had already spilled what sounded like the entirety of his body fluids all over his bedroom carpet, or so the police report said.

It was the police scanner that had clued us into the fact that a crime had taken place at Jacobs' apartment. We didn't get the most interesting details that way, of course, but it was far easier to hack into the local precinct and read the filed police report than it had been to get information out of the FBI office. I glanced at my crew over the breakfast table, where Bruno was reading off the details. Maybe I should have thought better of including Casey in this part, since the description of the body was pretty graphic. She sat quietly, taking bites of the sugary cereal Bruno preferred every now and then and drinking her coffee, while Boris read off more of the details of the crime scene.

"–and a bottle of some brand of wine called Belladonna on the nightstand, and–"

"Belladonna?" Oh, lord. I was tempted to have some myself, after hearing that. The guys looked at me in commiseration.

"You knew she was gonna make trouble some way, boss," Bruno said.

"It could have been worse," Boris added with a shrug.

"What are you guys talking about?" Casey asked, not understanding our moment of enlightenment. "Is this about the wine?"

"Yep," I said with an epic eyeroll. "That particular wine is only made in Louisiana, and only for the Assassins' Guild." It was pretty bad wine, too – Louisiana was good for a lot of things but growing decent wine grapes wasn't one of them. Still, tradition was tradition. "Every now and then, they gift it to friends and allies. The only person in New York I can think of who'd have a bottle of that wine on hand is Odessa Drake, leader of the Thieves' Guild."

"So Odessa Drake murdered Special Agent Jacobs?" Casey asked.

"Or she had a member of the Assassins' Guild do it for her. Either way, she's messing with us." And I thought we'd gotten past the bad old days. More fool me.

"With you," Boris corrected. "She couldn't care less about the rest of us, more fool her. Her obsession has always been with you." It was true. Our fathers had both trained under the Black Fox, had been friends for years. Now her father was dead, and he'd left Odessa in charge of a failing guild, tasked with seeking the immortality that he himself had so desperately wanted. She'd come through, in her own way, but now she was trapped in a role that she didn't really want. Odessa Drake didn't give in to anything with good grace, and we'd had our little tiffs in the past, but they'd mostly been settled. Nothing said "truce" like a roll in the hay. Still, she liked to make mischief, especially with me.

"I'm going to call her."

"Do it in the garage please, boss," Bruno said. "That way you won't deafen the rest of us."

"I said call her, not yell at her," I said, affronted.

"Boss. C'mon."

Fair point. I headed into the garage and stopped dead in front of the deconstruction site that was Danny Rand's gorgeous car. The engine was spread out in pieces across a blue plastic tarp, and I couldn't even see the bumpers or tires. "What the…" I stuck my head back into the apartment. "What are you doing to Danny's Ferrari? I thought you said you were just cleaning it!"

"I need to test out some upgrades!" Bruno called back, a smile breaking across his craggy face. "Thought the best place to experiment would be with somebody else's ride, and trust me, they're gonna turn out great."

"You thought… the best place…" It was so easy to forget sometimes that Bruno was just as weird as the rest of us – he just hid it better. "You better be able to put this thing back together."

"No worries, boss!"

Oh, I was plenty worried, but I'd handle that later. Danny Rand wasn't going to hunt down random associates of mine and cut their throats, after all. Odessa – well, she'd already proven her willingness there. I shut the door and called her on the number I would definitely never admit to anyone outside my crew that I had.

She let it ring four whole times before she picked up, the

thieving wench. "Felicia," she purred. "To what do I owe the pleasure?"

"Oh, you know. Just checking in, seeing how it feels to be an evil, murdering demoness in human skin," I replied cheekily.

"You'd know as well as I would."

"Oh come on, Odessa. I know you're behind the death of Special Agent Jacobs. What I want to know is *why*." Because honestly, we'd barely been at each other's throats lately. This seemed too random. "Are you trying to force me to fetch you the apple like everyone else?"

Odessa laughed. "Felicia, really. When have I ever done anything like everyone else? Sure, I'd like the apple." I could hear how her voice sharpened, going a little lower, a little more earnest – yeah, I bet she'd like that apple. I knew just what she'd ask, too. There was more than one path to immortality in the world, after all. "And I'm more than a little offended that you're chasing it around at someone else's beck and call, when you know I'd be more than happy to shield you from that sort of rudeness. But I have no intention of employing, bribing or forcing you to get it for me. That's not the kind of relationship I want us to have."

Oh my god, was she … jealous? "We don't have a relationship outside of mutual antagonism and a one-night stand."

"Mm, you can tell yourself that," she said doubtfully, "but the truth is, you knew just who to call when you found out the agent was dead, didn't you?"

I held back a curse of frustration. "Pretty wasteful, leaving an entire bottle of wine there."

"I had to make sure it stood out. Besides, leaving that bottle behind was no loss. It's not a very good wine."

What do you know? We agreed on something. "Why bother, though? The job I'm working right now has zero to do with you, and zero to interest you."

"It interests me *because* you're working it, Felicia," Odessa said. Her tone was dark, possessive. It was slightly thrilling, but more off-putting. "I still think about you a lot, you know. I watch you, just like you watch everyone else. We both have plenty of work to do, but you're my *favorite* job, Felicia. I always make time for you, but I don't feel like that's being reciprocated. Didn't we promise we'd do better? Be more honest with each other? And yet you didn't feel like you could come to me for help?"

She *was* jealous! I suppose I should have seen it coming, but there were parts of Odessa Drake that were still opaque to me. "I didn't even think of it," I admitted. "You know that I like to work alone."

"You don't work alone, though," she pointed out.

"Oh please, Boris and Bruno don't count."

"And some random teenager who ingratiated herself so well you're working this job with her," Odessa shot back. "Which doesn't make me happy. When I'm not happy, I get thoughtful."

More like vicious.

"And right now, I wanted to make sure your life was a fraction as hard as you've made mine over the years. So!" Her voice brightened. "Enjoy getting information from a dead man. I suppose you could always employ a necromancer, but–"

"Oh, go to hell." I ended the call before she could monologue anymore and stared up at the ceiling for a long moment, fighting my urge to kick something. I wasn't wearing my suit boots, just socks, so I'd probably hurt myself if I tried. Stupid Odessa and her stupid fixation with me and her stupid willingness to kill people for stupid reasons.

Well, fine. That avenue was closed, permanently. I'd just have to confront the Maggia more directly to get the information I needed about Dalton Beck.

Honestly, how hard could it be?

CHAPTER SEVENTEEN

"Is the entire Maggia on vacation or something?" I demanded forty-eight hours later, frazzled after another day of running down leads only to come up empty handed. I *never* came up empty handed, never – it was a condition I loathed almost as much as I loathed nostalgia. The past was nothing but a memory, and the future could only be properly ushered in if you had the tools you needed to challenge it, but right now? My toolbox was empty.

"What about their pharmacies?" I asked Boris while I paced back and forth across my living room floor. I thought better when I was moving. The Manfredi family, out of all the local Maggia powerhouses, had the heaviest hand in the drug trade, and one of their fronts was a chain of pharmacies throughout the city.

"There's been no sign of backdoor dealings at any of them for the past three days, from what I can tell," Boris said, sounding put-upon. "I would have told you if there was. We could try interrogating some of the employees, but none of them are known family members."

I turned to Bruno. "What about St Nicholas Church?" I had fond memories of that church – I'd gotten married there once. Well, fake-married to Spider-Man when we took the place of Maggia heirs who were meant to fight each other to the death, all while breaking into their secret crypts and making off with a cool million bucks, but still… Good times.

"Not a service, a christening, or a funeral for the past three days," Bruno said. "Sorry, boss, but I got nothin'. Not even any chatter from the other families, and you know how they'd normally jump on an absence from one of their rivals."

"Well, what happened three days ago that made a group of tough guys like the Maggia decide to run and hide?" I asked, still pacing. "That's not anywhere close to their MO."

"Um… the special agent guy died?" Casey tried. She, unlike me, was capable of sitting still. She'd buried herself as deep in her oversized hoodie, which I was certain now was her father's, as she could. I could barely see the tip of her nose, but what I did make out was reddish.

Oh, dang. She'd been crying again.

I couldn't, couldn't, couldn't deal with tears. Seeing someone crying made me turn and run faster than anything but costume jewelry and symbiotes, but ever since our pursuit of Dalton Beck had run up against a wall of silence, Casey had been very quietly crying herself to sleep at night.

We all tried to cheer her up in our own ways. Boris showed her how to make a new type of bomb, Bruno watched a Browns game with her, and I showed her a meditation that the Black Fox had forced me to learn that was good at convincing your run-of-the-mill psychic that you were nothing more than a tree.

The only thing that would really cheer her up, though, was making progress on her father's kidnapping.

"Special Agent Jacobs died four days ago thanks to Odessa 'look at me, look at me' Drake," I said. "But..." Actually, maybe we were onto something with this. "Think bigger," I said out loud, leaning over to touch my toes before arching into a backbend and touching my heels. Oof. My supraspinatus was tight today. "What happened three days ago that could be concerning enough to the Maggia that they decided it was best to lie low? What could spook an entire criminal organization into going underground for so long? Not just the Manfredis, but all of them."

"Something big," Boris murmured, steepling his fingers beneath his chin like a proper villain. All he needed was the fluffy white cat, seriously. "Something capable of taking them down. What are their enemies up to?"

"Um..." I didn't really rate as a proper Maggia enemy. It took an organization to fight the families, and that meant– "Oh. *Oh.*" I lifted my feet off the ground so I was in a handstand, then lifted one of my hands as well and pointed at Boris. "See what the Kingpin has been up to lately. Wasn't the Owl bringing him the golden apple?"

"Intriguing," Boris murmured, his fingers flying over the keys. "I can't find word of any great boons coming his way lately. If anything, it's the reverse – he seems to have holed himself up in his offices downtown after a fight with... the Owl?"

"Ha!" I couldn't help but laugh as I switched hands. "No honor among thieves!" Everyone in the room turned and looked at me. "I mean *those* kinds of thieves, not us! They're amateurs, we're tops! I'd never betray you all, you know that!"

"Just keep diggin', boss," Bruno said, but he was smiling as he said it.

"Apparently it was quite the battle," Boris said. "The Owl is a biter, it seems, but in the end the Kingpin triumphed."

"I can imagine." Those nasty sharp teeth, how they jutted forward in his jaw like a makeshift beak… honestly, some of the people in this community took their professional names waaay too seriously. I might be Black Cat, but you didn't see *me* licking myself and knocking random artifacts off shelves while I was on a job.

I stood up, stretched, then walked over and flopped down next to Casey on the couch, curling around my favorite cushion. "Odds are that the Kingpin hasn't used the apple yet, then."

"Maybe, maybe not… but it seems that no one knows for sure," Boris agreed.

"Then the Maggia are right to be worried." I didn't like Wilson Fisk, but even I had to admit he was a smart guy. "If he's mulling over a big wish, it could mean very bad news for the Families."

"Good reason for 'em to keep outta sight, then," Bruno said. "Why poke the bear? Get Fisk to focus on the other things he could ask for and leave 'em out of it."

"So where do we have to go to find them?" Casey asked, getting right to the heart of the matter. "Where does the Manfredi family live?"

"They own a bunch of apartment buildings and such here in the city, but they actually live in–"

"Hold that thought," I said to Bruno, then turned to Casey. "Let me make this clear first. Under no circumstances are you to go to the Manfredi compound and start demanding answers, do you understand me? If you so much as move from this apartment without being in my direct line of sight, I will turn you over to CPS and the FBI and as many other acronyms as I can think of before you can blink. There will be *no* repeat of that stunt with Special Agent Jacobs against someone who could do you serious damage, not under my watch." I was willing to bet that wherever he was, Dalton Beck would prefer I *didn't* find him if I didn't also keep his daughter alive and well.

Casey pushed her hood back – the better to see her scowl at me, it seemed. "That's not fair!"

"Who says I have to be fair?" I shot back. "My father was incarcerated for most of my life while my mother let me think he'd been killed in an accident, and I wasn't able to get him out until he was dying of cancer and it was too late to have any sort of meaningful reunion with him. Was that fair? Was it fair of my mom to keep the truth from me?" I plowed on, not in the mood for interjections. "No, it wasn't! Of course it wasn't! But that's not the point. My mother did her best to keep me safe, and I was an adult by the time I decided to start taking serious risks."

"You're not my mother!" Casey shouted, standing up. I stood up too.

"I don't have to be your mother to tell you how it is and expect you to toe the line!" I shouted right back.

"You're barely letting me do anything at all!"

"I let you steal information from the freaking FBI *and* meet with an informant, what more do you want?"

"I want my *dad back*!"

Casey was off in a whirl, stalking over to my bedroom and slamming the door behind her. I heard something fall off a wall.

I was about to follow and yell at her some more when Bruno caught my shoulder.

"Leave her alone for a bit, boss," he said, his tone soft and kind. "Give her a chance to get herself under control."

There was another crash.

"Oh, I should stand out here and take it while she destroys my things because she's butthurt about me not letting her go and get herself killed?" I demanded, crossing my arms.

"Inaction seldom suits the young," Boris said, from the table where he'd pulled out a complicated-looking timing unit and was messing with the wiring. "Stillness feels like failure. Compliance reeks of timidity. Obedience is anathema."

I narrowed my eyes. "Are you talking about her or about me?"

He cracked a grin. "The fact that you have to ask is telling, but I'm talking about Miss Beck right now. Your situation was similar to hers, but do keep in mind – you still have a mother."

"Casey's got no one else," Bruno added. "Nobody but her dad. Gotta figure the stress is making her a little crazy."

Oh. Well, that was… hmm. I felt my inclination to march over to my room and storm inside fade away. "Fine. I'll give her some space while she comes to her senses. Honestly, though." As my anger subsided, so did some of my early optimism. "If they're holed up inside of their home base, we're screwed."

The Manfredis had lived in New York for a long time, and their home, which was a little way north of the city, was entrenched – by which I meant literally sunk into the ground in places. These people and their underground lairs, honestly… I think they'd had the original buildings retrofitted to work as bomb shelters in the fifties, and they'd never gone back after that.

It would be hard to infiltrate on the best of days. If the entire Manfredi family was holed up in there, all of them armed and on edge thinking that an attack from the Kingpin might be coming at any moment… well. I'd heard of worse odds, but only when it came to snowballs and hell.

"We gotta get them to come to us somehow," Bruno said, sitting on the back of the couch, his big hands folded in a way that let him twiddle his thumbs. It was one of his "thinking" tics, but from the frustrated look on his face, it didn't seem to be helping much right now. "Make 'em think we've got something they need, or at least want."

"But what does Silvermane want that we could provide?" I was about to start my constructive pacing again before there was suddenly a knock on the door. Not on the front door – access to that was controlled by an elevator that required a caller identify themselves on the bottom floor. And it definitely wasn't Casey knocking on *my* bedroom door. No.

This knock came from the door to the garage.

CHAPTER EIGHTEEN

What. The. Heck.

I stared at the guys. They stared back at me, Bruno's hand creeping toward his gun while Boris's went to his nearest grenade. "Not in the house," I scolded them. We did *not* have shootouts and explosions at home.

Whoever it was knocked again, very politely. I pulled up the video feed on my phone. It was… "What? *Seriously*?" I marched over to the door, threw it open, and was greeted by a handsome smile in a square-jawed face that I couldn't see the rest of, thanks to the red helmet. The little horns on top of it caught the light as Daredevil ducked his head in a nod.

"Black Cat," he said in a friendly tone of voice. "Or should I say, Felicia?"

"Daredevil," I replied, in as unfriendly a manner as I could muster. "Or should I say, Matthew Murdock, professional pain in the butt? And you can stick with Black Cat – Felicia is for friends who don't invite themselves into my house."

His smile widened. "I'm sorry I couldn't call ahead. I don't have your number, and this is time-critical, so waiting for you to be in the mood to open the door wasn't a good option." He gestured at the garage. "You really need to do something about your external security, it was laughably easy to redirect."

I pouted. "Even the motion detectors?"

"Oh, those were the easiest part. You should just get a brand-new setup at this point."

"When I want your critique of my security measures, I'll ask for it." Although clearly I *did* need a new system when it came to access through the garage, because... good grief.

"Aren't you going to ask me inside?"

I rolled my eyes. Daredevil was one of those "friend-of-a-friend, pulled a job with him once, maybe-sort of-kinda seduced him to get ahead" acquaintances. He wasn't a guy I would actively seek out unless I was in dire straits, but he wasn't a parasite-laden, unforgivable jerk either. More to the point, he wouldn't come to *me* unless he had something worth talking about. Daredevil understood that time was money – it was probably a lawyer thing.

The fact that he was here now was actually a little worrisome. Super heroes didn't seek me out, not if they weren't Spider-Man. What had brought Daredevil to my door?

"Does the eyeroll mean yes?"

"How did you even know I rolled my eyes?" I said, nonetheless stepping aside so he could enter. He stepped carefully, not because he had to but because I knew he was casing the joint, so to speak – detecting angles, individuals, and places he could ricochet his batons off if he needed to. "And don't tell me you can hear it."

"I can hear it."

"What did I *just* say?"

"I can't hear your eyes move," he clarified. "But there's a particular tone of voice that often accompanies that expression, and when combined with a sigh like you produced, the odds were better than ninety-three percent."

"How many of those data points are your law partner? Because Foggy by himself is not a representative sam–" My door suddenly opened, and both Matt and I turned our heads in that direction – me because I wanted to see if Casey was done with her hissy fit, and Matt because he was nosy.

Casey didn't say anything, just squeaked and slammed the door shut again.

"What's that all about?" I muttered.

"Um, I think... I think she's a fan," Matt said.

"How can you tell through the soundproofing?" Were *any* of my security measures useful with this guy around?

"It's not *that* good. And the fact that she's whispering 'omigosh it's really Daredevil' to herself in there is kind of a clue."

I whapped his upper arm with the back of my hand. He didn't hit me with one of his batons. Nice and friendly, so far. Boris and Bruno were staying out of it, exactly as they should, although both of them had weapons out in easy-to-reach places. *Aww, backup. So sweet.*

Back to business. "How about you stop listening in on the teenager and explain to me why you're here. I've got a lot to do, and I don't need another red-suited crusader getting in the way."

"I take it you've had a run-in with Spider-Man recently."

"Tony Stark, actually," I said snidely. "Now talk, mister."

"Fine." He focused on me. The hairs on the back of my neck

stood up – it was a little eerie, staring into the suit and knowing that he wasn't staring back. "I'm here about the golden apple."

Oh my god. "No," I said, turning away from him and flouncing – yes, flouncing, because I deserved it – over to the couch. "Nope, no, not a chance. I am *not* getting the apple for you. I am *done* chasing down that *freaking* apple for people who ought to know better, and–"

"Is it really in the Kingpin's hands?"

I sighed. "How should I know?"

"Because from what I hear, you were there when the apple was stolen from the Hammer mansion."

Someone had loose lips. "Where did you hear that from?"

"Oh, around." His smile was back, charming and patently false. Forget having the devil in them, Murdock men must have the souls of used car salesmen to be so blatantly conniving. "Is it true?"

He'd know if I lied. That was my absolute least favorite thing about Daredevil, hands down. "Yes, I was there. The Owl stole the apple from Sasha Hammer and glided out of there like his tailfeathers were on fire. He said he was planning on selling it to the Kingpin, but I can't say for certain that he did."

"But you've seen the news."

"Yes." Again, there was no point in denying it. "I know that our dear mayor has been holed up in his office for three days, ever since the Owl stole the apple. I don't know any more than that, though, and I don't care."

Murdock walked over to me and leaned his hip against the back of the couch, crossing his arms. "You don't care that the Kingpin might have control of a powerful magical artifact that could wreak havoc on all of New York City?"

I shrugged. "I think if he was planning on doing something dumb like that with it, he'd have used it already."

"Which means he's planning something smart with it," Daredevil pointed out with the air of a lawyer poking holes in my deposition. Could he hear pouts? Because I was pouting at him hard right now. "And if he is, imagine the sort of damage a man like him could do with the kind of power the apple offers."

"If he's still got it – which hasn't been verified lately that I know of," I emphasized, "then what's to say he hasn't already used it on one of those smart things and wants to keep a low profile?"

"The horde of people trying to break into his office, for one."

Ha, inconclusive at best. "What makes you think a mob knows anything other than how to be a mob?"

"There are mutants in that mob. Psychics."

"Oh." Well, OK, that was a little more conclusive. Psychics were hard to fool. It could be done, of course. Black Fox had taught me that the most important skills a thief could have were deflection, deception, and determination, and fooling a psychic utilized all three. It wasn't easy, but a focused mind could manage it.

Wilson Fisk might have a mind that was up to the task, but I doubted all of his cronies and hitters could say the same.

I shook my head. *Don't get off track.* "It sounds like you already know, or at least strongly suspect, that the Kingpin has the apple. What does that have to do with me?"

"Well, I was going to appeal to your better nature and ask you to help me take it from him before he has the chance to destroy millions of lives…" I spluttered with laughter, and he sighed. "But I think now the better path is to offer a straight trade. You help me get the apple away from the Kingpin, and I'll help you get a meeting with Silvermane."

My laughter ended as quickly as it began. "How did you know I want a meeting with Silvermane?"

"No comment."

I stood up from my couch and came around to confront him, hands on hips. I heard my guys scooting their chairs back, ready to engage if a fight broke out. "Just how long were you eavesdropping outside my door?" I asked coldly. "Is that the behavior of a man of the law?"

"Desperate times call for desperate measures."

"Oh yeah? And if I refuse to help you, what are you going to do? Set the Punisher on me? Send the Hand my way?"

"Why would you refuse?" There was that perfect, and perfectly fake, smile again. "I'm just trying to give you what you want in exchange for something *I* want."

No, he didn't get to reframe the situation so fast. "By being no better than a *spy*, nothing more than a damn–"

My bedroom door suddenly opened again, and Casey ran out. She ran straight to me and wrapped her arms around my waist. I was so startled that I let her. Murdock seemed startled too, if the way he took a step back was any indication. "Um..."

"Please." Casey looked up into my eyes, her face full of longing. "*Please*, please Felicia, do this. Please do it. You said we need to meet with Silvermane and there's no way to break into their place, so please do this. For my dad." Fresh tears spilled down old, salt-laden tracks. "*Please*."

She was pulling the crying card again – not only that, she was crying in front of Daredevil. I could only hope it was discombobulating him as much as it did me. "It's not that simple, Casey. We—"

"It can be," Daredevil interjected. "Look, I promise I don't want the apple for myself. I have absolutely no interest in it, other than to ensure it doesn't stay in Fisk's hands. Other people, criminals even, I wouldn't worry so much, but Fisk?" He shook his head. "It's just too dangerous, and it's going to get more dangerous the more pressure he feels to make a wish."

"How can I trust you?" I asked. "When you say you don't want it for yourself. How can I be sure you're telling me the truth?"

Daredevil seemed to slump a little. "Felicia, come on. Do you really think I'd give in to the temptation posed by an *apple*? Don't you know how Catholic I am?"

"You might use it if you thought you were helping someone else."

"No." He shook his head. "I know myself better than that. Wrath might be the deadliest of my personal sins, but pride is right there behind it. Always thinking I know best, making decisions without talking them over with others…" His smile wasn't broad, bright, or even a little fake this time. It was the smile of a man who understood how easy it was to send your life off the rails, and how hard it could be to get it back on track. "I won't go that way again. I can't risk it. But I can't let Fisk use the apple to hurt someone either. So…" He held out a hand. "Do we have a deal?"

"You swear you've got a way to get me a meeting with Silvermane?" I clarified.

"I do if you don't mind getting your paws a little dirty."

Now it was my turn to grin. "That's more like it." I took his hand. "Deal."

Casey sagged against me with relief. "Thank you," she said, first to me, then to Daredevil.

"Thank *you*," Daredevil said, inclining his head to her. Casey blushed and let go of me, stammered something incoherent, then ran back into my room and slammed the door shut again. This time, I was pretty sure it was embarrassment. Ugh, crushes were the *worst*. Especially when they ended with me being successfully manipulated.

"So. What do you have in mind when it comes to getting that apple out of the Kingpin's hands?" I asked, because I knew without a shadow of a doubt that Murdock wouldn't come here without a plan. He was as much of a control freak as any of us – more, even, because being blind made him hyperaware of his surroundings.

"Well," he said speculatively, scratching the side of his jaw with the end of one of his batons, "I'd say we infiltrate the mayoral building, but it's pretty well surrounded at this point."

"Meaning you tried already and failed."

"It *might* mean something like that," Daredevil agreed. "I did get close enough to hear what he was planning to do next, though. He can't stay holed up in his office forever, and he's not ready to make a decision with the apple yet. Or at least he wasn't an hour ago."

"Ah-*ha*." I knew it, I knew if a guy like the Kingpin had the apple, it would still be in play. "Such big brains, and as soon as they get something with the capacity to give them whatever they want, they freeze."

"Too many possible permutations," Daredevil agreed.

"Too many ways for things to go wrong, or right. It's choice paralysis, and it's working in our favor this time. As for what he's got planned next, well…" He nodded his head toward the garage. "How do you feel about taking a little drive?"

CHAPTER NINETEEN

It's not every night you race down the highway in a sexy stolen – I mean *borrowed* – sports car, with a good-looking man at your side, the wind in your hair, and the excitement of a huge score to look forward to.

"Yeah, baby!" I crowed, pushing down harder on the gas pedal. When the Kingpin decided to move, he moved quickly, and got traffic in both directions on the highway shut down while he and his posse fought their way out of downtown Manhattan. Of course, by the time they were on the road I was too, and thanks to a little helpful application of bad luck that sent the police car blocking our entrance into a surprise tailspin, we were quite close to the Kingpin's convoy. Three armored cars – please. What kind of amateurs did they think they were dealing with?

I glanced at Daredevil and laughed. "Isn't this the best?"

"The engine is *not* making happy sounds!" Daredevil insisted. He was surprisingly tentative in a moving vehicle – maybe things were going by too quickly for his senses to really get a bead on them. I could understand how that would be disorienting. I also completely didn't care.

"It's from an upgrade! I'm *sure* Danny is going to love it once he gets used to it."

"What kind of upgrade?"

I sharpened my gaze on the convoy ahead. Three cars, so the middle one most likely held the Kingpin. Well then. Time to thin out the pack. "I'll show you." I touched the onboard computer and pulled up the menu for "specialty items." One entire side of it was dedicated to a single big, glowing red button. "Woot! Here we go!" I pushed it.

Time suddenly seemed to slow. Even the wind seemed to settle, which I knew should have been impossible since we were traveling faster than ever now, but it was true. The steering wheel didn't shift so much as a millimeter under my hands, but the car jumped forward along the road like a bullet shot from a particularly large gun. We roared into battle like a lion, and I remembered the blue button for activating the new shielding just in time for us to smack into the rear of the back car without destroying Danny's bumper.

Hitting another car that hard at these speeds had only one outcome – disaster. For them, that is. Our kinetic energy transferred beautifully, thanks to the resilience of our energy shielding, and the armored car's rear end flew up into the air. It managed to coast for a hundred feet or so on just its front two wheels before the driver finally spooked and tried to use the steering wheel.

The car swerved, shivering across four lanes of traffic before the driver finally made a fatal mistake, turning the wheel too far to the right. I triggered my quantum rig at the same time, and rather than coming down on all four tires, the car rolled straight over onto its roof, then barreled off to the side of the road until it hit the guardrail and burst into flames.

We left the wreck in our dust, the passengers inside of it abandoning ship moments before the car went up in a blazing fireball. "Wow," I said, glancing in the rearview at the light show. "It's like the Fourth of July."

Daredevil didn't say anything. I glanced at him. "You OK?"

"Fine." His jaw was set so hard I was half afraid he'd chip a tooth. "Can we focus on the Kingpin, please?"

I tipped an imaginary hat. "One Wilson Fisk, coming right up." Eh, what did I care that Daredevil wasn't much for conversation on our little road trip? I was sure my plan was *way* more fun than whatever he'd had in mind. We were about to jerk a big fish right out of the water. I refocused on the rear car and checked the power gauge for our little booster rocket setup. Awesome, we still had a little over half the charge ready. I punched it, and–

Our leap forward ended almost as quickly as it began, with the lead car in the Kingpin's convoy doing an absolutely *badass* spinning turn, clearing the way for Fisk's car even as it swung around to come into position behind it – backward. Yeah, *backward*, with the front of the car facing us. I don't know if an AI was controlling that thing or if Fisk just happened to be employing a stunt driver, but I *did* see the twin guns extend straight out from below the front bumper of the thing.

"Hang on!" I shouted and jerked us hard to the left just as the other car began to fire. Bullets chewed into the road, sending up a brilliant shower of sparks while I punched our special power-up button again. We raced forward, getting up next to Fisk's car and leaving his rear guard behind us. I got ready to engage the shield and bump them off the road when the car I'd *just* gone to the trouble of evading did a donut – another one – at over a hundred miles an hour and came in right behind us.

"You need to move," Daredevil warned me, his hands pressed so hard to the dashboard I could hear it creaking in protest. "Those are fifty caliber rounds. If they hit us–"

"Yep, we're screwed, got it." I'd already triggered the car's roof to come back up, but that wasn't tough enough to provide much protection in a firefight. This car wasn't shielded all the way around; it didn't have the battery life for that kind of protection. I could focus it on the back of the car, but it wouldn't last for long. Judging from the manic grin I could make out on the driver's face, they had a *lot* of bullets. "OK. Brace yourself, because this isn't going to be fun."

"What's not going to be fu – *uuuuuuhh!*" Daredevil reached out with both hands to keep himself from faceplanting into the dashboard as I jammed on the brakes. A second later the car behind us ran into our rear shield at over a hundred miles an hour.

They didn't just crash – they *launched* over Danny's car, the entire front end of their SUV crumpled from the impact as they turned three full circles in the air, coming to a crashing halt on the blacktop ahead of us, spinning around on the driver's side of the vehicle like a top before finally coming to a halt.

Well, that had worked great! But now we needed to catch up with Fisk again. I did zero to sixty in approximately three seconds, leaving even more smoke and rubber inlaid on the ground behind us. These tires would definitely need to be changed out before we gave the car back to Danny, but they were doing us proud right now.

We were closing in on the Kingpin, and he didn't have an entourage with him anymore. All we had to do was... wait a second, what the heck were *those*?

They looked like a little fleet of commercial quadcopter drones, done up in basic silver and black. Four of them took up positions at the corners of the Kingpin's car, while four more flew back to array themselves in a line between us and our target. In perfect sync, red lights activated in front of them, and a second later–

"Whoa!" I hit the brakes again, barely stopping the car before we impacted a line of lasers powerful enough to make the road burn where they hit. The lines began moving toward us, and we had *not* upgraded Danny's car well enough to withstand attack from laser-wielding drones. Something for the next package. I put the car in reverse just in time to avoid burning out the engine, and we roared back along the road – in the opposite direction from where we wanted to be going.

"Drones?" Daredevil asked.

"You got it. Geez, everyone's so high-tech these days."

"Can't you bad-luck them?"

"I can try." I tried to focus my ability and drive at the same time, but it was no use. "Here, you take the wheel for a second."

"Uh, Black Cat–"

"Just keep us going straight! We won't hit the other car for another fifteen seconds at least." I set the controls so the speed would stay constant, then climbed out and on top of the car. Our course wobbled for a moment, but Daredevil could be counted on to come through in a pinch, and he steadied us out.

I crouched down on the roof of the car, focused on one of the drones in the center of the formation, and activated my quantum probability pulsator. The drone suddenly seemed to lose control of one of its motors, going into a spin that ran it into the drone to the right of it. Both of them careened off course, lasers still firing, and took out their neighbors before crashing and burning.

One of them also nearly took off my head with its dying lightshow. I heard a few of my hairs sizzle as the laser passed by and smelled them burning. It wasn't bad enough to leave me with a bald stripe down the middle of my head, though, so I counted it as a win.

"Black Cat! Any time!"

"Coming!" I slid back into the car and got us going in the right direction again. We were way far back from the Kingpin now, though. I could barely see his SUV in the distance, which meant using our rocket booster again. I looked at the power – down to a quarter of the battery left. If I used it all on speed, we'd have nothing left to spend on a shield when we got in close.

"Fortune favors the bold," I murmured, and I pushed the button. We shot forward, everything around us becoming a blur as we closed the gap. By the time the battery pack ran out of power, we were close enough to make a real go of running the Kingpin off the road… or would have been, if the drones flying above his car didn't set up a different sort of laser array – one that made a fence-like structure around his entire SUV, not quite touching the pavement so it didn't interfere with their driving, but enough that we wouldn't be able to sneak beneath it and bash his rear bumper.

I prepared to get on the roof again, but all of a sudden Fisk's car slid across three lanes and down an exit ramp. I was barely able to follow in time to make it, and suddenly we were in a world of twists and turns and, worse yet, other cars and pedestrians. I'd probably get someone killed if I tried to put Daredevil in the driver's seat again.

"Shoot. His car is surrounded," I said, banging one hand on the steering wheel in frustration. The computer console made a frowny face at me.

"I can hear the drones," Daredevil confirmed, grabbing his cane. "I've got it."

"Got what?"

"Just drive. Keep us as close to them as you can." Then *he* was up and onto the roof. I held the car steady, only veering once to go around a hideously slow Oldsmobile. Up ahead, the running inferno that was the Kingpin's laser shield was causing plenty of superficial damage to other vehicles, but it didn't look like anyone had been injured yet.

"Whatever you're going to do, do it fast!"

The grappling-hook end of Daredevil's cane came shooting through the air and hit the right corner drone, snagging and crushing it simultaneously. The broken drone vanished toward the road for a moment, then a second later was whipped up and into the other rear drone so hard they both disintegrated. The two in front were already changing their tactic, moving to defend the back of the car, but Daredevil had their number now. One more quick launch-and-smash, and he'd taken them both out of the game.

"Nice," I murmured. Now we just had to stop Fisk's car, and then we could– "Holy crap!"

A huge metalloid creature had just landed in the middle of the Kingpin's roof, denting it severely. The SUV swerved, slowed, and ran off the road to the right, going straight between two gas pumps before smashing through the plate-glass window of a corner store. The wreck didn't even phase the creature that had caused the crash, which held itself steady on the roof with one huge metal hand. It was wearing a set of dark gray fatigues, and, backlit against the brightness of the corner store, I could see that its head was oddly squashed and rectangular.

Daredevil jumped back down into the car. "What *is* that?"

"I think it's... an android," I said, stunned and not afraid to show it. Androids showing up out of nowhere? Time to apply the brakes. "In fact, I think it's the Awesome Android."

"Awesome Andy?" Daredevil looked puzzled. "He doesn't seem like the type to take this sort of action on his own. And Fisk isn't known for being anti-robot. Why would he–"

We paused while Andy ripped the roof off the SUV. Literally ripped it right off, like it wasn't reinforced alloy designed to withstand superhuman impacts. A second later a new set of drones came whizzing out of the night, each of them firing their laser at the Awesome Android, but whatever he was made of was too tough to be chewed up like the road had been.

Two more androids, not quite as big as Andy, showed up, fighting the drones off while Andy reached inside the car. Andy's arm emerged holding onto the apple – and onto the Kingpin, who was gripping it tight and shouting something even as he fired round after round of ammo into Andy at point-blank range. From inside the shop, a dark-haired woman screamed as one of the drones burst into flames beside the cash register.

The apple began to glow. Oh my gosh, was it going to happen? Was I going to see an apple used in real time? And what would Wilson Fisk spend his wish on?

But it wasn't meant to be. The bullets might as well have been made of cotton candy for all the effect they had on the

Awesome Android, and he ripped the apple out of Fisk's grip with contemptuous ease, then picked the Kingpin up by the back of his suit jacket and threw him into the ruined store. He didn't even acknowledge that we were there, just flew into the air, his two backup androids rising with him, and jetted off into the twilight. The surviving drones raced after him, and then Daredevil and I were left staring at a car full of groaning goons, an unconscious Wilson Fisk – not dead, I was sure, not after that display of potato chips broke his fall – and sirens incoming.

Police. I didn't do police. "Ride's over," I said to Daredevil. "Time for you to get out. We might not have gotten the apple, but it's safe to say that the Kingpin definitely didn't get it. I'll expect to hear from you about our deal tomorrow."

"You drive a hard bargain, Cat," Daredevil griped, but he got out of the car. "I guess clean-up duty is on me."

"You guessed right!" I congratulated him. "Thanks for a fun evening, let's do it again sometime!"

"Let's not," he said, but he was smiling, so I decided to be flattered instead of offended. I drove back home feeling quite pleased with myself, actually – as drives went, it had been one for the record books, *and* I'd tested the shielding system on the car so successfully I hadn't even scratched its paint, *and* the Kingpin hadn't gotten a chance to use the apple. Not really because of Daredevil and me, but still, that was something. The question was, who had the apple now?

CHAPTER TWENTY

"The Mad Thinker!" Boris burst out the moment I entered the apartment, swiveling toward me from his kitchen chair. His computer was out in front of him. "It's got to be the Mad Thinker! With that kind of coordination with other androids during the attack itself, he's the only person it could be."

No waiting from my personal geek squad. "The Mad Thinker. Interesting." He was one of the Fantastic Four's nemeses, not quite up there on the level of Doctor Doom, but smart enough to be a real pain in Mr Fantastic's rear, which I appreciated. "He's the probabilities guy, right?"

"You mean the greatest experimentalist to grace the field of probability theory with his presence since its very inception? The man who, thanks to his brilliant self-programming methodology and eidetic memory, pioneered the field of AI-enhanced robotics with his android creations?" Boris laughed and rubbed his hands together with glee. "Forget *using* the apple – the Mad Thinker is the sort of genius who will be able to take it apart! He has the intelligence to break something that seems magical down into its constituent scientific elements. I guarantee that if he maintains his grip on the apple, within the week he will find a way to make his own!"

Ooh, it looks like we have a fanboy. None of that diatribe in favor of the Mad Thinker sounded particularly good to me – and honestly, who gave themselves the moniker *Mad* Thinker, it was like he was trying not to be taken seriously – but then again, it wasn't my problem. I'd never tangled with the guy before, and I honestly didn't really care who the Mad Thinker was; what I cared about was that he stayed out of my way. The Fantastic Four could have him, as far as I was concerned.

Yeah, that "hands off" approach had been working so well for me lately.

"Lots of people use robots," I pointed out, carefully pulling off my gloves and tossing them on the table. It had been a long night, and I was ready to get out of my admittedly amazing suit, sit back with a glass of good wine, and relax for a while.

"*Robots* are not *androids*," Boris ranted, looking on the verge of pulling his hair out. "Is Vision a mere robot? Ultron? Nimrod? Lady Deathstrike?"

"Um, in at least two of those cases, I'm thinking yes," I said, just to wind him up. It worked – my henchman loosed an inarticulate cry of rage and despair, spun around in his rolling chair, and went back to his computer, muttering imprecations about my intelligence the whole time. I felt accomplished. Boris was a man of strong emotions, and sometimes he couldn't be happy if he didn't have something to rail against.

I turned to Bruno, who was sitting on the couch watching a game. "I'm sure you were monitoring the car," I said, "so you saw that the shield worked great, but the low battery power is a problem. Can we recharge them off the car's engine?" I wanted to get all the tests in with Danny's high-prestige vehicle that I could before giving it back. Mine were mostly practical – his was all about style and speed.

"We could do that, but it'll eat up a lotta gas," Bruno said, scratching his scruffy chin. "Be better if we could build something into the car to extend the battery life. There's a lotta work going on with hydrogen fuel cells right now that could be interestin.'"

"I don't want a car that's going to blow up if it gets tagged by a bullet."

"That's not how hydrogen fuel cells work, boss, but I'll keep it in mind." He nodded his head toward my room. "Just an FYI, but you might want to go talk to Casey."

I frowned. "What's wrong with her?"

"She got a little shaken up watching the car chase."

"Oooh, did you save the video?" Of course Danny Rand's car had cameras to help it back up, pull forward, park, do donuts – it basically took care of driving for you, if you let it. Bruno had tapped into it to give him real-time footage of our little race this evening. It was easier than me trying to relay the whole escapade while I was trying to pull it off, not that they could have done much to help from back here. Still, it was nice to know my team was with me, however silently.

"Yeah. She got kinda ... *concerned* for you a time or two."

I scoffed. "Concerned for her meal ticket, you mean."

"No." Bruno's solemn head shake gave me pause. "Concern for *you*. The kid likes you, boss. She looks up to you. Just ... don't tease her too much, all right?"

"All right," I promised. "I'll be nice." Actually, speaking of nice ... "Can you pull some footage for me while I clean up?

I've got a hunch I'd like to follow up on." A hunch I wouldn't be sharing with my team before I verified it, but I'd learned to trust my instincts when it came to things like this.

"Sure thing, boss. What do you need?"

I told him, then walked over to my room – my own room, for heaven's sake – and knocked on the door.

"What is it?" came the sad, tiny voice of a girl feeling distressed. Well, that just wouldn't do.

"It's meeeee," I announced. "And I'm coming in, so you better not be wearing my platinum stilettos. Those shoes cost over a million dollars."

There was a pause, and then– "You have million-dollar shoes? God, you're *gross*."

Ah, petulant teenage voice coming back into play – that was more like it. I stepped into my bedroom and found that my bed had been turned into what amounted to a nest. Every blanket I owned was piled on it, every pillow was stacked there, and in the middle of it all was Casey, still in her hoodie, looking at her phone instead of me. The hood was pushed back, though, giving me a clear view of her eyes, which weren't moving. It was a decent bluff, but not good enough.

"Hey." I sat on the edge of the bed. "What's up?"

"Nothing."

"Oh yeah? What are you watching?"

"None of your business."

"No posting to social media from my home," I reminded her. I was sure she wouldn't, but I had to get it out there.

"Duh." Casey rolled her eyes. "Like the feds aren't watching my accounts. And throwaways are just a hassle."

"Good." I could continue to pry in a roundabout fashion,

but I thought there was more to be gained from the direct approach – certainly more quickly. "So, what do you think of my driving skills?"

"Oh my god, you're insane!" Casey burst out. "Why did you go after the *laser drones*? They shoot freaking lasers! They could have burned your head off! I don't even know how they *didn't* burn your head off!"

"Just lucky, I guess."

"Shut up! And then another set of drones, and you let the guy who *can't see* handle them? What the, how could you – you tried! I mean, you could say you tried after the first car, you could say you tried before the drones got involved. And Daredevil is a good guy, right? He would still help you talk to the Manfredis even if you didn't take down the Kingpin, as long as you tried."

"Maybe, but–" I tried to interject, but Casey was on a roll now.

"And, and then! After all the lasers and crazy stunts and them crashing into a gas station, you didn't even get the apple!"

"Getting the apple wasn't the goal for me or for Daredevil," I reminded her. "Keeping the Kingpin from using it was."

"But you didn't keep him from using it, the android guy did," Casey said, undeterred. "So you technically didn't do what he asked you to do, but he's still helping you, and you knew he would. So why…"

"Why what?" I asked gently.

"Why do something so dangerous?" she said at last, finally looking me in the eyes. "Why risk your life for a stupid request from a guy you don't even like, when you could have backed

out when it was safer? What if you died? What would happen
to your crew, to all your stuff? What would your mom think?"

Oh, we were treading on dangerous ground now. I needed to
be careful… but I also needed to be honest. "Casey." I crossed
my legs and faced her fully. "First off, it wasn't as dangerous as
it seemed. Daredevil isn't my biggest fan, but he wasn't about
to let me take a laserbeam to the head if he could help it, and
vice versa. Second, I *like* a little danger in my work. It makes
things more fun. No, I don't want to die in a road race with
the Kingpin, of all people, but believe me when I say there are
worse potential ways to go."

"Duh," Casey said, rolling her eyes. Ah, good, that was *much*
better. "But that doesn't mean it's a good way to go, either."

"No, that's true. But I had contingencies in place for if things
got really bad." I gestured down at my suit. "I've survived a
whole lot of stuff thanks to the tech stuffed into every inch of
this, not to mention my probability rig. At the worst, I would
have had to ditch the car and let the Kingpin get away."

"Would Mr Rand be mad at you if you crashed his car?"

I laughed. "Probably not. Danny is honestly one of the most
laid-back people I know. He would ask if I was all right, but I
doubt he'd even ask me to pay for it."

"Because he's nice, or because he's a billionaire?"

Ha, way to be precise. "Because he's nice. There are plenty of
jerkhole billionaires out there who would charge me for their
car, and the gas that was in it, and their mental suffering while
they were at it. All of which are good reasons to be careful when
it comes to stealing from billionaires."

Casey looked thoughtful. "What would Tony Stark do if you
stole from him?"

"It depends on the day," I answered honestly. "As long as I gave him a puzzle to go along with my thievery, he'd let it go." I had personal experience with that, from when I broke into his Nanoforge and fabricated a custom suit that took him on a wild chase all over the city. Good times.

"Getting back to the point," I continued, "I know it probably looked and sounded scary while I was out there, but I had it under control. I'm still in when it comes to finding your dad, and with Daredevil owing us a way to make a meeting with the Manfredis happen, I promise that we'll keep doing our best." I shrugged. "What else *can* we do, after all?"

"Grab a stupid golden apple and wish for it to tell us how to find him," Casey grumbled, looking away from me. She bit her lower lip so hard the flesh turned stark white. I tapped her on the chin.

"Careful."

"That's what I would do if I found the golden apple," Casey said, letting go of her lip but still looking away. "I wouldn't ask for money or stock picks or how to take over the world or any of that. I would ask how to find my dad as soon as possible, exactly like that, with no room for the dumb thing to misunderstand me."

Well, that was… incredibly specific. I had no doubt that a lot of people out there had spent some time pondering what they would say if and when they came across a golden apple, but I hadn't thought Casey would be one of them. I thought she was laser-focused on finding her dad, to the exclusion of daydreaming – but then, was it daydreaming if she was dreaming about finding her father?

Hmm.

"I see you've made yourself right at home," I said, happy to change the subject. "Where am I supposed to sleep tonight, huh?"

"Um." Casey blinked her big eyes. Butter wouldn't have melted in this child's mouth. "Gosh. I hear the couch is really nice, y'know."

"Imp." But she wasn't wrong either, and besides, I had some work to do that required more screens than I had in my room. I grabbed a change of clothes, did my toilette in the bathroom, and by the time I stepped out again she was fast asleep.

Boris and Bruno had moved on to their own bedrooms by the time I came back out to the main room, so I had the place to myself. I settled in at the table, pulled up footage from three different events I'd participated in recently, and set facial recognition software to work on them.

The results came in surprisingly quickly. Only two faces turned up each time. Mine, and the face of another familiar person.

Ah-ha.

Now that I had a face to go on, I could expand my search. I'd had enough run-ins with the apple so far that I felt the need to know more about it. With this new piece of information, I had the chance to learn things that no one else knew.

I started with the widely known events in Shanghai, Madrid, and Sydney, and refined the identification algorithm more each time. Once I had that, I turned my puzzle-solving skills to Casey.

It was harder because she lived in Nowhere, Ohio, but she was a fiend for social media. Her Instagram and TikTok were rife with posts dating back to right before she'd found out her father had gone missing. I put my algorithm to work on her files and made myself a cup of chamomile tea while it searched through her accounts, then through her friends' accounts. Nothing. I expanded it to include expanded footage in her town, and five minutes into that search I got a hit.

There, in a park two blocks from the Beck family home, was the mystery face. And sitting on one of the swings, looking down at something in her hands with a dumbstruck expression, was Casey.

One more piece fell into place. Now I just had to talk to Casey about it… when she wasn't exhausted and on the verge of an emotional meltdown.

Eh, she was a resilient kid. Tomorrow, then.

I settled back on the couch, satisfied with myself and the world at large. Tomorrow was going to be great.

CHAPTER TWENTY-ONE

"What do you mean, he wants the car back?" The last thing I expected after I woke up with a crick in my back from sleeping on the couch – I should never have let Casey convince me to sleep there – and spectacular bedhead was Danny Rand knocking on my proverbial door, asking for his car back.

Bruno shrugged. "I dunno why, boss, but Rand's left three messages in the last two hours asking about it. Maybe he saw it on the news."

"Shoot." I was going to miss this car. I'd have to see about stealing one for myself someday soon. "Fine. We can take it when we go to get Daredevil's info on the Manfredis, and he can make sure it gets back to Rand. It's in good enough shape to go back, right?"

Bruno shrugged. "The leather's nicked in a few spots, and there's a little paint damage here and there, but he doesn't seem like the kind of guy to look too closely."

"Excellent." I pulled out my phone to figure out what to text Daredevil. I knew he used text-to-speech software, probably with the volume turned way down, but... eh, the prank was still worth a shot.

Had a great time last night. Two is fun, but wouldn't three be better? Bring your friend with the iron grip to our rendezvous at ten. I promise to make it worth your time.

Hopefully he'd read that somewhere in public, and blush as red as his hair. I also sent a text straight to Danny, because I wasn't a jerk, telling him to contact Matt to find out where we were meeting, and that I'd bring his ride there.

Pigtails successfully tugged, now it was back to business. I'd been debating whether or not to talk to Casey about what I was almost sure of this morning, or if I should put it off for a while. We still had a couple of hours before the meeting, though, and I *did* have to spend some time in my actual bedroom getting ready this morning.

I walked over to the fruit bowl and picked out something pretty, then headed for my room. I knocked, and a second later Casey called me in. "I brought you a snack," I said, shutting the door behind me and tossing the fruit to her at the same time. She caught it from her spot on the edge of the bed, and her open expression immediately shuttered.

"I know they're old school, but I love Golden Delicious," I said, crunching down on my own. Mmm, so good. "Don't you? I mean, I'm sure it's not as nice as the last apple you had in your hands, but this is the best I've got."

Her expression didn't change. "How did you figure it out?"

"It wasn't that you gave anything away," I assured her. "You've done a good job keeping it close to your chest, but I'm one of the best there is at ferreting out secrets." I didn't tell her about the person I'd seen on the periphery of the park with her. That was *my* secret for now, and not one I was inclined to share with anybody. "My question is, what did you ask for? And how did it lead to me?"

Because it had to. With someone else, I might think they'd wished for something different and then had buyer's remorse once they realized they could have done something truly meaningful with their chance, but Casey was so fixated on her dad that I couldn't imagine she wouldn't try to get him back immediately. "Did you not know he was gone by then, or–"

"I knew." Casey tossed the apple down on the bed, her blank expression becoming one of pure distaste as she wrinkled her nose. "I didn't know much before that, though. They told him to lie to me about it, tell me it was a work trip instead of coming back for the trial. He did, and I believed him. He said he'd be back in a few days, and I believed that too, which was dumb but I totally did. My dad… he never lied to me, before. He never lied about his past, he never lied about what was happening to my mom when she died. He just didn't.

"When the FBI called me and told me that he was missing, they said they were sending someone to take me into 'protective custody' until they found him." She huffed derisively. "Total crap. That's just another word for foster care, and there's no way I'm doing that. Not when my own dad is still out there. And I *knew* they would screw up getting him back, I just *knew* it, and I was right!"

"You sure were." Wow, I'd barely had to pull to get all of this out of her. She must have been dying, holding onto a secret like this. "And then you found the apple?"

She nodded. "I was already planning on going to New York," Casey said. "Had a bus ticket bought and everything. I was cutting through the park when I saw the apple. It was after the first few had been found, so I knew what it was. I thought maybe it was a joke at first, but then I touched it." Her look became a little haunted, eyes glazing as she stared straight forward, looking into the past, not at me.

"It spoke to me. It said I could have anything I wanted, know anything that I needed to know. That I could experience life through new eyes. And my brain… it just, like, got stuck on that." Casey bit her lip, talking around the tension of her teeth. "All I could think of was seeing my dad again, and when I finally asked my question, I asked …" She looked up at the ceiling, her eyes welling with tears. "I asked who the last person my father had seen was, instead of how to save him. And it said he saw you." Casey shook her head. "God, I'm so *stupid.*"

Oh, hon. It was an unfortunate bit of phrasing, but it could have been a lot worse. I sat down next to her and put an arm around her shoulder. I'd have to wash the bedspread if we kept soaking it in tears every twelve hours. "You're not stupid."

"I am! I should have asked to become an all-knowing badass with unlimited money who could find her own father!"

"I think if you had, the chances of you finding your dad would have gone way down." I'd been thinking about this for a bit, actually – why none of the people who'd found and used apples had enjoyed their largesse for long. "Magical items like this are tricky, and none of them are ever what they seem. Ask me how I know," I added. "I was almost possessed by a piece of magical tree once."

Casey wiped her eyes on her sleeve. "What?" she asked faintly.

"Yeah, a tree." Yggdrasil the World Tree more specifically, but she didn't need to know the details. "Wild, right? And it told me it could give me everything I ever wanted, showed me all these pretty pictures of me in power, with all the money I could ever want, all the prestige. Even all the lovers I could desire, with everyone in my life I'd ever wanted all wanting me back."

Casey frowned. "That seems kind of evil."

Ha, *she* got it instantly. "No kidding. Either the thing was going to take away peoples' free will, or it was going to make simulacra of the ones I was actually interested in. Either way, nothing I was willing to deal with, and if one part of the deal looked bad, then the whole thing was probably bad. So I chose to pass."

"I wish I had done that. Or… I don't know. Done *something* better."

"Honestly, Casey." I gave her a little squeeze. "I think you asked just the right question. I mean, you managed to get me on your side, and that's no mean feat."

She looked up at me, eyes wide with hope. "You mean you're still going to help me? Even though you already know the answer to how I found out about you?"

"I don't believe in leaving a job undone." And there was a second mystery now, one that was alluring enough to grab my attention and keep it. Money, jewels, tech – those might be the bread and butter of my existence, but for pure pleasure, the best thing I'd ever found to scratch my itch was a good puzzle. And this time around, the puzzle was thinking of a way to use the golden apple without getting screwed over.

It didn't hurt that this one was connected to a fascinating magical object, either. I *might* have been starting to come around on the apple thing. I thought I might see a way to make use of it without hurting myself. I'd want to confirm – if I got the chance, if the Mad Thinker didn't use it up himself – but Boris was usually right when it came to his idols. If he thought the Mad Thinker would take the chance to take the apple apart and see what made it tick, so to speak, then it might still be out there.

That was a question for another day, though. "Come on," I said, standing up. "We've got a meeting in an hour, so go get some breakfast while I get ready for the day. And you *are* taking the couch tonight," I added, pointing my finger at her. "No big eyes, no trembly lips, no sob stories to get out of it."

"Sure, boss," Casey said, smiling even as she rolled her eyes. She walked out of the room with a skip in her step.

"I *am* the boss!" I called after her.

"Okaaaaaay."

"Brat," I muttered, then headed for the bathroom. I had barely enough time to make myself presentable, and I wasn't going to waste another minute of it.

CHAPTER TWENTY-TWO

With Bruno tailing us in my Benz, I drove Casey and me to the legal offices of one Matthew M. Murdock, Esquire, also known as the luckiest lawyer alive because he had friends who wouldn't let him fail at his day job and put up with his night job. Just thinking about the amount of emotional energy it would take to handle Daredevil on a regular basis made me glad we kept each other at arm's length. He was fun for a night, but his wasn't a face I wanted to see first thing in the morning.

I parked Danny's Ferrari out front, which was as good as a death sentence for the poor thing if I left it alone in Hell's Kitchen for more than a few minutes. Or it *would* have been, if Bruno hadn't modified the shield system to, when activated by the key fob, act as a close-lying force field that would prevent anyone not only from breaking in, but also from so much as keying the exterior. Still, it was probably best I keep a watch until Danny could take over.

Bruno had a lot of respect for this car. I hoped Danny appreciated it half as much. Speaking of...

"We're outside," I said, stepping onto the street. I immediately knew my presence had been felt – a lady just knows these things. "Come on down, gents."

"Can he hear that?" Casey asked, shutting her own door.

"He knew it was us the moment we got within a five-block radius," I replied with a smirk. "He's probably waiting for Rand to show up. We can–"

"Hey, baby." Aaand cue the first jerk looking to make trouble. It took some real swagger to approach me when I was wearing these heels. "Lookin' fly up against that car. Wanna take me for a spin?" he said with a leer.

Of course, swagger was less than nothing in the world of traits I respected. "Ooh, so tempting, but no. I think I'd rather you gouge your own eyes out."

"That's not how that saying works, is it?" Casey asked.

"It's how it works with me," I said, grinning at her. She grinned back. *Excellent, I've just found my new straight man.*

Meanwhile, my would-be paramour was feeling neglected. "Look, you don't come onto my street lookin' like this and expect not to have to share a little of what you got," he said, patting his hip meaningfully.

This gentleman had run right past "dangerous" and straight into "suicidal." I got ready to trigger my rig; with bad enough luck, he'd end up shooting himself through the foot before I had to dirty my hands by actually touching him.

"You better be careful," I said, shaking my head. "Or Daredevil is going to get you."

The punk got even further into my space. Much closer and I'd be smelling his breath, not just his rank body spray. "Don't try to scare me off, woman, everybody knows he only comes out at night, so – *ow*!"

"Oh, whoops!" Matthew Murdock stumbled from the aftershocks of smacking his cane hard enough against the back of this jackass's knees to buckle them. He looked for all the world like a stumbling blind man who'd just made an innocent mistake. "Gosh, sir, I'm so sorry about that. I was just coming out here to meet my friend, I didn't expect anyone else to be with her."

"He's not with me," I said. "In fact, I think he was just leaving."

"The *hell* I am!" The guy got back to his feet ready to start throwing punches, if the awkward way he was bouncing on his feet was any indication. "You think you can play with me like that? Think again, you blind mother–"

"Uh-uh." One of those jumping fists was caught in the ridiculously strong grip of Danny Rand, and it stopped the tough guy mid-bounce. "I don't think so."

"Hey, get offa me, man!" The guy tried to pull his hand away. No luck. "Let go!" Danny didn't move an inch, not even when the guy started using his other hand to help. Finally, once anger had been replaced with fear, Danny let go. The former tough guy fell backward so hard he did a roll, and ended up flat on his back five feet away. He got up and ran off a second after that, and Casey started to laugh.

"That was awesome!" she said. "It's like slapstick, but better, because it's real! Grab me now, I want to see if I can pull away." She thrust her hand at Danny Rand, who looked a little blinkered.

"Um…"

"Casey, we're on a timetable," I reminded her.

"Oh, right." She lowered her hand and stepped back, smile slowly vanishing.

"It's not that pressing, right?" Danny asked, always a sucker for a sad face.

"That depends on Mr Murdock here," I said, turning my eyes to him. How did he always manage to make a smirk look charming? It was one of life's little mysteries. "What've you got for me, counselor?"

"Why don't we discuss this in my office?" he said. "Where there are fewer people around to fail at hitting on you."

Ha. "There's always someone around for that."

"There would be if Foggy was in right now, but he's taking some client statements, so I have the place to myself."

"Sure." I glanced at Casey, then at Danny. "You can stay down here with him, as long as he promises not to drive off and leave you."

"I wouldn't!" Danny protested at the same time as Casey said, "Awesome!"

"It's sweet of you to let her have her way," Murdock remarked as we headed up the stairs of his shabby little building.

I shrugged. "She's had a tough time lately. She deserves a chance to be a goofy teenager for a little bit, and who better to bounce goofy off than Danny?"

"Yeah, good point." He opened the door of his office for me. "Coffee? Tea?"

"There's no need to schmooze me, I'm not one of your clients." I did accept the bottle of water he held out, though. "Talk to me. How am I getting a meeting with Silvermane?"

"By offering him the one thing he wants more than anything else right now."

Great, now we were playing a riddle game. "Which is? Hurry it up, Murdock, I don't have all morning."

Matt tilted his head, ready to lay on the condescension. Great. "What else could it be but his son?"

"Ah." Actually… that made perfect sense. There were a few flaws with the plan, though, the most obvious of them being, "No one knows where he's being kept during trial, though."

"His location is changed daily so that the Maggia never know where to break him out of," Matt acknowledged. "But I happen to know that after trial adjourns today, he's going to be sent to the Manhattan Detention Complex."

"The Tombs." Not an incredibly secure location, but a challenging one all the same since it was part of the Civic Center. That meant there were a lot of people around to poke their nose into places it didn't belong, and a lot of eyes to evade.

"I also know," Matt went on, "that Joseph Manfredi has requested new counsel. He thinks his lawyers aren't being aggressive enough. He's going to be interviewing several candidates tonight, and one of them is a lawyer with this firm." He handed over a business card with the name *Mallory & Associates* on it. "If you can take their place, you'll get access to him."

"Well, well." That was honestly more than I'd expected to get out of Better Off Red, here. I tucked the card into my purse. "Thanks for the tips, Murdock. I'll make the most of them."

Matt smiled again – not his lawyerly smirk, not this time. This was the dark, toothy grin that Daredevil liked to give people right before he kicked them into next week. "Have fun with that. In fact – oh." He pushed to his feet. "We should get downstairs. Now."

I immediately headed for the door. "Is Casey in trouble?"

"No, but–"

I didn't wait, just ran downstairs in less-than-elegant fashion. My heart was pounding when I burst out onto the street, looking at…

Looking at the "tough guy" Danny had run off earlier, who'd apparently come back with three friends. All of them were lying unconscious on the sidewalk.

Danny scratched the back of his head self-consciously while Casey stared at him with fresh hero worship in her eyes. "Um… it's all good, we're fine," he said.

"You can give a guy a secret identity," I muttered, motioning to Bruno, who'd hung back by a block. "But you can't make him keep it. Good grief."

"They were insistent," he protested. "And rude! I didn't want Casey to have to listen to that kind of language!"

"All right, whatever, it's – stop laughing!" I whirled on Murdock, who was snickering behind his hand. "You're no better, Mr 'Oh no I'm blind, how did I hit all those pressure points?' We're out of here." Bruno pulled up and I opened the back door for Casey, then got into the front seat myself. I held out a hand toward Danny, his silver pendant dangling from my fingers. "You lost this at the Gala, by the way."

He beamed at me and grabbed it. "Oh hey, thanks! I was wondering where that ended up."

"You're so welcome," I cooed. Murdock looked like he'd swallowed a lemon. Excellent, my job here was done.

Casey rolled down her window and waved.

"Bye!" she called out. "Don't forget to follow me on TikTok, OK?"

"I will!" Danny called back. "And thanks for bringing my car back, Felicia."

"No problem. Oh! Be careful with the upgrades, they take some getting used to!"

"Um… upgrades?"

On that quizzical note, Bruno got us out of there. "Where to, boss?" he asked while Casey quietly flipped out in the back seat over her latest super hero encounter.

"Home," I said. I glanced in the direction of Centre Street, where the detention complex was located. "We've got a job to plan and not a lot of time to plan it in."

"What kind of job?"

I smiled. "Tonight, we're stealing Joseph Manfredi."

CHAPTER TWENTY-THREE

In the end, the hardest part about getting our target out of the Manhattan Detention Complex was figuring out which lawyer from Mallory & Associates would be coming to meet with Joseph and making sure we took their place. A little digging on Boris's part revealed that his would-be lawyer was a guy named Ray, which wasn't the best name for me to try and inhabit, but it wasn't the worst either.

"I could be Mr Mallory instead," Boris offered. "I promise to do my utmost to ruin his reputation."

"He's already a complete scumbag who makes the world dirtier just by breathing," I said apologetically. "It's hard to sink much lower. And I'd rather have you running our lookie-loos from across the street. You're sure the radar can penetrate the building?"

We had recently become the proud owners of some cutting-edge equipment that had "fallen" off the back of a Department of Defense truck, right into our laps! It allowed us to literally look through walls and track the people moving in them, which was totally illegal in every way, shape, and form – except when it was being used in search and rescue operations, which is what the creators of said tech had originally designed it for. As far as I was concerned, this was one more step on the road to rescuing Dalton Beck, so it counted.

Boris scoffed. "Child's play. It's not even lead-shielded. With a ten-minute head start, I'll have a map that leads straight to where Mr Manfredi is cooling his heels between interviews."

"Perfect." I turned to Casey. "Are you still sure you want to help out with this?"

Her jaw jutted forward a little. "I'm sure."

"Because you don't have to."

"I *know*. You already said that."

"And I want to emphasize, again, that there are other ways to get this done. You don't have to go crawling through some vents just on my say-so, we could–"

"Actually," Bruno said with a slightly apologetic air, "this really is the best way to do it with such tight timing, boss. Ain't gonna get a better chance at this guy than the Manhattan Detention Center – it's in a civilian building, and it's not retrofitted to account for super powers or anything. Boris really oughta run the equipment if you're on the con, he's the best at it, and I'm too big to fit in those ducts."

"See?" Casey said. "You *need* me. And I promise I won't do anything you don't tell me to do, this time."

With our timeline so tight, my hands were tied. Unless… "I could ask Spider-Man to do it."

All three members of my crew looked at me like I was insane. "You wanna bring that boy scout into this–"

"There's no need to invite him to see how our brilliant machinations work–"

"I climbed straight up your building, I can totally do this!"

An entire chorus of "no's," in essence.

"Fine," I huffed. I hadn't been all *that* serious about it, after all, but I still regretted the loss of a chance to spend more time with him. Peter would come if I asked, I was certain. He would help me, no matter what, and then…

Then he would feel terrible about breaking a criminal *out* of federal custody, when the world was so much safer with him *in* federal custody. Peter definitely wouldn't agree with my plan to exchange Joseph Manfredi for Dalton Beck. No, I couldn't bring Spider-Man into this, no matter how much I wanted to.

Well, Casey had wanted to play a bigger role in the team. Nothing like going from stealing data from the FBI to sneaking into a secure detention facility to really make you feel like part of the gang.

I glanced at my phone. "All right, everyone, suit up. Bruno, make sure you go over using the special screwdriver in case Casey needs to get through a vent cover, and for the love of all that's holy, *tell* me we've got a few noise dampeners we can stick on her." I wasn't going to trust Casey's safety to her ability to crawl through a vent in complete silence. We couldn't all have catlike reflexes.

"I got it taken care of, boss," Bruno assured me. "We'll handle it. And I'll be helpin' her through the whole way." He reached out and ruffled Casey's mousy hair. She batted at his hand, but she was smiling.

"All right, then." I leaned both hands on the table and looked at my crew, a grin spreading across my face. This was going to be fun. "Let's go steal a criminal."

•••

There was something about the sound of a stiletto heel striking the ground that I loved. As footwear went, the style was far from forgiving, but you didn't indulge your love of elevating yourself over everyone around you as much as I did without training yourself to love stilettos too. In a world where body language was as important as anything you ever bothered saying out loud, footwear said a lot, and these shoes? They practically screamed "badass coming through, move aside or get squashed."

I walked inside the Civic Centre at a brisk pace, moved straight past the front desk and over to the guard sitting to the side of an elevator at the far end of the lobby. It was kept separate from the other elevators in the building and was the most foolproof way to get up to the seventh floor, where the Tombs began. A few seconds behind me, Bruno walked in with Casey, both of them dressed like tourists.

"Let's go see the view from the top!" Casey said excitedly, like she was ten instead of fifteen. "Can we, Dad?"

"Sure, honey." They headed for the regular elevators, Casey's backpack swinging from one hand.

"What the – this ain't the Empire State Building," the guard muttered, getting up from his chair. I intercepted him before he could accost the rest of my crew.

"I'm here to see my client," I said briskly, flashing my new and very shiny ID card in the man's face. "I believe he's expecting me."

The guard blinked, looking up at me with the wide eyes of someone experiencing a vision. Whether it was a good one or a bad one remained to be seen. "Um… sorry, who are you, miss?"

I flipped a strand of dark brown hair off my shoulder and glared at the guard. "Can you read? Is that not a requirement for this sort of work any longer? My name is Ray Mallory, and I want to see my client right now."

The guard looked down at the tablet he'd been holding on his lap. "You don't look like no Ray," he said after a second.

"Short for Ramona," I snapped, "and you try shouting that at a law office and see how fast people listen to you. Look–" I glanced at his nametag "–Teddy, I didn't come all this way at this time of evening to be stopped by the patriarchy giving me the third degree, and if you don't let me up to see my client right this instant, I'll be bringing a lawsuit for–"

"OK, OK! Geez, lady, ain't no patriarchy here." He reached around behind him and scanned his card. The elevator door opened with a *ding*. "Just doing my job, you get me? I expected a guy, you ain't a guy, my mistake, end of story."

"It had better be," I said, nose in the air as I entered the elevator. It really *had* better be, because the actual Ray Mallory was currently lying in the trunk of his own car sleeping off a dose of pentobarbital.

The elevator was slow and smelled faintly of cheese. I rolled my eyes at my wavy reflection in the dingy steel doors. This facility could use so many upgrades, and it could make them all once I was done here. There weren't even any cameras in the elevator, for crying out loud… although I had a feeling that that was more because the white-collar criminals who waited out their sentencing here had the occasional visitor who'd rather not be identified.

The Tombs were a pit, but they were a pit with Wi-Fi, televisions, and private bathrooms. It was like being in a roadside motel instead of a prison, perfect for secret assignations like mine.

"All right, here we are…" I heard a clatter over my com, then Bruno said, "I think we're ready to get started. I'm gonna lower you down slow, OK, Casey? Keep the goggles on, they're gonna show your map. Boris will guide you to where you need to be with 'em."

"OK." Casey sounded nervous, but not scared – the perfect combination of emotions in a beginner. I felt proud just listening to her rappel down a tube of steel-sided ductwork.

The door opened. I stepped out of the elevator into a white, Spartan room that seemed to take security a *little* more seriously than the guy downstairs did. There were two people here, not in guard uniforms but in black security gear. The woman stepped toward me with a wand while the man immediately demanded, "ID and briefcase."

"Here." I held both up, making sure the briefcase was unlocked and ready to go. It was full of paperwork – stuff I'd taken off the real lawyer, so it all looked official. The guard snatched them out of my hands, taking both things over to a desk and scanning them with a computer.

"Hands up," the woman barked. I raised my hands in the air, confident they wouldn't find anything untoward. My gear was top of the line for a reason.

After another second of scanning, the woman lowered the wand and picked up a tray. "Jewelry off."

What? "What?" I asked, not even having to pretend to be outraged. "Why should I leave my jewelry out here?"

"Can't have you bringing any potential contraband into the unit, ma'am," the woman intoned.

"Jewelry isn't contraband, it's *accessorization*."

"Could be given to prisoners who could use it to buy favors. Contraband." The woman shook the tray. "Jewelry here, or you don't go in."

"This is utterly draconian," I snapped even as I reached up to undo my right earring – which was also my com. For Pete's sake, this was supposed to be a *civilized* prison; it's not like I was flying out to the Raft. I wasn't going to be able to listen in on my crew anymore. I wouldn't know exactly when Casey was making her move, or how much time I needed to stall with Joseph. "Absolutely draconian. I'll be speaking with your manager."

"I copy you," Boris said, picking up on my code phrase. "We have things under control. Estimate removal beginning in ten minutes." Then I couldn't hear any more, because my earring was off and in the ugly plastic tray. I removed the other, then my necklace, then my rings.

"There," I snapped. "Are you satisfied?"

"Shoes too."

"What?"

"Could be used as weapons." She shook the tray again. "Shoes. Now."

"If I get an infection from having my bare feet on this floor, I'm suing."

"Yeah, yeah. Tell it to the judge, sister."

A minute later, barefoot and genuinely furious about it, I was shown into a small room pretending to be a lounge that was clearly just another version of a cell. Every piece of furniture, bad as it was, was screwed to the floor – and there were no cushions on anything, not even the couch. "Nothing but a bench with pretentions," I muttered, sitting down on the edge of it with a grimace. The security camera in the corner of the room blinked at me, and I rolled my eyes back at it.

Two minutes after I sat down, the door opened again, and Joseph Manfredi stepped into the room. He wasn't barefoot – he had some kind of cheap, cardboard sandal on, and he was still wearing his nice Cavalli suit from the trial. It was a strange dichotomy, but then again, there wasn't a whole lot about this situation that *wasn't* strange. I'd forgotten that the Manhattan Detention Complex, while nicer than most of the other prisons in the city, was still a prison. It wasn't going to be caviar and lobster for Joseph, even if he was a big deal.

The door locked behind him, and Joseph Manfredi, aka Blackwing, aka the leader of Heavy Mettle, stared at me with one raised eyebrow. He wasn't a classically handsome man, not like his father had been in his youth, but he had nice, regular features, thick brown hair slicked straight back – *so* Maggia, honestly – and the inoffensive expression of a slightly stunned golden retriever. "I might be hallucinating," he said a moment later, "but I was under the impression that Ray Mallory was a man."

"You were mistaken," I replied smoothly, getting up and crossing over to hold out my hand. He shook it, a gentleman even in handcuffs. "But I forgive you."

"No," he said quietly. "No, I don't think I was mistaken. But I might like to be, depending on what you've got on…" He looked me up and down, then smirked. "On *offer*, shall we say."

I smirked right back. "Oh, I think I've got just the thing to interest a man like you. Why don't we have a seat and talk about it?" I needed to stall long enough for Casey to get to us. I had the feeling it wasn't going to be hard – Joseph was clearly bored out of his mind and more than willing to chat.

"Sounds good to me." He gestured toward the two chairs beside the plain steel table. "I'd offer you a drink, but unfortunately this isn't a very hospitable place."

"I'm sure we can do something about that," I said, sitting and crossing my legs artfully. Eyes went down to them, then back up to my chest – yep, I'd get this guy to follow me anywhere in a few more minutes. "I don't think The Tombs are the best place for you for the duration of your trial, Mr Manfredi. I think we can do much better."

"Eh, they're not so bad," he said with a shrug as he sat down. "A big improvement over some of the holes they've stuck me in so far. You think you can make a deal with the judge about that?"

"Perhaps. Or…" I let my voice trail off, lowered my eyes and batted my eyelashes a little. Joseph couldn't look away. "We can bypass the judge entirely."

He swallowed hard. "Uh… how?"

Now came the pitch. I could drag Joseph out of here if I needed to, but it would be so much easier to get him downstairs and into our getaway car if he came willingly. Since I didn't have any idea when Casey was going to show up, I decided it was better to move fast.

"This trial has been dragging on for quite a while," I said. "And the longer it goes without the star witness coming to the stand, the longer you're going to be in limbo."

"Rather be in limbo than back in a hole," Joseph replied. "This is a step up, from where I'm sitting."

"And when the judge declares a mistrial?" I pressed. "When

he decides that without Dalton Beck, he can't adequately assess the truth of your statement and sends you back to your hole permanently?"

Joseph frowned. "That's not how the law works. That's not what's going to happen. Without Firestrike to run his mouth off against me, the judge will have lack of sufficient evidence to prove the conviction and I'll be off the hook."

"Oh, that's… such a cute thought." I shook my head. "I didn't take you for an idealist, Mr Manfredi."

"What are you talking about? I'm–"

"While Silvermane has a lot of sway with New York's judiciary, Judge Reem is deep in the Kingpin's pocket," I said briskly, folding my hands on the table in front of me and leaning in. I was about to state some patently false things, and while I could lie like a champion, it was always easier to sell the fake Monet when the client was a little… distracted. "Wilson Fisk has no reason to be kind to anyone from the Maggia, but he's particularly salty toward your father. There's no way you'll be going free at the end of this, no matter what. Either Firestrike comes out of hiding and sells you up the river again, or Reem sends you back to prison to await 'further evidence' or something like that."

Joseph was full-on scowling now. "So what, you're telling me I'm done either way? This goose is cooked?"

"Not at all, Mr Manfredi." I smiled. "I'm just asking you to think a little… outside the box, as it were. There are a lot of opportunities out there for a man of your skills and connections." He actually had little of either, unless I was hankering for someone to control a colony of bats for some reason. Which – hey, never say never, but I needed to lay on the compliments here. "Especially with the support of your family behind you."

Joseph scoffed. "What are you talking about? I don't have Pop's support – never did."

I shook my head. "Your father is getting older," I said quietly. "Starting to look back on his life, starting to regret certain things. He's got lineage in mind, and most of your old competition is dead. Your father wants to give you a second chance."

I'd rarely seen a guy get flummoxed so fast. "Really? He said that about me?"

"Absolutely." *Not.* "And he's done waiting around for the law to do the right thing and let you go. After all, it was nothing but circumstantial evidence and a known traitor's testimony that got you put away in the first place! And you haven't acted against your father in any way since you've been inside. Silvermane is ready to make amends, Mr Manfredi." I heard a very faint scratching in the ceiling above me, and my practiced smile became real. "All you have to do is say yes."

Joseph looked at me like I'd just offered him the Holy Grail. "Yes," he said after a moment. "Yes."

Hook, line, and sinker. "Then let's do this!"

CHAPTER TWENTY-FOUR

A second later, a ceiling tile was pulled out of the way. A second after that, two full-face gas masks dropped down onto the table between us. I just barely caught a glimpse of Casey's eyes behind her own mask before she was off again. At the same time, I began to smell something in the distance... something truly foul.

"All right," I said, standing up and tugging the ends of my hair to make sure the wig was nice and tight. "It's time to go, Mr Manfredi. I suggest putting that mask on – it's going to get pretty unpleasant in here before long."

He did as I said, and a moment later we were both snug in the protective embrace of our face masks, with my crew's dulcet tones back in our ears. "Welcome aboard, Mr Manfredi," Boris said, sounding a little too gleeful. "I hope you're not too attached to that suit. It's going to stink to high heaven once my special smoke bombs filter in."

"Forget his suit, what about mine?" I complained. "I *like* this one."

"That shade of blue is very last year," he replied. "You'll have company in three… two…"

Sure enough, one of the guards unlocked the door and staggered in a moment later, his gun drawn even as he weaved. "What the… how did you…" he gasped before falling to the ground.

"Oh, I know, it's awful," I commiserated, going over to him and pulling off his shoes. Then I stepped across his prone body and out the door. "Be glad it knocks you out too, so you don't have to smell yourself."

I led the way down the hall to the entryway, opened the door, and found the other guard already unconscious. Joseph went straight for the elevator, but I stopped to look for my things.

"Get a move on, Ray!" Joseph called out, decidedly on edge.

"Just a moment…" Where had that wench put my jewelry?

Oh ha, in her *pockets.* How she'd been planning on getting away with keeping it I didn't know, but it certainly did away with any sympathy I might have had for her. I couldn't put my gear back on right now, but I was happy to have it in hand again. I slipped on my stilettos – at least she hadn't put those in her pockets, or worse, on her feet – and handed the male guard's shoes to Joseph.

"Put these on, please. We want to look as inconspicuous as possible once we get to the bottom level."

He kicked his cheap sandals off and slid his feet into the shiny black shoes, then held out his cuffed hands. "These are pretty dang conspicuous."

"And we'll get you out of them as soon as possible," I said soothingly. "In the meantime, we'll just do this." I slid off my jacket and draped it over his lower arms. "You're such a gentleman to hold that for me," I cooed, and got the predictable smile I'd expected. "All right. Shall we go?" I led the way into the elevator and pushed the button for the bottom floor.

"We're still going to have trouble once we get down there," Joseph said, jumpy with energy now that we were really moving. He had a look on his face that was half hope, half agony, to quote one of my favorite novels.

"Trouble," Boris chuckled. "There's trouble all right, but not for you. God pity the men who try and prevent a teenage girl from teenagering."

"Is it good?" I asked Boris.

"It's fantastic. Worthy of an Oscar. You'd never know she was the same precocious rug rat who'd been crawling around the arteries of the building just a few minutes ago. Couple that with the general call to evacuate that's about to go out thanks to the smoke bombs, and you'll be able to walk out as free as birds."

Joseph looked confused. "What?"

The elevator *dinged.* I stepped out in perfect confidence, and was hit with a level of volume that was generally only reachable by opera singers and certain specialized mutants.

"–DO YOU MEAN I CAN'T?" Casey demanded from where she stood at the front desk. She'd gotten into her second ensemble faster than any quick-change magician and was now dressed in an adorable outfit – borrowed from me, of course – and wearing makeup, a wig that turned her into a honey blonde, and an expression that could have curdled milk faster than a cup of lemon juice. "I'll have you know I'm an *influencer!* You should consider yourselves *lucky* that I'm even in your crappy building for this shot, and I'm not going to be denied my status as a meme goddess just because you say it's *illegal* to take *photos* in the–"

"Miss," the guard who'd abandoned the elevator said, "it ain't all illegal, just the parts with the signs that say 'no photos.' All you gotta do is–"

"DON'T YOU TRY TO TELL ME WHAT TO DO!" She stomped her foot and caused a fuss, and a second later Joseph and I slipped out one of the side doors, which was open thanks to some tinkering by Bruno, who was standing there waiting for us.

"Howdy, boss," he said, then wrinkled his nose. "Ugh. I always forget how bad this stinks. Good thing you moved fast in there, otherwise they'd have sniffed you out."

"Yeah, the smell never gets better," I commiserated. "But I brought a change of clothes for the car." I'd brought my suit, actually – I wasn't walking into a meeting with Silvermane without all of my options available, and that meant being Black Cat.

"You bring a change for me too?" asked Joseph as I walked him toward our car. Boris was already there, crouched in the front passenger seat like a spider stalking his prey as he deftly parsed through the surveillance he'd gathered of the building.

"I left a lookie-loo in place just in case," Boris said as I got close enough to talk without shouting, "but it appears as though it isn't necessary. Both guards are still down and out, although concentration of the gas has already dissipated by fifty percent." He stroked his chin thoughtfully. "Perhaps I should go a little lighter on the active ingredient."

"You're the expert," I said, opening the back door and motioning to Joseph, who climbed inside, but looked a little put out.

"Are you planning on answering me?" he asked as I got in with him. I could see Casey coming from the corner of my eye. "I could really use a change of clothes before we meet with my father. I don't want to see him for the first time in so many years smelling like the back end of a horse, you know?"

"I absolutely do know," I said, grabbing my jacket from his arms. Gosh, Boris was right about this shade of blue.

"Not to mention these cuffs," Joseph went on with a perfect inability to read the room. Lord, this poor boy was dense. No wonder his father hadn't bothered with him for so long. "I can't see my pop looking like I'm a prisoner."

"I hear what you're saying," I told Joseph, then deftly ripped one of the sleeves off my jacket.

"Hey, what–"

"But I also think you've fundamentally misunderstood a few things about this relationship," I continued, and ripped the other sleeve off. "The big one being that, well, you're still a prisoner, Mr Manfredi. You're just *mine* instead of *theirs*."

He gaped at me. "What are you… no, *who* are you?"

I smiled. "I'm Black Cat." Then I rabbit-punched him on the side of the head hard enough to knock him out, then tied his cuffed hands to the "oh crap" handle above the seat using one of my sleeves and blindfolded him with the other one.

There. He should be down for a while. Still…

I buckled him into his seat for good measure. Safety was my middle name.

"Is that him?" Casey asked, a little breathless from running to the car. She jerked the blonde wig off her head and dropped it onto the floorboards. "Is that Silvermane's son?"

"Meet Joseph Manfredi," I confirmed, "and for heaven's sake, don't throw that on the ground like it didn't cost hundreds of dollars. Good wigs are expensive."

Casey rolled her eyes. "But you're rich."

"Not an excuse!" I picked the poor thing up, then took my own wig off, fluffed them both, and placed them into the briefcase I'd brought along purely for show to my meeting with Joseph. I loaded it into the trunk of the Escalade, then followed it, tugging the specially installed curtains closed to give me some privacy while I changed.

"He looks like a regular guy," Casey said, sounding disappointed. "Not, like, a criminal mastermind or anything."

I laughed. "Even when he *was* a crime boss, Blackwing was never a mastermind. Petty crimes were more his forte than bids for real power in the underworld, and he wouldn't have known what to do with that kind of power if it fell into his lap anyway."

No, Joseph Manfredi was never the son his father wanted, but he was the only one the old man had, and I hadn't exaggerated the depths of Silvermane's distaste for his current heir. That there was a retrial at all spoke to the fact that Silvio Manfredi was reconsidering his son's exile – Joseph didn't have the clout to pull that off on his own, but Silvio had deep pockets and liked to meddle. I hadn't lied about that part.

I just hoped he was interested enough in what I was offering to hear me out. We were heading into a make-or-break moment. I needed this to work. *Casey* needed this to work. She needed her father back, and I needed to solve the puzzle and come out on top. Being the Black Cat was synonymous with never giving up, always having one more life to turn to when the one I was living was attacked or blown up or beaten to a pulp. I was resiliency incarnate, and sometimes it was so tiring I could barely face lifting myself out of bed in the morning.

I smoothed the high-tech fabric of my uniform in place over my shoulders, feeling it hug me close, align with my muscles, prepare me for greatness. I sometimes – rarely, but sometimes – wondered what it would be like to put the Black Cat persona away for good. To be someone else, *really* someone else, not Felicia Hardy. Just a woman, living a life of ease off the profits I'd already made – profits that could keep me comfortable for a dozen lifetimes at this rate. No expectations of perfection or perfidy, no needing to be a little faster, a little stronger, a little better… just being. Sometimes, that sounded like paradise.

Usually it sounded like hell, though.

I closed my eyes and flexed my hands, feeling my claws pop out of the gloves. Beautiful, powerful, and deadly – that was my winning combination, and I'd ride that train until I died. I shook out my hair, put on my mask, then moved the curtain back and rejoined Casey and Joseph, who was still unconscious.

"You did great," I told her. "That was an excellent spoiled princess performance. A-plus, would totally watch you rant again."

"Thanks." She looked down, but I could see the satisfied smile on her face.

"You're a natural at this," I continued. "You've already come a long way from the charade at the FBI building." Honestly, when she wasn't – very reasonably – obsessing over her father, she was a dream to work with, just the right age to pull off a lot older or a lot younger, still curious enough to learn new things quickly, still malleable enough to take instruction without letting her ego get in the way… that had been the Black Fox's biggest problem with me. I never liked admitting I didn't know anything, and it had taken some hard lessons to get me to see the value in learning to take instruction graciously.

Flattering people into telling you their secrets was something of a specialty of mine now.

Our conversation dropped off as we headed further out of the city, all of us becoming more serious as the reality of what we were about to do pressed in. It was a good plan in theory – drive to the Manfredi compound, present Joseph at the gate, offer him up in exchange for Beck, and make the swap. There were a lot of assumptions present in there, though, and the saying "no plan survives contact with the enemy" might be cliché, but only because it was so true.

"Are there run-flats on the car?" I asked Bruno.

"Yep," he replied. "Got one of the force fields in this car, too. Directional, like the other one, but the battery's a little bigger. We can weather a blast from a rocket launcher if we need to."

"That's what I like to hear. Speaking of rocket launchers… Boris?"

"Of course I brought one," he snapped, "what kind of plebian do you take me for? It's in the back next to the spare tire."

I smiled. "You boys think of everything."

By the time we got to the Manfredi mansion, the sun had long vanished, and Joseph was finally awake. "What the…" he groaned. "What's going on here?"

"Exactly what I promised would go on," I told him. "We're about to meet with your father." *I hope.* "Get ready to put on your happy face, Joseph. Daddy's going to want to see a big smile."

He scoffed. "If you think that, then you don't know jack about my father." He tilted his head then, turning his blindfolded eyes toward me. "Or do you? Are you really Black Cat?"

"In the flesh," I assured him.

"I should have known from the start, with the level of sass you were packing," he said dryly, then sighed. "So what's the play here? What do you actually want?"

"You'll find out when Daddy does, Joseph," I promised. "And hey, we're here, so it seems like neither of us will be waiting for long." Bruno stopped the car about five meters back from the elaborate wrought-iron gate in front of us. It circled the entire Manfredi compound, and was only the first line in their defenses.

Before I could even get out of the car with Joseph, it began to open. Hmm. "Bruno... I think it's best if the three of you stay out here," I said.

"But–"

I cut Casey off. "No buts. Whenever a Maggia boss rolls out the red carpet, that's when you should be wondering what they've got in store for you. I'll be fine on my own."

"Yeah, but will I?"

I ignored Joseph's plaintive remark and turned to Boris. "Can you fire the rocket launcher through the gaps in that fence?"

"Without a problem."

"Good. Then keep the engine running and keep your ears open, because Joseph and I have a date with destiny."

"You have a date with a crusty old curmudgeon in a cyborg body who'd as soon kill you as look at you, you mean," Boris said.

I shrugged. "Destiny takes many forms." I untied Joseph's hands and led him out of the car, then took off the blindfold once I was sure he couldn't see Casey anymore. No sense in letting him get a better look at her than he had to.

"Let's take a walk," I told my companion, looping an arm through one of his bound elbows.

"Eh, might as well," he said with a sigh. "After all, what do I have to lose but my life?"

"Good attitude," I chuckled, and we headed into the Manfredi family compound together.

CHAPTER TWENTY-FIVE

The moment we passed the gate, floodlights erupted around us, illuminating everything in our path and lighting us up clearly. A sniper would have absolutely no trouble targeting us now. It sent a chill down my spine, but I kept my pace steady and my gaze firmly fixed on the mansion ahead of us.

The mansion, unlike the grounds, was still shrouded in complete darkness. There wasn't a single light outside from what I could see. Beside me, Joseph snorted.

"God, the old man never changes."

"What do you mean?" I asked.

"He's used the same tactics with this place for years," Joseph said. "Put visitors on the spot, make them feel vulnerable, then emerge from the darkness like the shambling zombie he is and try to scare them. He doesn't need a lot of light to be able to get around, you know. Freaking earthworm."

"There's really no love lost between you two, is there?" I asked – completely rhetorically, but Joseph answered me anyway.

"There never has been. You might end up real disappointed tonight, Black Cat – or real dead."

"Oh, I doubt that." If Silvermane was going to try and kill me, he would have started the party already. He was a patient planner, but once he got you in his sights, that patience tended to evaporate. It was how Spider-Man managed to get the better of him time and time again – Silvermane never could resist taking his shot the second he thought he could get away with it.

"Let's stop… right here." We were still within easy shooting distance of the Escalade, about twenty feet from the liminal space where the light ended and the shadows began. I waved into the darkness, smiling cheekily but keeping my probability pulsator at the ready.

"Hi there! I'm here to talk to Silvio Manfredi. I've got something he's interested in, and I promise it'll only take a few minutes of his time."

"Way to make me feel like more than a side of beef," Joseph muttered. I bumped his hip and continued.

"Come on, Silvermane, gentlemen don't keep ladies waiting."

A voice creaked out of the darkness, sounding as ancient as an iceberg and twice as cold. "I don't see any ladies here. Just a filthy little feline who needs to be taught some manners."

"You should know better than to even suggest it," I said, playfully scolding. "Cats are who they are. They can't help but be themselves. And if you don't want me to play with my prey before I kill it, you'll meet me in the light."

I didn't intend to kill Joseph, but Silvermane didn't know that. It was do or die time. How much was his son really worth to him? Joseph was as stiff as steel beside me, his eyes boring into the darkness like if he just stared hard enough, he'd summon his father to him. I felt an unwelcome pang of empathy. I knew all about having complicated emotions for a father.

A second later, Silvermane stepped forward into the light. As a man, he'd been average height; as a cyborg, he stood seven feet tall, and his metal body had to weigh close to five hundred pounds. He had a classic robotic look to him, with visible cable "muscles" and armored glass protecting fragile spots, particularly the beating heart that was clearly visible in the center of his suit. It certainly drew the eye, in a grotesque kind of way, and if he wanted to highlight his vulnerabilities, who was I to say no? I bet if I focused hard enough, I could use my quantum probability pulsator to get the pump that regulated his heart to malfunction.

Don't get too excited. You can still get through this without bloodshed. "Silvermane. How delightful to see you alive and well, after all the buzz I heard about the Maggia being afraid of the Kingpin's plans."

"Don't try to play me, Cat," Silvermane said, crossing his massive metal arms. "I know perfectly well that the Kingpin doesn't have the apple anymore, and I know you're part of the reason why."

I nodded graciously. "News travels fast. You're welcome, by the way."

Silvermane shook his head. "You didn't do it for me, so don't expect any gratitude. All that little show you and Daredevil put on has gained you is… *latitude*, instead. A meeting, rather than a funeral. So get to the point."

No small talk, huh? Fine. "I'm interested in a man named Dalton Beck. I have the feeling you know where I can find him, and I'm willing to trade your son for Mr Beck's safe return."

There was total silence for a moment, and then Silvermane smiled. It wasn't a nice smile. Beside me, I saw Joseph's shoulders slump a little.

"Well, that's a novel idea," he said, his voice almost a drawl. He was dragging it out on purpose now that he knew the terms. "And it might have worked on me a week ago. My son is marginally more suitable to take over for me someday than my current heir-apparent, and a man's got to think about the future. But now? Now that's not good enough. Nowhere near good enough. If you want the location of Dalton Beck, then I'm going to need more than the questionable freedom of my deeply misguided offspring." He shook his glass-encased head. "No. If you want Dalton Beck, then you have to get me the golden apple."

Of course I did. *Of course.* I wasn't even surprised anymore – why bother with surprise, when everyone in this whole stupid city had one thing only on their mind? "You do know who had it last, right?" I asked.

"Numerous sources say it's the Mad Thinker."

"And you think he hasn't used it already?"

Silvermane barked a laugh. "He's called the Mad *Thinker* for a reason. Where you and I see an object of power, he sees something to be ripped to pieces in the hopes of understanding it better." He held out his hand, and a holographic display sprang to life on it. It was a recording of a news anchor from last night, which almost immediately switched over to footage of the Mad Thinker himself, brown hair thinning at the temples from repeated tech attachments there, eyes wide and wild as he stared into the camera.

"To all who might try to defy my will, know that your

attempts will be fruitless. I have hidden the golden apple in an interdimensional vault inaccessible to everyone but me! With my great mind and all the minds I control turned to its study, soon I shall learn the secret of the golden apples and create them for myself! *Infinite* wishes! *Infinite* power! The world itself shall fall at my feet, and the universe shall swiftly follow!"

The news feed ended, and Silvermane turned off the hologram.

Well, shoot. That sounded like typical super villain bravado, but a mind like the Mad Thinker's might actually let him pull it off. I wasn't about to let Silvermane see my unease, though. "Eh." I shrugged. "I sincerely doubt he can do any of that."

"I don't care if he can, I care that he's going to destroy the apple in his attempt." Silvermane grimaced. "Who takes a perfectly good opportunity like that and wastes it on experimentation?"

"You *do* recall the part where the apple brings disaster on anyone who uses it, right?"

He waved a hand. "Probably exaggerated, but even if it's not, I have contingencies in place for that kind of thing."

Meaning he had people he could threaten into wishing for what he wanted and taking the heat on themselves, at the expense of their lives or families or… god, there were so many ways to manipulate someone into using the apple for you. It's what *I* would have done, now that I had more time to think about it.

But that was immaterial. "Hmm. How about instead of me getting you the apple, you give me Firestrike and I don't kill your son in front of you?"

Joseph stiffened, looking at me with a comically betrayed

expression on his face. I winked at him. "Sorry, honey, but all's fair in love and bargaining." Not that I had any intention of killing him, but the play was worth a shot.

"Kill him if it makes you feel better, but I'm not giving up the location of Firestrike."

Aaand the play had failed. Curses. This guy was shockingly cold when it came to his only child. Time for some digging. "Why are you even keeping Dalton Beck around?" I asked. "How is he of any use to you?"

Silvermane rubbed his metallic hands together. "I haven't lived this long to simply throw away things that might be of value someday. I knew someone would come sniffing around for Beck, and that I'd be able to use him for more than just delaying Joseph's trial. I didn't figure on you, but I'll take the win."

"How do I even know he's alive?" I asked, and heard Casey gasp over the com. Surely she'd thought of this possibility already. "How do I know you're not bluffing?"

"I might be," Silvermane concurred. "But there's no way for you to know for sure until you bring me the golden apple. I'm not one to underestimate your skills, Black Cat. I don't want to make an enemy out of you. A *greater* enemy out of you," he amended after a moment. "I just want that apple, and I want you to get it for me. There's no other way for you to find Dalton Beck. He's hidden from psychics, he's hidden from surveillance, he's even hidden from *me*. Just one speck in a sea of specks, until I decide it's time for him to reappear. You get me?"

God, villains did love their monologuing, didn't they? "I get you," I said with an eyeroll. "Fine. The apple for Dalton

Beck. You'll hear from me soon." I took Joseph's arm again and turned us around to walk back toward the car.

"You're not even going to shoot him just once?" Silvermane called out after me. "After going to the trouble of getting Joseph out of prison, and having all of it coming to nothing?"

"I haven't lived this long to simply throw away things that might be of value someday," I replied, enjoying the way his wrinkled face became even sourer for a moment. "Don't call me, I'll call you. Toodles!"

We made it back to the Escalade without getting shot at, which was nice. I'd take anything nice at this point, honestly. "Well, that was useless," I said as I opened the door for Joseph. I could be genteel when I wanted to be.

"I can't believe you expected anything different," Joseph said, grunting a little as he levered himself up into the car with bound hands. "I can't believe *I* expected anything different. I should have known you were a fraud as soon as you started saying nice things about that dirty, rotten, son of a–" He glanced at Casey and finished up, "Gun. Son of a gun."

"He certainly looks like what would happen if a robot and a semiautomatic had kids," I agreed.

"What are we–"

I silenced Casey with a stern look before she could say anything that Joseph Manfredi didn't need to be hearing. "Back to the Civic Centre, Bruno," I said. "We'll drop Mr Manfredi off there."

"Back to that place?" He made a face. "You can't pick a nicer jail? Or better yet, just let me go?"

"Sorry, but I'm not going through all of this for things to end in a mistrial," I said. "And if you don't like the Detention

Center, there's always the Manhattan Correctional Facility, or – hey, when's the last time you did a stint in Rikers?"

Joseph winced. "Geez, no need to be so hostile."

This guy didn't know hostile, but he was going to if he kept complaining. Fortunately, he was as meek as a lamb when we left him blindfolded and bound outside the Civic Center. I think hearing his father say out loud just how little he thought of his son had knocked the last of the stuffing out of Joseph. It was a little melancholy, but then, when the alternative was making your dad proud of you by being a truly terrible human being, I was more in favor of a little paternal disappointment.

By the time we got back to the apartment, Casey looked like she was moments away from tears. Her arms were crossed tight in front of her chest, and she was biting her lower lip so hard I was a little afraid she was going to sink her teeth right through it. "That's it, then," she said, sitting on the edge of the couch and staring at the floor. "There's no hope."

"When did I say that?" I replied, sitting down beside her. "There's always *some* hope."

"I heard what the Mad Thinker said! He's keeping the apple in a whole other dimension! There's no way you'll be able to steal it back."

"Listen to you underestimate me time and time again," I said, shaking my head. "I think I'm insulted. The Mad Thinker is brilliant, for sure, but he's no Dr Doom." And there were workarounds for even the most brilliant of targets – namely, finding equally brilliant people to help me get what I needed to break those targets. How did I get those people to work with me? A combination of flattery, pressure, and poise, usually.

And one thing was for sure. "I'm going to get that apple," I said, looking Casey right in the eyes. "I'm absolutely going to get it." It was more than just for Casey now – it was a matter of professional pride. And once I had stolen the apple, well...

Anything was possible.

CHAPTER TWENTY-SIX

The first step in going after the apple was finding out who was *already* going after it. I imagined that at this point, especially after the Mad Thinker's very public rant about his intentions, there were super heroes lining up to be the one to keep him from using it. Wilson Fisk with a wish was one kind of devastating – a crazy genius with unlimited wishes at hand was a whole other bag of cats, so to speak.

The Mad Thinker, also occasionally known as Julius, from what I was able to find out – go figure, he totally seemed like the Little Caesar type – was, like a lot of villains, obsessed with the Fantastic Four. Honestly, if I was part of a group that drew baddies in like crows to carrion, I'd quit the band. Maybe that was one of the reasons I worked better being a solo star. I had my crew, but they didn't draw the kind of attention that a super hero did.

There was only one person I cared to talk to from the Fantastic Four, and that was Johnny. Lucky for me, he always took my calls. I dialed him up and waited for paydirt.

It went to voicemail instead.

That was odd.

"Are the Fantastic Four in the middle of a battle?" I asked out loud. "Or maybe some kind of, I don't know, diplomatic mission or ribbon-cutting?" My people all immediately checked their favorite devices – Boris looked at his computer, Bruno opened the newspaper, and Casey started scrolling on her phone.

"There are no new sightings on social media for any of them," she said. "Not since Sue Storm apparently got into a heated argument at a PTA meeting last night."

Oh, I bet she did. I couldn't imagine the fear that came with teaching the child of Sue Storm and Reed Richards.

"Nothin' in the society pages about an event for them," Bruno said.

"From the look of the security footage near the Baxter Building, they haven't left the facility this morning," Boris added. "But several rather important people have come to visit *them* instead."

"Oh?" I walked over to his side so I could look at his screen. "Do tell."

"At seven o'clock this morning, Iron Man showed up." The screen fuzzed out for a moment. "And you see that interference in the recording? That's a side effect that occurs approximately twenty-two percent of the time when Doctor Strange is using his magic to flit about the place."

"You've catalogued the glitches that occur when Doctor Strange uses his magic?" I had to admit, I was impressed.

Boris sniffed. "It's only reasonable to know what might go wrong when we end up dealing with him on such a regrettably regular basis."

He had a point. I stood up and crossed my arms thoughtfully.

The Fantastic Four, Iron Man, and Doctor Strange... what did they all have in common, apart from unattractive streaks of self-righteousness?

New York addresses. They were big name, hometown heroes, and this particular golden apple was a hometown problem. That made the Mad Thinker their problem, beyond him being a regular thorn in the Four's side. They were probably all holed up together having a very serious meeting, with lots of pregnant pauses and big words being thrown around. I could practically hear it already.

Might as well hear it in person, then.

"Well." I smiled brightly. "It looks like I'm going to be paying the Baxter Building a little visit."

Casey shot to her feet. "Can I come? I've always wanted to meet The Thing!"

"Sorry." I ruffled her hair. "Not this time." She pouted. "If it's any consolation, I don't think I'll be there for very long." Heck, Sue would probably fumigate the place once I left. Getting in would be a hassle, especially if Johnny wasn't answering his phone.

Good thing I had a plan for that.

Doordash. Grubhub. Resident restaurant delivery drivers. I was giving them all a workout this morning, as I called up a dozen restaurants within a mile of the Baxter Building and made orders for food to be delivered there. Good food, too; I wasn't crass enough to send them soggy sandwiches and rubbery eggs. I gave a standing order to each delivery driver to ring the doorbell, say a phrase, and leave it on the stoop.

Bagels: "Courtesy of Black Cat."

Pizza: "From the Black Cat."

Shawarma: "Black Cat sent this."

The hot dog vendor from down the street I paid extra to move his cart shouted out, "Hey, Ben, there's some broad in a cat costume paying for your lunch, and if you leave my hot dogs to get cold on your doorstep like the rest of this stuff, I ain't selling to you again!"

That one did the trick. The door opened a crack and the Thing's gravelly voice called out, "Aw c'mon, Jakey, don't be like that! It's not my fault this lady is off her rocker."

"Crazy or not, you better not disrespect my food like you are everything else," Jakey the hot dog vendor snapped, hoisting one of his boiled beauties up high. "These are *gourmet*. They deserve better than drying out in the sun!"

The Thing paused. "Um… is the broad still around?"

That was my cue. I poked my head out from around the corner of the front door. "Hi, Ben! Long time no see."

He sighed the sigh of the put-upon. "Geez, Black Cat, don't you know how to take a hint?"

"I've never had much luck taking hints, I'm afraid," I said, reaching out for one of Jakey's hot dogs and passing it to Ben as I stepped inside. "Besides, I'm under the impression there are some big brains doing some hard thinking in there. They need fuel."

"How do you… nope." He shook his heavy head. "Never mind, I don't even want to know how you figured that out." He looked a little mournfully at his hot dog, then ate it in two big bites.

"Best in the city," I said, and took the tray of the other six from Jakey as well. "I'll get these, you get the rest of the stuff,

OK?" I slipped past him into the foyer before he could stop me and began to walk in the direction of Reed's biggest lab. "We wouldn't want any of it to go to waste."

"Hey, you can't just... *hey!*"

I made it another ten feet before Attempted Interception #2 came my way, in the form of the delectable Johnny Storm. He was in his official costume and looked unexpectedly serious.

"Felicia, you can't be here," he hissed under his breath at me. "We're in the middle of something big, and–"

"Ah, you haven't found the Mad Thinker yet, then," I said sagely.

Johnny's jaw dropped. "How in the world did you figure that out?"

"By being an incredibly annoying busybody," came the voice of Attempted Interception #3, aka Susan Storm, aka The Invisible Woman. She looked as lovely and professional as ever, and more uninviting than I'd ever seen as she stood in the doorway of the lab.

I smiled at her just as brightly as I had at Ben, because I knew it would only annoy her even more than it had him. "I just keep my ear to the ground, that's all."

"I don't care. You're not getting in here."

"I think I could be a big help."

"I think you're dreaming."

"Sue, c'mon," Johnny said, flushing a little as he looked between us. "She was a help last time, wasn't she?"

"Only because of that freak occurrence with Blastaar. The answer is still no."

"I've been closer to getting the apple than any of you this past week," I pointed out.

"Because you were trying to steal it for yourself, I daresay."

"That's not fair," Ben called out from behind the pile of boxes in his arms. "We know Tony was behind one of those tries. Shoot, Johnny, give me a hand here, I'm about to lose the tacos–"

"Got 'em!"

"You might as well let her in," a familiar voice called out from inside the lab up ahead. "Black Cat's curiosity is legend, after all. I'm sure you'd prefer we know exactly where she is to her snooping around somewhere we can't see."

Aw, Doctor Strange stepping in for the win.

Sue made a sour face, but turned away from the door and walked deeper into the building. I followed, hot dogs in hand, and walked through the layers of hallways and open rooms that made up their awkwardly architected building until we got to Mr Fantastic's enormous lab, complete with the now-covered portal that had let the interstellar villain known as Blastaar through the last time I was here.

He'd proposed to me. Kind of – in that "hey, I'm gonna carry you off and make a concubine of you" way. So sweet. I'd had to run him over for it.

I turned to Doctor Strange and hoisted a hot dog in his direction. "Hey, Doc. Care for a bite?"

He inclined his head. "I'll hold out for a bagel, thanks. How have you been since we last met, Miss Hardy?"

Since we fought against a symbiote invasion together after I tore you out of their magic-leeching prison, you mean? "A heck of a lot better than I was back then," I said frankly, and he smiled. "How's Bats?"

"He's doing well. You should stop by sometime. I'm sure he'd love to see you again."

Bats had been a big help to me more than once. I wasn't much of an animal person, but I made an exception for spectral, talking basset hounds with better manners than most people I'd met. "I'd love to see him too."

"Are we done with the hellos yet?" Reed asked, always blunt enough to dull the sharpest edge. He wasn't even looking at me, just staring at a complex 3D hologram of something weird and twisty, like someone had grabbed a handful of spaghetti and thrown it into the air, then froze time and took a picture. Tony was standing next to him, but he gave me a little wave, then inhaled deeply.

"Oh my god, is that shawarma? Did you bring shawarma?" He came over and started to dig through the bags that the Thing was still holding.

"Back off, Shellhead," Ben grumbled, slipping the shawarma bag off his arm and handing it over before Tony ripped it.

"Best shawarma in the city." I threw him a wink. "Plus hot dogs, pizza, and plenty of other things to tempt your tastebuds."

"Are you seriously going to let her bribe her way in here with food?" Sue asked, crossing her arms as she stared at the group of guys busily chowing down on my offerings.

"Better than her breaking in," Reed said absently, the only one, apart from us girls, not eating anything. "Strange, these pathways aren't making any sense. There shouldn't be this gap here."

Doctor Strange shrugged as he reached for a bagel and schmear. "That's magic for you."

Reed sighed. "Be helpful."

"It's a random gap, and the only thing we know about it is that it *will* occur, not where or for how long. Think about it in terms of quantum physics and–"

They started in again, and I sidled over to Tony, whose mouth was only mostly full. "No luck finding the Mad Thinker, then?"

"Nope, not a glimpse," he said, sounding part glum, part impressed. "We're pretty sure that he himself isn't in New York, or even the United States, which makes the issue of jurisdiction particularly thorny. Of course, it doesn't really matter where he is, because he can control his androids from anywhere, and the last we saw they were the ones with the apple."

He took another bite. I graciously waited for him to chew and swallow before I asked, "So what are you looking at over there, then?"

"Oh. That's one of Strange's ideas, actually." He gestured at the spaghetti tangle. "The Mad Thinker boasted that he was holding the apple in a different dimension, which – not impossible in and of itself, but hard to pull off without leaving some ripples. Strange was able to locate the pocket dimension he thinks the apple has been stowed in, even map it to an extent, but…"

"But?" I prompted. "I mean, that's good, right? If you know where it is, you can go in after it." Or at least that was how it had worked whenever I went dimension-hopping, which was as infrequently as possible. They tended to be ludicrously dangerous places where you might lose your mind, your soul, or both before you found a way out.

Tony sighed. He looked tired. "It's not as easy as walking through a door, Felicia. Different types of dimensions are accessed in different ways, and *none* of them are safe. To try and step into this one without knowing more about it, or about how it's made and maintained, would be suicidal. Couple that with the fact that it seems to repel all magic except for the apple, which it was probably created around, and it would be a bad idea to send Stephen in."

I nodded. "OK, that explains why he's not going after the apple. But what about the rest of you? You've all been to different dimensions at one time or another, haven't you?"

"That doesn't make interdimensional travel fun," Tony grumbled. "Besides, I said we know *where* this place is. Enough for Reed to get a picture of it, even." He gestured at the spaghetti again, and I moved in closer, looking at it from different angles. There was a faint golden glimmer in the center of it. "Knowing where it is doesn't mean we know how to get into it. It's like looking through a telescope at a star – we can see the star, but none of us has a spaceship to get there."

I raised an eyebrow.

"I mean, OK, yes, I do have a spaceship but – look, it's a metaphor, OK?"

"There has to be a human connection out there keeping the door open," Reed said, tapping his forefinger against his upper lip before glancing at me. "Otherwise we wouldn't have been able to find it ourselves. Without being seen, it would in practical terms cease to exist. It's a variation on Wigner's quantum entanglement paradox that–"

"Whoa." I held up my hands. "Let me stop you right there. I don't need to know the gory numeric details."

"Killjoy," muttered Boris in my earpiece.

"I just need to know the broad strokes. So this place exists, but you can't find it without the Mad Thinker, and you don't know where the Mad Thinker is yet. Right?"

"Actually, we're also looking for the Owl," Johnny said.

I frowned. "Why?"

"Because he ain't been seen since he tangled with Fisk," Ben said from where he'd just polished off the rest of the tray of hot dogs all on his own. "And these guys think he's got the kind of brain that might be good at holdin' a dimensional door open, or some crap like that."

"It's not crap. It's a very viable theory," Reed said. He sounded a little offended. "Knowing the Mad Thinker the way we do, it makes far more sense for him to pass the risk on to someone else rather than take on any for himself. It's evident in everything he does – look at his reliance on statistics and probability, and his use of the Awesome Android and others to handle the physical work. Why wouldn't he also outsource the mental heavy lifting? And the Owl has a very advanced neural network that makes him perfect for this kind of task."

Hmm, that made sense. Of course, it also made their problem even more abundantly clear. "I take it you don't know where the Owl is, either."

"We've requested assistance from several psychics who might be able to help us find him," Sue said, finally deigning to speak to me instead of just glaring. "So far they haven't had any luck, but one of them is on their way here now. Once they're on site, things should be much easier to coordinate."

In other words, *bye, Felicia!* I could take a hint.

Not without twisting the knife a little bit first, though. "So you need to get a psychic to find the Owl, or the Mad Thinker, who then might be able to help you figure out how to get to the dimension this apple is being held in, which might *then* enable someone to go in after it." They nodded. "Why not just close the dimension and leave the apple there? Didn't you just say that the place stops existing if you can't see it or something?"

Tony shook his head. "It would be a decent play if the dimension wasn't already being used as a container, but this one has the golden apple in it. It's like leaving an unexploded bomb in someone's back yard. Sure, they might live there for years with no problems, but then one day it rains or they decide to plant a garden or there's a shiver in the space-time continuum, and the next thing you know – *kaboom*." He did the exploding fist gesture for emphasis, but his face was dead serious. "I'm done leaving bombs in people's backyards, Felicia."

Aw, so responsible. I patted him on the cheek. "I get it. Welp." I sighed heavily. "I suppose I'm just not going to be of any use to you here."

"Not at all," Sue said.

"But the food is great," Johnny added. "Thanks for that."

"You're welcome." I flipped my hair and put on my "sad but determined not to show it" face. "I guess I'll go, then." I started to walk toward the door.

"Felicia."

I stopped and turned back to look at Doctor Strange. "Yeah?"

"Why are *you* so interested in the apple?" he asked.

I smiled. "Oh, you know me, Doc. I love a good puzzle. Especially when it comes in gold."

Sue scoffed, and Tony grinned. That's right, shallow, shallow, shallow me. Don't think twice about it, friends. Don't think twice. "Enjoy the lunch," I added, and then I was gone.

Gone, but with all the pieces I needed to take the next step, especially after I'd made sure to get a good picture of that spaghetti tangle with my microcamera. A psychic was a good idea – although all but the most powerful could be shielded against if you knew the right techniques or had the right equipment. This group of heroes knew some phenomenally powerful psychics, though. Once they found the Owl, they'd be hero-ing on to their next step in a flash.

Which meant that I had to get there first. Lucky for me, I knew just how to do that.

CHAPTER TWENTY-SEVEN

One of the key components of any good heist was coming up with the right distraction. Misdirection was a classic gambit for everyone from street magicians to Wall Street stooges and even the titans of tech: get 'em lost in your Terms of Service and get permission to harvest their data. In my case, a distraction meant having "Felicia Hardy" seen out and about with Bruno, while the real me enacted the next part of our plan without being watched by the super heroes I'd just left behind.

It was a given that they were going to watch me. I didn't trust them to believe I'd given up any more than they trusted me to actually do so. You got paranoid in this business pretty fast, and it was almost always justified. I needed to give them a show, something blatant enough to draw their attention without making them commit to interfering. It was a fine line. Lucky for me, I had a double on hand.

"Ow!"

"Hold still and it won't go in your eye!"

Not an incredibly realistic double, but she'd have to do.

"Why are you putting eyeliner on me anyway?" Casey

whined. At least she managed to hold still this time – one poke with the pencil was enough, apparently. "You hardly wear any!"

"That's true," I said. "But makeup is about more than looking pretty. It's about drawing the eye to the things you want people to see. Haven't you ever watched makeup tutorials on YouTube? Don't you know about contouring?"

"No," she said sullenly.

"Well today, you learn." And she hated every second of it, but two hours down the road, with the application of the correct padding, clothes, and wig, I was staring at a reasonable facsimile of myself with pride.

"You look great."

Casey took a tottering step before falling onto the side of the bed with a grimace. "I feel like a baby giraffe in these heels."

Yeah, that could be an issue. "Don't walk around much," I advised. "You don't even have to get out of the car. Bruno can just drive you around in some conspicuous places. Definitely make it look like you're taking pictures – that'll get their attention for sure. And here." I grabbed a pair of oversized sunglasses off my dresser and handed them to her. "These will keep people from noticing you rolling your eyes constantly."

She started to roll her eyes – again – then stopped and huffed a sigh. "I get it."

"Do you? Because it's time to commit, Casey." I put my hands on her shoulders and looked her in the face. *My* face, almost, but underneath the makeup mask was a teenage girl who was desperate to get her father back, and knew that if we didn't get the golden apple before the hero brigade did, that she'd lose him forever. "You have to sell your part of the charade like you've never sold anything before in your life. You have to keep them off my back so I can do what I need to. If they find me too soon, it's game over. This is important. I'm not sidelining you with this job, I promise."

"I know." She almost bit her lower lip, then stopped herself. She squared her shoulders, smiled a brilliant smile, and cocked one hand on her hip. "I've got this," she said, and she had my intonations down perfectly.

"You're awesome," I told her, then looked at Bruno. "You got your route picked out?"

"Regular tour of the Big Apple coming up, boss," he confirmed, but he looked antsy. "You sure I can't do more?"

"You're doing plenty," I assured him.

"It doesn't feel that way."

"Listen to her, you dolt," called Boris from where he was feverishly studying the three-dimensional map of the pile of spaghetti I'd managed to photograph earlier. "The time for muscle is over. Now let us enter the arena of the *mind*."

"Does that mean you're finding me routes through that mess?" I asked, checking my own reflection one more time. I was the one wearing the honey blonde wig today, and I'd dressed like a bike messenger. I had my suit in my backpack, though – arena of the mind or not, it never hurt to be prepared.

"I'll have several mapped out for you by the time you get to the Owl."

"Big talk," Bruno said.

"At least *one* of us can use polysyllabic words, you enormous–"

"Let's not get bogged down in arguing about nothing today, all right, gentlemen?" I said, grabbing my bike helmet. Safety first. "We've all got a job to do." I checked my phone, where the person I was heading toward had been sitting for the past hour.

Still there. Good. "Let's get it done."

I let Bruno and Casey go first, gave them a five-minute head start, then raced out of there on my bike like I was two lengths behind the lead rider of the Tour de France. I was careful to keep my head down, avoiding looking directly at any of the storefronts and traffic lights so their cameras didn't get a clear picture of me. I figured it would take me about half an hour to reach my destination, a mixed residential and commercial street close to the Hudson, but underestimated the effect of my nerves and got there, panting, in twenty minutes.

I made the final turn onto the block where my target was, then slowed down and pulled out my phone, where Boris had linked a security feed that centered on the elegant, dark-haired woman I'd met once before as she sat at a café, sipping her second espresso and perusing a book. Still there. As I watched, the image of her on screen lifted its head and looked in my direction. It was half invitation, half challenge.

I never did back down from a challenge.

A server brought another drink to the table moments before I sat down across from her. She put her book down, then pushed the drink in my direction.

"For you," she said, her smile as beautiful as the rest of her. "I believe it's your favorite, isn't it?"

A dry cappuccino with a dusting of raw sugar over the top of it. Delicious. "It is. How did you know?" I asked, picking it up and taking a sip. Mmm, so good.

"You're not the only person who likes to scope out the competition," my companion said with a wink.

I hummed thoughtfully as I glanced at the book on the table. It was a dog-eared copy of *The Iliad*. The last of my suspicions fell into place. I gestured toward the book. "Reminiscing about the good old days, Eris?"

Eris, Greek goddess of discord, laughed brightly, her long brown neck arching as she threw her head back. "Oh, *very* good," she said after a moment, tucking a coil of hair behind her ear. "You've really put some thought into this."

"It's obvious when you think about all the clues," I replied. "Once I realized that I'd seen you at every golden apple heist I've been part of so far, and found video footage of you at another one, it wasn't hard to figure out who you are. You've used golden apples to such great effect before, after all. Why mess with a clear winner?"

"Our apples caused all sorts of problems for many different mortals," she said, then shrugged. "Although I will say that none of the other apples achieved quite the fame that my ploy did. That Homer, what a gem."

"Well, you're staging quite the comeback now," I said. "But I have to wonder... why? Why now?"

Eris tilted her head, her eyes so piercing I felt like I'd been run through with a spear. "Why not now? It's been such a long time since I've played, after all, and there's no injunction against meddling in the affairs of mankind."

"People are suffering as a result of your playing," I pointed out. "At least one person has died."

"And you don't care," she replied blithely. "Don't expect me to believe a speech about the greater good from you of all people, Miss Hardy." She had a point. I didn't start caring about the apple until it impacted someone I knew personally. If I were a better person, I might feel ashamed about that. As things stood, it was enough for me that I cared *now*.

Eris leaned forward, setting both forearms on the table and lowering her voice. "I've watched you, you know. I saw you putting the pieces together, I felt your gaze upon me whenever the apple was passed from carrier to carrier. I felt your interest, and I return it. You're a fascinating person, Felicia." She smiled coquettishly. "For a human. I would get to know you better, if you'd let me."

Excuse me, a powerful, beautiful, stupidly attractive person wanted to get to know me better? Sign me up… except I had a feeling that there was more to this than met the eye.

"What's the catch?" I asked.

"Does there have to be one?"

"There does." I knew it like I knew myself. "You're still running a game, and until the game is over, you're not going to get distracted. That means whatever you did with me would be a part of that game." I shook my head. "I'm a player, Eris, not a pawn."

She stared at me for a long moment, garnet eyes sparkling, before finally leaning back again. "Your loss, γατάκι," she said, but there was a hint of admiration in her voice. "Back to the game, then. Yes, selfish people are paying a selfish price when it comes to my apples. Believe it or not, I don't even have to intervene to make that happen. Whether they suffer or not is entirely up to them, based on their wish."

"Is it?" I asked. "Even with the Mad Thinker being the one holding the apple?"

Eris stared at the street consideringly. "His genius with computers and such is rivalled by very few. I suppose if anyone can break Hephaestus's encryptions and decode the apple, it would be Julius. I'm rather surprised, honestly – I didn't expect the apple to survive for so long in this city, and yet people keep holding onto it instead of using it."

"New York is the ultimate city of opportunists." I could attest to that. "It leads to a lot of holding and thinking and plotting how to get more out of whatever it is you've got. The people who've had the apple so far, they're people who know how to plan for the future."

"Mostly to their detriment," Eris pointed out. "The apple has changed hands nearly a dozen times already. Mostly at the Gala, but you've seen the others."

"I have." Which was quite the coincidence. Or… was it? "Do you believe in fate?"

Eris chuckled. "Belief doesn't enter into it for me. I've met them numerous times."

Right, the mythology angle. "And are they your friends too, like Hephaestus?"

"It always pays to have friends." She reached across the table and touched the back of my hand with her fingertips. They were feverishly warm, but she wasn't even sweating. "What about you? Why are you *really* here, Felicia? To stop the Mad Thinker from decoding the apple? To use it for yourself?" She smiled, and her cheeks dimpled. "Or to be a hero, perhaps?"

"I guess you'll find out once I get my hands on it," I said, with only slightly more bravado than I felt.

"I look forward to it," Eris said, leaning back and standing up. "I'd like to ask that no matter what course you take, you make the solution a final one. There are all sorts of ways to get what you want, after all."

We'd see about that. I stood up as well. "Care to give me a hint on where I can find the Owl?"

To my surprise she nodded her head toward the building across the street. "There used to be a speakeasy in the basement of that flower shop," she said. "The last owners of the building were going to feature it in tours and had the whole thing modernized, including getting it rewired. Then they went bankrupt, and the new owners boarded the place up."

But it was still there. Convenient. I inclined my head. "Thanks," I said.

"Thank you for making my time in New York City a little more interesting, Black Cat. I'll be watching you." Eris turned around, took two steps, and –

I lost sight of her. She didn't seem to vanish, it wasn't like she went "poof!" and evaporated in a cloud of smoke, but the place where she'd been standing a moment ago was simply… empty.

CHAPTER TWENTY-EIGHT

God tricks. So she was watching me, huh? Well, I'd do my best to put on a heck of a show, then. "Did you get all that, Boris?" I asked quietly.

"I'm looking up the specs for the building across the street right now," he said briskly. "Do yourself a favor and get changed. The heroes are more suspicious than usual, and you're their focus this time. They're converging on Casey, and she won't be able to keep fooling them for long."

I strolled across the street and into the flower shop, closing my eyes briefly as the blissful cool and sweet scents washed over my body. I walked past rows of gardenia, rose, carnation, and baby's breath as I headed for the bathroom, away from the sole employee manning the register. It was surprisingly spacious in there, and I was into my suit in almost no time.

I tied my hair back, staring at my reflection in the mirror as I went through my final check. My suit was performing at top efficiency, my claws were sharp, my grapnel ready, and my batons repaired and prepared. Plus, ha, I had a dose of bad luck ready to go at all times. I didn't know what I was stepping into, but if it meant a fight, at least I wouldn't be emptyhanded.

We'd see how prepared I was for the other eventualities.

"Where to next?" I asked Boris. I could hear the clerk's voice pick up, no doubt talking to a customer.

"Down the drain."

"Down the – what?"

"You need to get to the cold storage room where they keep the flowers," he clarified. "There should be a large drain in the floor there. Move the grate and follow it down. Once you get to the main pipe, look for a door."

Oh, great. "A tour of the sewers, really?"

He made a *pfft* sound. "Would I send you into the sewers if there were any way I could avoid it? Nonsense. You'll find the basement entrance well before the drain drops to the main line of the sewers."

"I should never have doubted you." I slipped out the bathroom and toward the back of the store. I was on camera now, but it couldn't be helped – and I bet no one was looking at the security feeds right now anyway. I pushed aside the long, stiff pieces of hanging plastic that separated the storage room from the rest of the shop, and it got downright cold.

"Whew. Glad I'm not sticking around." It was dark back here, and damp underfoot. The bunches of flowers were nothing more than looming silhouettes, devoid of color, and the sweetness of their scents was muffled by the chill. It was far less enchanting than the shop out front, that was for sure.

I got to the drain, pulled the heavy iron grate up and set it aside, then shined my flashlight down into the dark. There was plenty of space for a person to fit – even a little ladder. "How do you reckon the Mad Thinker set up a base down here without anyone noticing?" I asked as I began to descend.

"Using his androids, undoubtedly. They can take all sorts of shapes, after all. Why not turn them into beasts of burden to haul his equipment along the very sewer route we more fragile beings must strive to avoid? You're almost there."

So I was. I hopped the last few feet down onto the ground, grimacing a little at the wetness and the earthy *squish* of it beneath my boots. "Door, door…" To my left was a solid brick wall about a dozen feet away, but to the right – ah, there. A pile of bricks, neatly stacked, and in front of them a newly installed, solid metal door. It looked like the opening to a bank vault.

Fortunately, I had plenty of experience with bank vaults. I headed over and inspected it, running my fingertips around the edges as I probed for weaknesses. It was a very good model of door, unfortunately. The keypad was resistant to solenoid interference, it had a cobalt plate to help prevent drilling, and even if you could drill through, the relockers would fall into place, giving whoever was in there plenty of warning that I was coming. That was *if* I had my safe cracking tools on me, which I didn't. Still… I felt the fresh concrete again. Mmhmm. Figured.

"Curses," Boris muttered over the com. "I should have anticipated something like this. It's not impossible to get through, but we'll need–"

Ka-chunk. He went silent as I grabbed the handle for support, braced my feet against the walls on either side of the door, and heaved backward. It only took a few seconds for the door to pop free. It was heavy, but not so heavy that I couldn't handle it in my suit.

"That's the problem with doing masonry in the sewers," I

said tightly as I carefully set the door down to my right. "It takes forever for the cement to dry."

Of course, ripping the door out of the wall wasn't a quiet method, so the Owl undoubtedly knew someone was coming. Hopefully he wasn't armed. I slipped through the hole like a shadow, ready to trigger my pulsator at the first sign of trouble.

As my eyes adjusted, I realized that I'd overthought it. The Owl was there, but he didn't know I was coming – he didn't appear to know anything at all about the outside world. He was sitting back in what looked like a dentist's chair, wearing a heavily wired headset that connected him to a series of server banks. The room hummed with the sounds of running machinery, including a dehumidifier – it was much drier in here, undoubtedly better for the computer equipment. There was one small light hanging right above the Owl, and it illuminated a face that appeared rapt, mouth moving silently, eyes twitching like caged mice beneath his closed lids. Whatever he was seeing, it fascinated him.

We were right, then. The Mad Thinker had connected the Owl's mind to the pop-up dimension where he'd stored the golden apple. He might be using the Owl to do the bulk of the decryption work, or perhaps just turning him into a conduit for the computers to use, so they could do the heavy numeric lifting. Either way, I wasn't going to leave him plugged in like this.

Because it was *my* turn to be plugged in.

I had to move fast. The minute I cut the Owl's connection to the pocket dimension, the Mad Thinker would probably be warned. I could have androids on me in minutes. "Tell me you've worked out the spaghetti map," I said to Boris as I plotted my next move. The busier I kept, the less time I had to feel nervous.

"As soon as I know where you enter, I'll know where to tell you to go." He sounded a bit grim. "Let's hope my voice can reach you in there."

"Fingers crossed." I inspected the wired headpiece setup a little closer, but it looked like a standard lift-and-dump, with nothing drilled into the Owl's skull or anything like that. How fortunate. I got my double set of super-strength cuffs, gag, and blindfold – otherwise known as my party pack – ready, took a final slow breath as I flexed my fingers, and then–

Quick as blinking, I had the headset off the Owl. He seemed unconscious, but I wasn't taking any chances. I slapped the cuffs on his ankles, turned him over and cuffed his wrists, then finished wrapping him up and laid him down in the corner in under a minute. "Sleep tight, Leland," I muttered before sitting down in the chair myself. I grabbed the headset, which was blinking with a warning red light that I didn't like, and slid it on before I could have second thoughts.

This was my first time taking a swan dive into a magico-psychic dimension designed by a literal madman in order to keep his ill-gotten gains out of reach, and I had to say, I didn't care for it. All of my senses went haywire, my brain trying to orient me in a place that defied orientation. It felt like I was spinning out of control, subject to forces that were too strong for me to control, or even understand. I was out of my depth, so far out of my depth. I couldn't do this. I needed to–

"–get out of there. Cat? Black Cat? *Felicia?*"

It was a familiar voice, somehow penetrating the damp blanket of dismay that had overtaken my mind. The panic settled, and I regained my ability to think. Slowly, the spinning resolved into a single bright singularity in front of me. It felt like I was staring at something so far away I couldn't reach it, but then… why couldn't I? Because something was giving me an arbitrary sense of distance in a place where physical distance was meaningless? Screw that.

I reached a hand – oh hey, I had hands again, that was cool – toward the singularity, imagining it as something I could bring closer with ease, like a grain of sand. It resisted at first, but eventually I got my mind around it, then brought it to me and dropped it over my mental self, turning the midnight blue of my surroundings into bright white, like something straight out of a Matrix movie.

It was stark in here, but not silent. I could still hear the hum of the computers if I focused, only inside this place it was more like water rushing by, an entire river of data being transmitted. Was this the computers trying to break down the golden apple's programming? Even as I detected it, though, the sound began to die off, like the aftermath of a battle before the sirens started. All around me, the whiteness became tinged with a golden glow.

Welcome, stranger.

Oh, that voice… I could sit and listen to that voice for hours, maybe days. It was the most beautiful thing I'd ever heard, and I'd heard plenty of alluring sounds before. This was elevated above all those somehow, a voice and a force and a feeling all at once.

"Black Cat! You need to communicate with me. Don't make me send Bruno in there after you."

This was *not* the same voice as the one I'd just heard, but it was even more welcome. I cleared my throat – once I remembered I had a throat – and said, "I'm here, Doc."

"Felicia?"

How did I vocalize thoughts when my brain was so thoroughly separated from my vocal cords?

Why did it *have* to be separated from my vocal cords, actually? Why not be able to use my actual body in addition to my mind in this place? I tried again, focusing intently on the body that felt like it wasn't really a part of me anymore. "I'm... here... Doc."

Dang, that was hard. And *loud* – the entire dimension seemed to vibrate with the force of what had to be no more than a whisper in the real world. I coughed.

"Ah, I hear you now. You sound – oh, but of course. We should have anticipated having trouble with typical communication, under the circumstances." Boris *tsked* himself. "All right, we'll assume things are going swimmingly unless you say otherwise, then. Is there any sort of identifier you can give me for your location within the dimension?"

Gosh, was there? I looked around with a little more attention to detail. I'd brought this place to me... but that didn't mean I'd created it. This whole place had existed before I got here, and even though my mind was different from the Owl's, I'd managed to access it. That meant the map I'd seen might not be useless. How could I visualize where I was, though, when I didn't understand anything about this place?

Well, actually... I understood one thing about this place. I understood *me*; I'd gone through hell and back to make sure I knew myself back to front, inside and out. Facing yourself was never an easy thing, but the pain was worth it. Especially if it meant I might not be lost in this place.

I thought about myself *hard*, zeroing in on my place in space and time. Space and time – ha, they could go jump off a bridge, because they couldn't hold me down, couldn't hold me back. I was here because I wanted to be here, and I was staying until I got what I needed. I never gave up, I never gave in, I always had another plan, I was *Black Cat* and I was proud of who I was, and this dimension could bow down in acknowledgment or it could give up the game right now and hand the apple over.

Clever girl.

I suddenly saw myself, floating in a stark white space, only… tiny. As I watched, the space resolved into a thread, which became one strand of many, a tangle of infinite possibilities, vaguely resembling the plans I'd seen in the Baxter Building but so much more complex. The section of the tangle that held the apple was on the far side, seeming almost impossibly distant. How was I going to negotiate these strands that far? How was Boris's map going to help me at all?

It wasn't. So I needed to find a new way. First, I needed to soothe my backup. "I'm… on… it."

Boris sniffed haughtily, but it carried a relieved edge to it. "Fine, I see how it is. Just know that I'm monitoring your vitals every moment. Don't get lost over there, or I really will send Bruno in after you, and you know how claustrophobic he gets underground."

Oh, I knew. I didn't fancy getting pried out of this machine by a guy on the verge of a nervous collapse, so I'd better get this done myself.

All right, I needed to get from where I was to way over there… and there were what looked like about a thousand hallways between me and the spot that glowed with the light of the apple. Even if I raced this version of me as fast as I could think, I still had to deal with the architecture of the dimension, and I didn't care to into any invisible walls at top speed. So how did I get there?

I had to use *my* experiences, my reality, and impose it as best I could on what I was looking at. If the architecture of the dimension was stable, then I needed to use that stability to my benefit. I'd come in here, so it was penetrable.

I was going to need a ride.

CHAPTER TWENTY-NINE

As soon as I thought it, I had it – my latest joy ride, courtesy of Danny Rand's generous forgetfulness. The Ferrari growled under me, raring to be on the move. But the car itself wasn't enough. It needed a shield, a version of the same one in the real car, only *this* one –

A glittering forcefield extended from the car, sparkling like a million diamonds. I laughed – that was more like it. Now, to plan my route.

If I took the path of least resistance, then I was actually fairly close to where the golden apple was resting. Our strands didn't touch right now, but that didn't mean they couldn't. I just needed to bring my passage along with me. I was the point of the needle, and the threads would connect once I brought them together.

I envisioned that point out in front of me, shaping the diamonds into a drill that would power me through whatever I ran into. Then I oriented my new ride in the direction of the golden apple, setting my visualization of the map in the dash where I could see it, and flexed my fingers on the wheel.

"Yipee-ki-yay, mother–" The car accelerated so fast I lost my voice as I drove us straight into the closest sidewall of the thread we were currently in. I felt it the moment we impacted – it resisted my interference, almost *resented* it. This place had been built by a mad genius, so resentfulness was baseline along with narcissism, but I was a literal unstoppable force right now. It took some gritting my teeth, but then we were through, and I was–

In nothing. In the middle of *nothing*, a nowhere place, and there was nothing at all around me, the absence of color and thought and life and–

Oh god, I was going to die, I was going to die, I was going to–

Only die if I couldn't *pull it together, Felicia!* I wasn't going to lose my mind in this place. I came here to win, and I was *going* to! I visualized tugging the severed thread wall along with me, attaching it to the front of the car and carrying my own reality along with me as I checked the map again. I was heading right for the spot where the golden apple was located. I'd be there in no time if I–

I hit another wall, then another, sliding through them like a needle and bringing my thread along with me. Each new passage was different, one a thousand different colors that made me wince to look at them, another pure black with the smell of iron and an uncomfortable echo, and another painted with beautiful portraits of beings I didn't recognize but felt like I should. None of them had the apple, though. I had to keep going… but it was getting harder to keep moving. My mind provided my momentum, and my mind was getting tired of psychically punching its way across this dimension. *C'mon, c'mon…*

Finally I hit a wall so hard that it bent against the hood of my car instead of breaking. I gritted my teeth and gunned the engine, sending smoke up from the tires until the flexing surface in front of me finally cracked down the middle. I roared into a new kind of room, a vast hall with a single, golden light in the center of it. *Bingo.* I had finally found the end of the labyrinth.

"Wow," I said, just for the pleasure of hearing my own voice for a second. "Here I am."

Here you are.

I shivered as the power of that voice washed over me. I stepped out of my car, confident that it still existed even if I wasn't looking directly at it, and moved toward the golden light. I could see it, but I couldn't seem to focus on the apple itself. "Where are you?"

I'm with you, Felicia. You just have to look a little closer.

I shook my head. "Do you talk to everyone in riddles?"

Everyone worth talking to, yes. Everyone else hears nothing but their own selfish desires.

I turned in a circle, making sure I wasn't missing something obvious. "What's so wrong with having selfish desires?"

Nothing at all. I exist to give people what they want, selfish or not.

"But you don't like to do it."

I have no personal feelings in the matter, but my makers do. You've met one of them. What do you think she would say?

I already knew what Eris thought of most of the people who'd played her little game so far. "I think I know what she'd like me to do, but coming from someone who's indulging herself just by playing this game, I'm a little skeptical that she's genuine. Why can't I see you?"

I thought you would want to avoid what I've shown all the others.

Well, now I was curious. "What was that?"

Their selfish desires, of course.

A flood of information came at me from all sides, all at once. I saw skyscrapers, luxury jets, enormous mansions filled with beautiful people, expensive cars and jewels to die for. I even saw one person with a crown on his head and a scepter in one hand, and a wave of people kneeling down before him.

Oh yeah, I recognized him now. That was the guy from Madrid.

"But you didn't give them these things," I pointed out, closing my eyes for a moment. When I opened them again, the images were gone. "They got money instead."

Money is easier to manipulate than physical objects and adulation. When I offered it as a first resort, they all took it, assured that their true desires would soon follow.

"That's very tricky." It almost felt like cheating, except there were no set rules to cheat.

My makers would call it efficient. And money, of course, is an ephemeral thing, simple to create in this world. You know that already, don't you, Felicia?

I did. Still. "So you're not actually bound to give whoever is wishing for something *exactly* what they want."

The more rooted their desire is in the physical world, the longer it takes to bring it to fruition. That is the nature of my magic.

That must be the real reason the Kingpin's apple was still there to be stolen – he was going for something complicated and needed to give the wish time to work. "So if I asked to be, oh, say, the queen of New York City, that could potentially take a long time."

Days at least, in which you would need to maintain control of me at all times. It's the reason the Mad Thinker decided he was better off decoding me, rather than relying on my assistance.

"Interesting."

But you have no wish to ask for such trite prizes, do you? You already reign in New York City. You're the queen of thieves, and not even Odessa Drake can say that with as much authority as you can.

"True," I said. "And if you think you're going to be able to get away with offering me everything my heart desires, think again. I've already gone through that with–"

Yggdrasil, I know. It offered you the physical, mental, and emotional sustenance it thought you desired in exchange for the use of your body. Power over those who would seek to subdue you. Vengeance against anyone who had wronged you. Money, influence, rare treasures – all the trappings of greatness.

But Yggdrasil made a fatal mistake.

It certainly did.

I would never presume to offer you the love of others, Felicia Hardy. Black Cat. You know the true cost of love – you know that it must be earned if you're to ever trust it. Everything of real value must be earned. Friendship, respect – these are the things you covet more than anything else, and treat more reverently than any of your treasures.

"And they're the things you can't give me," I replied firmly.

I wouldn't say that, exactly. While I can't give you these things without cheapening them, I can offer you the chance to earn them for yourself.

All of a sudden, Captain America was right in front of me. Geez, even the way he stood was inspiring. "I gave you a mission," he said, as straightforward as ever. "Save Doctor Strange from the symbiotes. All our other heroes, our greatest fighters, were subsumed by the horde. I didn't know if you could do it, Black Cat, but I had to try. You were all there was left."

I'd... wondered, afterward, if that was the real reason Steve Rogers had turned to me in his time of need. Just because I was there, not because I was as slippery and resourceful as he had claimed.

"But you did it," he went on. "Turns out you were just the person for the job. You've got the heart of a hero inside you, Felicia Hardy. Your thieving exterior serves a purpose, but you could have a much bigger one. You're smart, you're strong, and you're creative." He took a step forward. "You could be an Avenger."

"I always knew you could." I whirled and saw Spider-Man standing to my right. He took his mask off, and then there was Peter Parker, the man of my dreams. The man I knew I could never have, the man I would never be able to compromise enough for. Except...

Except...

"You could be a real hero," Peter said, taking a step forward. Even though I knew in my heart he wasn't real, even though I knew all of this was being pulled from my own mind and dangled in front of me like a piece of yarn, I felt my resolve soften. I always softened around Peter.

"You could fight for good," he went on. "You could be greater than who you are now, earn yourself a place of honor." He took my hand in his and held it gently. "Be the hero you know you could be, Felicia."

Oh, my. This pitch was genuinely sweet, the exact opposite of the high-pressure sell I'd gotten from the shard of Yggdrasil. This drew on a piece of my heart that I'd tried to bury a long time ago, a piece that had always wondered not just how great I could be, but how *good*. I'd gone toe-to-toe with some of the mightiest heroes in the world, after all, and I'd come out on top more than once.

And I'd done that through trickery, through deceit, and by bending the rules to suit myself. That was how I liked it, and I wasn't about to change. Not even to become an Avenger, or to be the sort of woman that Peter Parker might consider a hero.

"Thank you," I said, squeezing his hand before letting go of it. "But no. I don't need to be a hero in order to reach my full potential. I could never be like… him," I gestured to Peter, "or like Captain America, without losing a special part of myself." I shook my head and took a step back. "No. I'm not that kind of hero."

If you say so. They both vanished, and in their place was the golden apple I remembered. The writing around the edge of it glowed warmly, "For the cleverest," in beautiful script twirling around as the apple gently spun in the air. *You don't wish for the opportunity to remake yourself, either for great evil or great good. What do you want, then, clever one?*

I reached out my hand and grabbed the apple. A thrill ran up my arm and along my spine, tantalizing me. The power I held in my hand was intoxicating. I smiled so widely my cheeks ached, glorying in my moment of unlimited potential. I knew exactly what I wanted, and who I wanted it for.

Then I asked my question. A second later, the apple answered me.

As you wish.

CHAPTER THIRTY

I opened my eyes to the sound of gunfire and arc reactor blasts overhead. *Shoot, they're already here.* Not only were the heroes here, they were battling it out with someone. The Mad Thinker had undoubtedly realized that the Owl had gone offline and sent someone in to check on him.

"–Cat? Black Cat, you need to wake up *now*, before they bring the building down on you!"

"I'm here, Boris," I said. I sounded a little hoarse, but not bad. "Mission accomplished. I'm heading back up."

"It's about time." He sounded more relieved than brisk, which meant he'd been worried out of his head. "You'll be walking into a firefight, so prepare accordingly. I can have Bruno on site in five minutes, if you prefer to go out the back door."

"Five minutes, huh? That's fast."

"Not so fast – you were down there for over an hour."

An hour? Wow, it hadn't felt nearly as long to me. Was time dilation part of the popup dimension's side effects, or the apple's? Had the apple been able to keep me from hearing Boris after that first time, or had my ears dissociated from my brain or something?

Geez, how did *anything* work in another dimension? I had better things to think about than being trapped in some magico-psychic treasure chest. There was another boom overhead, and a trickle of concrete dust on my face made me sneeze.

"Oh, for the love of…" I pulled the headset off and got up out of the chair, shaking the languor out of my limbs. The Owl was awake and shouting as loudly as he could around the gag.

"What's that? Sorry, I can't hear you over the booms," I said, pointing at the ceiling. "Let's go tell the cavalry to knock it off, huh?"

"Mm mple!"

"Hm? Maple?" I hoisted the Owl up over my shoulder, because I was *so* nice, and carried him into the secret hallway, then over to the ladder.

"Mm mmpple!"

"Oh, the *apple*, right!" I hoisted him out onto the floor first, then followed, putting the grate back where I'd found it because I tried not to be rude when I was infiltrating other people's places. "It's gone."

"HMMM?"

"Oh yeah! I used it, of course." I winked at him before I grabbed him by the ankles. "What, you don't think I'd go to all the trouble of digging it out of the Mad Thinker's hidey hole just to leave it hanging around, do you?"

The Owl lapsed into senseless mumbling, despair evident in every inch of him. I'd have felt a little sorry for him, if the guy hadn't tried to shoot my head off at Sasha Hammer's place. As it was, I was fine with him languishing in a pit of despair for a while.

The flower shop clerk was huddled behind the register with an expression on her face that was common for New Yorkers: half interest, half irritation. Yeah, we got this a *lot* in the city. I glanced outside, then down at my semi-conscious, entirely depressed burden and decided it would be better to leave him in here.

"Do you mind keeping an eye on this guy for me for a few minutes?" I asked the clerk.

Her eyes narrowed. "What's in it for me?"

"Them not bringing the roof down on your head," I said, jerking my thumb outside. "I'm the one who can get them to go away."

A particularly close blast rattled all the light fixtures. "*Fine,* whatever."

"Thanks a bunch." I dropped Leland's ankles, took a moment to check my hair, then walked outside into the sunlight. It was late afternoon, the golden hour, and it would have been absolutely lovely right now if not for the active firefight taking place in the middle of the street. The Fantastic Four were there, all suited up and battling it out with blank-faced, metalloid androids. Andy, the biggest one, was shouting in a familiar and, yes, rather mad-sounding voice.

"You can't stop it!" the Mad Thinker shouted through his android. "You may put an end to my investigation here, but you'll never be able to find the apple! I've hidden it so deep in the quantum multiverse that even if you find my lair, accessing the specific dimension it's stowed away in will be impossible." The android threw a van at Mr Fantastic, who bent around it like a boomerang before it was caught and hurled back at the android by The Thing.

"You're not that good at covering your tracks," Iron Man shouted from above, where he was using his repulsors to blast some dangerously fast androids out of the sky. One of them fell into a heap right at my feet, its components already repairing themselves. "We'll find a way in!" He shot two more androids at Doctor Strange, who swept them up into some sort of magical hamster cage that prevented them from moving.

The android in front of me was almost reassembled. *Nope, not gonna let that happen.* I took a running step forward and kicked its head so hard with my foot that the still-fragile neck attachment snapped clean in two. The head went flying into the fray, and the android's body made a pathetic *bzzt* noise and went still again.

No one even noticed. Ugh. I cupped my hands around my mouth and shouted as loudly as I could, "KNOCK IT OFF!"

I was a little surprised when it worked. Even more surprised when the first person to speak after my impromptu interruption was none other than the Mad Thinker himself, sounding absolutely furious as he focused the Awesome Android's eyes on me. "You! What are you doing here? You're not supposed to be here! I haven't accounted for you!"

Oh right, this guy lived his life based on probabilities and statistics. "What?" I stepped forward, hands on hips as I shook my head. "I think I'm offended."

"Preliminary data shows you're not powerful enough to have a discernible impact on my plans," the Mad Thinker went on through his mouthpiece. "Yet…"

"Mm, yep, it's the 'yet' that always gets you," I said sagely. "Sorry to be the one to tell you this, but I've already crashed your party, bud. Your apple is gone."

"That's… that's impossible."

I laughed. "I specialize in doing the impossible. Go ahead, check." I held one of my hands out in front of my face and popped my claws, idly inspecting them for damage. "I'll wait."

"No. *No!* No no no no no…" All at once, every android in the fray went still – like someone had just activated hibernation mode. The assembled heroes looked at each other, then at me.

Johnny was the first one to come over, because he had manners, unlike *some* people. "Black Cat, are you serious?" he said, eyes wide. "You found the golden apple?"

"Sure did." I held out my hand for a fist-bump, and he enthusiastically obliged.

"That's bull," the Thing called out. "If you used the apple, then what did you wish for, huh? I don't see no diamonds raining from the sky."

I winced. "Ooh, sounds painful. I think I'll stick with my original wish, thanks."

"Which was what?" Johnny asked.

I batted my eyelashes at him. "Honey, you know a lady never wishes and tells."

"What lady?" Sue said snippily.

"OK, you know what?" I rounded on her, hands on hips, but just as I opened my mouth to tell her just who the lady out of the two of us was, the androids came back online.

"Always! There's always *something* to throw off my calculations! I can't – and you – did it even – *ARGH!*" Every android grabbed their heads in sync and wailed along with their master. Even the broken one behind me tried to, grabbing for a noggin that was stuck in the rain gutter across the road. "No one should have been able to get in there! Once the connection with the Owl was broken, the portal to the dimension should have closed! How did you do it? *How?*"

Oh, huh. Wow. How *did* I get in, in that case? Maybe I'd gotten more of a godly assist than I realized. I resisted the urge to look around for a dark-haired bombshell and shrugged. "Just lucky, I guess."

"*No one* is that lucky! Your brain should be as scrambled as my security algorithms!"

"I don't know what to tell you." *But I do know what* not *to tell you.* I looked at all the heroes standing around, listening to me argue with a madman. "So hey, how about we wrap this up?" I gestured to the androids, who – as one – suddenly hummed with new life and lifted into the air.

"Always, *always* something to throw off my calculations," the Mad Thinker muttered, his voice coming through in surround sound from the mouth of every android on the street. "I'll have better luck with the next apple, though." They began to flee.

"Nope, no more apples for you!" Iron Man and the Fantastic Four headed into pursuit mode, which was fine with me. The sooner they were gone, the sooner I could get on with business.

To my surprise, Doctor Strange came over to me instead of flying off after his buddies. "Forgive my curiosity, but what *did* you ask for?" he said, clasping his hands together behind his back.

I was tempted to say "more wishes!" just to see what he did, but I already knew what people thought of me. At least Doctor Strange was polite enough not to out-and-out accuse me of selfishness. "Nothing that will bounce back on me," I said with complete sincerity. "In case you were worried." I winked, but he didn't take the joke.

"I was, in fact, worried about that very possibility," he replied. "But I can see that I should have trusted your judgment. You're very aware of your own capabilities, after all, and you have better judgment than the vast majority of people who've ever been offered that kind of power." He inclined his head to me. "I hope it works out well for you."

"Thank you," I said, reluctantly touched. "I appreciate that. Now, don't worry about little old me. Go capture some androids and stop the Mad Thinker from hunting down the next golden apple."

"Something tells me I won't need to worry about that," Doctor Strange said with a sidelong glance at the flower shop. He made a complicated symbol in the air and a moment later, the Owl lifted off the ground and floated over to him, still whining to himself. Then Doctor Strange created a portal in the air in front of us and stepped through, villain in tow. The magical glow vanished, and I was left alone on a street that had taken only mild damage – pretty amazing, for New York.

"Well, that was fun."

Correction: not quite alone. I turned and watched Eris step out of the flower shop, a single coral-colored rose in one hand.

"I could have done without all the drama at the end," I said lightly, pleased to see her again.

She laughed. "Could you, though? You love drama."

Eris already knew me too well. "Yeah, OK, that part was fun."

She stepped closer and took my hand, even though my claws were still extended. "That was an interesting question you asked of the apple."

"What, how to safely find Dalton Beck and reunite him with his daughter? Just righting a wrong."

Eris shook her head. "It was selfless."

"No, it wasn't." I'd – reluctantly – grown fond of Casey over her sojourn with me and my crew, and I didn't want to be responsible for making her an orphan when I had the chance to get answers for her at no cost to myself. The golden apple was designed to be a trap, a weird, semi-moralistic trap, and the only way to win the game was to take yourself out of the equation. A wish for myself could have been nice, but unequivocally winning was even nicer.

"You have a soft spot for that girl."

"Sure I do," I admitted. "She reminds me of me. She doesn't deserve what she's gone through lately, and this was my shot to help make it right."

Eris raised one eyebrow. "Sure, that's the *only* reason. The fact that the FBI is now offering a substantial reward for Dalton Beck's safe return has nothing to do with it."

I laughed. "I can have multiple reasons for doing the right thing!" Feeling daring, I squeezed her hand. "So, do you want to hang around for a while?" I tilted my head and looked at her from under my eyelashes. "You, me, a little discord – sounds like a lot of fun." I'd never run with a literal goddess as a partner before, but I was eager to try.

"Mmm, it does," Eris agreed, but after a second, she shook her head. "I'll take a rain check for now, though." She handed me the rose. "Go be a hero, Black Cat."

"Shut your mouth," I said, using the rose to bop her on the forehead. Eris grinned, then let go of my hand and–

And walked–

Wait.

How did she vanish so completely without making it look

like she was going anywhere at all? Must be a goddess thing.

Bruno and Casey pulled up in front of me a second later, and Casey darted out of the car barefoot, stilettos abandoned now that the jig was up. She hit me with a hug so hard I almost fell over.

"Do you mean it?" she babbled. "You asked where to find my dad? You really did? You swear?"

"Sure did." I wasn't entirely sure what state he was going to be in when we found him, but the instructions had been very clear. "Let's go get him now, huh?"

Casey burst into tears.

I stared over her shoulder at Bruno. *What do I do?* He rolled his eyes – the traitor – and mimed putting his arms around Casey and giving her a hug.

Ah, right. The tears had thrown me for a loop. I gave her a squeeze, then turned us both toward the Escalade. "Let's go get him," I repeated, and Casey made a weird little humming sound that I figured was the closest thing to "yes" I was going to get out of her right now.

I gave Bruno the directions the apple had given to me, and about an hour later the three of us were outside of an old, possibly abandoned warehouse, given the rusty look of the siding. The most incongruous note to the whole scene was a man sitting on a folding chair in front of the place, cap pulled down to shield his eyes as he calmly read a newspaper, like hanging out in the middle of nowhere for hours a day was his normal deal.

He looked up as we approached, his face going carefully blank. "Um. Hello there?"

"Hi!" I looked him over. Plain gray overalls and a canvas

jacket – this guy was no top-level Maggia stooge. "How much are you being paid to babysit this place?"

"A hundred bucks a day for the past week," he said, folding his newspaper.

"What else are you supposed to do here?"

"Not much," he said with a shrug. "Just call if someone who isn't a worker tries to go in or out. Not my job to stop 'em, though."

"Call who?"

He shrugged. "Same random guy who gave me the job, I reckon. He paid through the end of the week, and he stops by once a day to visit somebody in there." The man looked me up and down uncomfortably. "Sorry, but I gotta call you in."

"I'll pay you a thousand dollars to go on a bathroom break for the next five minutes," I said, fanning myself with a thin sheaf of emergency hundreds. I never went out without cash on me. "You can call when you see us leaving. I can pretty much guarantee your boss won't care by then."

"Um…"

"Take the deal," Bruno added in his most intimidating voice, and the man's reticence evaporated.

"Bathroom break, got it!" He grabbed the money from my hand and hustled off. I turned to Casey.

"Look around, but if you see someone who isn't your dad, avoid them. Bruno, you stay with her." She nodded determinedly, and we split up as we stepped through the door.

The place wasn't all that big, but it was full of ancient boxes, oily machinery, and enough nooks and crannies to hide a dozen people in the darkness. I worked my way along the left wall and got lucky near the back when I noticed a pair of boots sticking out from behind an industrial lathe. I ran over and saw they connected to a man in dirty blue jeans and a stained gray cargo jacket, wearing a half-mask that covered him from the top of the head to the bridge of his nose. The lower half of his face looked familiar, though.

I bent down and lifted up the mask, and even though his eyelids were closed and it was almost dark out, he winced.

"No light," he slurred. "Hurts m'head."

Light sensitivity, check. Whatever his keeper was dosing him with, it made him want to keep his eyes closed. There was a foul-smelling bucket in the corner, and wrappers from pre-packaged food spread across the filthy floor. Wow. Thorough, but so gross.

"Dalton," I murmured. "Time to get up."

"Who?"

Memory issues, check. Silvermane had done his homework with this drug. When a guy didn't remember his own name and didn't even want to look around to see where he was, how would a psychic stand a chance at finding him? And I had no doubt that whoever was tasked with keeping him alive knew the bare minimum about him, just like the guy out front.

"You're Dalton," I said. "And your daughter Casey is here."

"Casey?" Now *that* got a response. His arms, weak from disuse, pushed down against the floor. I helped him sit up. "Casey? My girl? Where is she?"

"*Daddy!*" Casey hurtled out of the gloom toward us, but she was surprisingly gentle when she wrapped her father up in an embrace. He hugged her back, pushing the mask the rest of the way off as he did. My heart warmed, despite my distaste for the location. It was time to get out of here.

"I... you..." He looked at me, utterly confused. "What?"

"I'll explain once you've slept it off," I said. "Bruno! A little help, please?" The sooner we were out of here and away from any Maggia watchers, the better.

CHAPTER THIRTY-ONE

There's something so satisfying about a job coming together in the end. Even if parts of it were an unmitigated clusterbomb, like finding Dalton Beck had almost turned into, the hallmark of a good crew was being able to carry the job off even when the deck was stacked against you. And boy, had we ever carried it off.

As soon as word got out that New York City's golden apple was gone – which, fortunately, none of the heroes had openly pinned on me – the usual suspects came back out of the woodwork, each one returning to their slimy ways. Silvermane didn't appear to have taken my "inability" to get him the apple to heart, but he also seemed done with his interest in his son, too. Once the FBI made it clear that their star witness was back in custody – which he *wasn't*, he was still at my place but they should be happy he'd deigned to talk to them on the phone – Silvermane withdrew his public support for his son and went back to doing what he did best: lurking on the crimped, criminal edges of the city, taking a bite out of the crust whenever he could.

It made me feel a little sorry for Joseph Manfredi. He'd made a bunch of dumb decisions that had led to even dumber mistakes, but to be publicly forsaken by his father, after the brief hint of hope I'd witnessed in his face… it sucked. No two ways about that. Maybe he'd get lucky and the feds would keep him in the Tombs a while longer after the trial was over, which, once Beck had testified again, was only a matter of days.

Then, four days after the rescue, it was finally time to say goodbye to Casey and her dad.

I decided they should go out in style, and used my reward money from the FBI – because heck yes, I'd claimed that reward, it was the *least* they could do – to pay for Casey and Dalton to do all the tourist stuff that the city had to offer, including a helicopter tour that took them right over the Statue of Liberty. If I also asked Johnny Storm to do a fly-by while they were up in the air, well, that was my business.

And the way Spider-Man had swung right over their heads while they were waiting to see a show on Broadway was also a total coincidence.

And if I'd pushed one of Nelson and Murdock's cards a little too heavily into Dalton's hand and informed him that these guys were the ones to work with if he ever needed legal help again, that was just networking. You never knew when you'd need a Daredevil at your back, after all.

"Such a softie," Boris jeered at me after I sent the father-daughter duo off to a lovely dinner at my favorite Italian restaurant. "I never figured you for having such maternal instincts, Felicia."

"Bite your tongue," I told him. "These aren't maternal instincts at work. This is just making sure that Casey can look back on her time here as more than just a long stretch of boredom punctuated by occasional, terrifying fits of adrenaline."

"Soft. So soft. You wouldn't be doing such a thing if you didn't like the girl."

"I do like her," I allowed, making myself another cappuccino – decaf, because it was late and I was trying to *relax* from a job, not work myself up for a new one yet – and flopping back on the couch. "I like how gutsy she is. I like that she wasn't afraid to come to a new place by herself and basically harass her way into a spot on this crew. I respect her... gumption, I guess."

"She's a tough cookie," Bruno allowed from the other side of the couch. He was ostensibly watching the baseball game, but it was already going so horribly for his team that he'd turned the sound off to spare himself. "Could be a decent trainee if you ever wanted to bring somebody in more permanently, boss."

"She had promise in the technical realm," Boris chimed in. "And a better grasp of the nuances of social media than I have any desire to attain. She would make for an interesting apprentice if–" An alarm began to go off on the table in front of him, and he startled, then slapped it onto silent and ran for his room. He slammed the door shut, and a few seconds later a muffled *boom* sounded from behind the door.

Before either of us could run over there, he cracked it again. Blue smoke poured out, and he was coughing, but he didn't sound like a person who'd just lost a limb to science, so that was good. "Nothing to worry about!" he called out, then coughed again. "Nothing but a little experiment I kept on the hotplate too long! Talk amongst yourselves, and above all do *not* enter this room!" He slammed the door again.

I glanced apprehensively at Bruno. "Well, Casey certainly couldn't be any more terrifying than Boris is."

"You got that right," he agreed, a pensive line etched between his eyebrows even though he was smiling. "Seriously though, boss. If you were looking to expand, you could do a lot worse than a kid like her. She's got a skillset neither me nor Boris have, she wants to learn more about the rest of it, and she's a decent mimic. Give her a while to work at it and she could pull off a way more convincing you. Get her a decent suit on top of that?" He shrugged. "She could be really good."

"She could be," I agreed. "She's definitely got potential." I didn't say anything else after that, too absorbed in my thoughts, and after a few minutes Bruno excused himself to "go cry about my team somewhere you can't watch, boss" and headed for his own room. I was alone, and it felt... strange.

I decided to head up onto the roof, adding a slug of bourbon to my mug before taking my drink with me. It was still early enough that the horizon held the faintest hint of orange from the setting sun. In the eastern sky, a few brave stars poked through the New York light pollution. High above me, a slender crescent moon gleamed like the edge of a silver coin, spinning slowly across the heavens.

I sat down and let it all sink into me: the beauty, the ugliness, the stink and the noise and the power and the promise, everything that came with this wonderful, terrible city. This was the kind of place I'd been born for, the only kind of place I'd ever really be comfortable. I craved the sounds and smell and sights, craved the presence of people around me, and the opportunities that arose when so many of them were jammed together in such a small space. I could never leave the city, not for long. Certainly not for the rest of my life.

Could I ask someone else to change their own life for this place, and for me? I didn't think so. Not right now, anyway.

Casey was still in high school, and she clearly loved her father. They'd be going back to Nowhere, Ohio tomorrow, and that was undoubtedly the best thing for them. This place certainly hadn't treated Dalton Beck well, and I could already tell he was itching to get out of here. But Casey...

She'd definitely enjoyed it. Enjoyed the chase, enjoyed the thrill, enjoyed the jobs. At least, I thought she had. I'd never considered taking on an apprentice before, and it wasn't something I thought I had time for right now either, but if it was someone like Casey... I could see it.

Don't set yourself up for pain. I'd learned that from my mother, and as hard a lesson as it had been for me, it was a good one. The fewer people you let yourself count on, let yourself open up to, the better.

And that's why you're sitting on a rooftop alone mumbling to yourself while almost everyone else you know is paired off, or with friends, or out there living their best and most heroic lives.

Eh. Maybe. I didn't regret any of my choices; regret was for suckers. Still, even though I'd turned down the golden apple's offer of a new path, that didn't mean there was no space for change in the future. Perhaps it really was time for me to rethink things, time for me to... to...

Wait.

Wait.

What the heck was *that*?

From this distance it was a tiny speck, but it was coming in fast. Something dark, dotted here and there with red lights...

Oh, you had to be *kidding* me.

I hurled my mug at the rapidly growing speck, connecting with a satisfying *crash* that sent the drone off-kilter. Then I activated my com as I dove over the edge of the building, landing on the balcony outside my bedroom after a perfect front flip a second later. "Incoming attack drone, guys, get your gear on and prepare some countermeasures! I think it might be the Kingpin's!" It took a real egotistical jerk to be this brazen, and he was way up there on the egotistical jerk scale.

"Of course it's the Kingpin's," Boris muttered, sounding alert but a little hoarse. "A brilliant man like the Mad Thinker knows how to let go of losing a situation and move on after he's been bested, but *nooo*, not the Kingpin! He holds a grudge tighter than a hangman's knot, that piece of–"

I entered my room and closed the door behind me just as the drone began to fire. Bulletproof glass for the win! It took half a minute for me to get into my suit, but by then the first drone had been joined by two others. They all decided to fire on my window, which – the glass was good, but it wasn't *that* good.

I ran into the main room and almost right into Bruno, who was holding several of his favorite guns. Given how good his aim was, they were my favorite guns too. "How many, boss?"

"Three so far, but–"

"Make that eight!" Boris shouted, running out of his room holding a tablet. "Approaching on all sides! These are a heavier caliber drone than the ones you encountered on the road, and what they lack in laser armaments they make up for in–"

Ka-BOOM! A rocket – a literal rocket – launched from one of the drones outside my bedroom window. It easily penetrated the cracked glass and proceeded to blow up in the middle of my room. The backlash sent all of us tumbling to the floor, but it was mostly just heat and noise, thankfully. Strategically low-power rockets… he wasn't trying to bring the building down, at least. That was good. I didn't want Mrs Yu's life on my conscience.

I was confident we could take out the drones, even if they were heftier than usual. The very fact that he knew where I lived, though… that meant this stage of the game was finished.

I couldn't help it – I laughed. Exhilaration fizzed through my blood like bubbles in champagne. I was ready to move on. "Looks like we're going to have to find a new home base, boys."

"What?" Boris's eyebrows rose like twin caterpillars. "Are you suggesting we let the Kingpin win?"

"I'm suggesting it's time for the Testing, Testing protocol," I said. Boris's eyes lit up. Bruno, on the other hand, groaned and buried his face in one massive hand.

"You gotta be kidding me," he muttered. "You know how much time I've spent upgrading those cars, boss?"

"And now you should pick your two favorites and get Boris to help you drive one of them out of here," I replied, and patted his shoulder. "It's going to be OK. We've got more than enough in reserve to restart somewhere nice."

"Quit trying to make me feel better." Nevertheless, he turned and headed for the garage, Boris trailing in his wake, feverishly working on his tablet.

"Give me two minutes!" I called out to him. "And a countdown!"

"One if you're lucky!" he called back.

One minute.

I could work with that.

The fire in my room was mostly put out by the suppression system at this point, although the smoke was still pretty thick. Better yet, the window was open there. I gauged the distance to the closest drone, which was buzzing pretty close now, then began to run toward it. As I ran, I triggered my quantum probability pulsator.

The drone's weapons system malfunctioned just as I leapt at it, guns clicking uselessly. I landed on top of it, and it immediately dropped two stories. The two drones closest to it refocused on me, but I had already used my grappling hook to grip the top of the building. A second later I was in the air, while the drone I'd just used as a stepping stone was shot into slag by its buddies.

"Thirty seconds," Boris said. I could hear the roar of an engine in the background.

I swung over the edge of the roof and began running for the opposite side of the building.

"Black Cat," one of the drones broadcasted in a menacing AI voice. The seven that were left buzzed closer to me. "You are surrounded. There is no way out of this except for surrender."

"Fifteen seconds," Boris said.

"No thanks!" I trilled, readying my grappling hook again.

"Surrender to the Kingpin, or prepare to be destroyed."

"Ten seconds."

"I'm always prepared for a good round of death and destruction," I said, panting a little as I neared the far edge of the roof.

"This is your last chance to reconsider. Otherwise everything you love will be destroyed along with you."

"Five seconds," Boris said gleefully.

"Very well. Your lack of reason will be your undoing. Three… two… one…"

I kicked off the edge of the building just as the very top of it began to explode, all of Boris's paranoid chemistry experiments finally coming in handy. Lucky for me, the program he'd installed to control the explosions sought out and registered our bio-signatures before starting, and began the destruction at the farthest point from us.

The drones? They weren't so lucky.

Four of them were taken out instantly, caught in the heart of the blast right over the center of the roof. Another two were crisped badly enough that they began to lose altitude almost immediately, and were soon careening down to the ground. The last one was sent flying back by the concussion, but not so far that I couldn't get a lock on it with my grappling hook. I rode that spinning drone like I was Mary Poppins and it was my parrot-handled parasol, finally getting close enough to the ground that I was comfortable letting go. Before the drone could recover enough to start shooting at me, a hole the size of a fist appeared in the middle of it, taking out the control systems. A second later, Bruno drove up in the Escalade, gun in hand.

"Need a lift, boss?" he asked calmly.

"You have the best timing," I told him, and jumped into the passenger seat. We roared off into the night just as the sirens began to close in on the building, Boris in the van on our tail.

A call came in over the com. I checked the number and picked up. "Hey, kid."

"Felicia, oh my god! Are you OK?"

Aww, she was such a team mom. "We're all OK," I assured her.

"I saw on Twitter that an apartment building was on fire and then I realized it was *your* apartment! Dad and I are leaving the restaurant now, we can come and meet you and–"

"Casey," I said gently. "Relax. Everybody is fine, and honestly, this isn't the first time my home has been blown up." It was almost nostalgic. "But you and your dad should get a hotel tonight, OK? And I'm sorry about your spare clothes getting burnt to a crisp."

"I'm wearing my favorite stuff anyway." She was silent for a second. "Will you still come say bye to me tomorrow?"

"I wouldn't miss it," I promised her. It might not be a home-cooked meal to send off her and her dad, but I could meet them at the airport. "Go finish your dinner and stop worrying about me."

"If you're sure…"

"I'm sure. Night, Casey." I ended the call, and Boris took over the dead air.

"Did you see that? Perfect proof of concept of my patented destructive-defense maneuvers! No home should be without the ability to blow itself up when threatened!"

"Don't think that's gonna catch on in the larger market," Bruno said, turning the car in the direction of one of our safehouses.

"In New York City? Are you kidding?" Boris chortled gleefully. "I'll make a mint!"

I let the boys argue as I leaned back, rolling the window down to enjoy the feel of the wind in my hair. I'd have to let Peter know I was OK. I'd have to figure out where to set up our next home base and plan some jobs that would help furnish it to our liking. I'd have to plan some sort of slap back against the Kingpin, because otherwise I'd lose all respect for myself – and he probably would, too. Sounded like it was going to be a heck of a lot of fun.

In the meantime, though, I was going to enjoy the thrill. This was me. These were my choices, and this was my life, and I loved every bit of it – even the parts that came with explosions and extensive property damage.

It was worth it. So, so worth it.

EPILOGUE

I stood outside the main entrance of LaGuardia with a pair of backpacks on the ground to my right and Casey to my left while her dad checked them into their flight. I was dressed down, my hair pulled up under a ballcap to reduce the risk that someone would recognize me. Casey was wearing her trademark hoodie and tights, her face mostly blank, but her lips pursed like she'd just bitten into something sour. I knew her well enough now to recognize that expression – she was trying not to cry.

Awww. I held out an arm, and after a few seconds' consideration she tucked herself underneath it and leaned into me. "I can't believe your place got blown up," she said for the tenth time since I'd told her.

"It happens in this line of work," I said. I'd come out of it none the worse for wear, and I was looking forward to redecorating, honestly. All my best stuff was safe in storage. "At least you weren't there for it."

"I wish we had been. Maybe we could have helped you."

"Probably not," I said with perfect honesty.

Casey looked up at me and rolled her eyes. "Then maybe at

least I'd have remembered to save my own Browns hat, since none of you did."

"I think that was a strategic move on Bruno's part," I confessed, and there was the smile I was hoping for. I glanced at the announcement board and saw that their flight was getting ready to board. "You better go catch up to your dad," I said. I reached into my pocket and pulled out a scrap of paper with a phone number on it and handed it to her. "This isn't my number," I said. "Those change all the time. This is my mom's number. She's had the same landline phone since the eighties, this will work forever. Just in case you need to get in touch."

Casey tucked the slip of paper into her pocket, her eyes shiny with unshed tears. "Thanks," she said. "I promise I'll never share it with anyone else, not even Dad."

That was what I liked to hear. Speaking of, though, I saw her father waving her way from inside the airport. "Your dad's ready to go. C'mere." We hugged, and she squeezed me tight enough to make the air rush out of my lungs. "Geez," I grunted. "Ease up."

"Toughen up," she said with a smirk, wiping her eyes as she picked up her backpack. "Say goodbye to the guys for me."

"You know I will."

She nodded, her feet shuffling in place like she didn't know which way to go. Eventually, though, force of will made her turn into the airport, and a few seconds later she was back with her dad. He gave me a nod, which the smart guy knew was all I wanted from him, and they vanished into the crowd of people toward security.

I stood in the mix and watched them go, saying goodbye to an unexpected but not totally unpleasant chapter of my life.

It had been… nice, having Casey around. More than nice, even – she was useful, she was gutsy, and she was fun. But with Silvermane sniffing around, and the Kingpin holding a grudge, and heck – for all I knew the Mad Thinker wanted his piece too – it was better to go it alone, but I'd miss her.

"Is this exercise in mawkish sentimentalism done yet?" Boris asked with a huff through the com.

OK, I wasn't *exactly* alone.

"Can we proceed to the next stage of our plan?" he went on. "Because I refuse to look at any more buildings with this myopic yeti until you get back. He wants a garage big enough to fit a fire engine but when it comes to lab space, he–"

"Hey! Just 'cause you and your mad science experiments might have to share a few outlets doesn't make the last spot a bad option."

"Share? *Share?* There were two outlets in the entire whole of the downstairs! *Two!* That's so underpowered it's criminal, and I know criminal! If you'd just take your grubbing hands off the extended garage–"

"We need space for at least four vehicles, doc. *At least.* What, you want to park some of my custom work on the street where anybody walking by can run off with it?"

"That's why I suggested installing the flamethrowers underneath the cars as a deterrent, but *noooo*, you said, that might cause a fatal accident. Fatal accidents are the entire point!"

"All right, boys, no need to argue," I said, turning around and heading for my car, which I'd left parked in the unloading zone, *oops*.

"I'm on my way."

I was headed into excitement, into danger, into downright peril – and that was just the New York housing market. Beyond that? We had jobs to plan, treasures to steal, and a whole community of super heroes and super villains to annoy at the same time.

Life was good. And now? It was time to spread a little... discord.

ABOUT THE AUTHOR

CATH LAURIA is a Colorado girl who loves snow and sunshine. She is a prolific author of science fiction, fantasy, suspense and romance fiction, and has a vast collection of beautiful edged weapons.

twitter.com/author_cariz

**AMAZING
SUPER HERO
ADVENTURES**

WORLD EXPANDING FICTION

Do you have them all?

MARVEL CRISIS PROTOCOL
- ☐ *Target: Kree* by Stuart Moore
- ☐ *Shadow Avengers* by Carrie Harris *(coming soon)*

MARVEL HEROINES
- ☐ *Domino: Strays* by Tristan Palmgren
- ☐ *Rogue: Untouched* by Alisa Kwitney
- ☐ *Elsa Bloodstone: Bequest* by Cath Lauria
- ☐ *Outlaw: Relentless* by Tristan Palmgren
- ☐ *Black Cat: Discord* by Cath Lauria
- ☐ *Squirrel Girl: Universe* by Tristan Palmgren
  (coming soon)

LEGENDS OF ASGARD
- ☐ *The Head of Mimir* by Richard Lee Byers
- ☐ *The Sword of Surtur* by C L Werner
- ☐ *The Serpent and the Dead* by Anna Stephens
- ☐ *The Rebels of Vanaheim* by Richard Lee Byers
- ☐ *Three Swords* by C L Werner

MULTIVERSE MISSIONS
- ☐ *You Are (Not) Deadpool* by Tim Dedopolus
  (coming soon)
- ☐ *She-Hulk Goes to Murderworld* by Tim Dedopolus
  (coming soon)

MARVEL UNTOLD
- ☐ *The Harrowing of Doom* by David Annandale
- ☐ *Dark Avengers: The Patriot List* by David Guymer
- ☐ *Witches Unleashed* by Carrie Harris
- ☐ *Reign of the Devourer* by David Annandale

XAVIER'S INSTITUTE // SCHOOL OF X
- ☐ *Liberty & Justice for All* by Carrie Harris
- ☐ *First Team* by Robbie MacNiven
- ☐ *Triptych* by Jaleigh Johnson
- ☐ *School of X* edited by Gwendolyn Nix
- ☐ *The Siege of X-41* by Tristan Palmgren *(coming soon)*